HEDONISM

LISE GOLD

MADELEINE TAYLOR

Lise Gold Books

Edited by Debbie McGowan

Cover design by Lise Gold Books

For real-life Athena

Love is composed of a single soul inhabiting two
bodies

ARISTOTLE

ONE

RUBY

The office is silent as I pace, reading through the merger agreement one final time. It's 11:47 p.m., and as usual, I'm the only one left on the fortieth floor of the Hughes Center. The cleaning crew left hours ago, leaving behind the faint scent of lemon polish and emptied wastebaskets. My desk is still a mess; they know better than to touch it.

My reflection fragments across the wall of windows: auburn hair falling from what was a neat chignon sixteen hours ago; green eyes shadowed by fatigue; Chanel suit wrinkled from too many hours in my ergonomic chair. I have dark circles under my eyes, my collar has lost its crisp line, and there's a smudge of coffee on my legal pad. I used to care about these things. I used to care about a lot of things.

"Section 7.2(b)," I mutter, scanning the dense text for the hundredth time. The words blur together, black ants marching across white paper. I blink hard, forcing my vision to clear. Sixty million dollars doesn't allow for tired eyes. "The Seller agrees that for a period of five (5) years following the Closing Date—"

My phone buzzes against the glass desk, cutting through the silence. Another late-night email from the other side's lawyer, trying to slip sneaky changes into our agreement while hoping I'm too tired to notice. Classic move, but an amateur one. I've been handling corporate mergers for almost a decade—I didn't build the city's most feared law firm by missing tricks like this.

I sink into my chair and pull up the document on my second monitor. My fingers fly across the keyboard, adding comments in track changes. I'm surgical in my approach to contracts, dissecting the clause and rearranging its innards until it says exactly what I want it to say.

The Las Vegas lights sprawl beneath my window, a glittering carpet of false promises stretching all the way to the mountains. The Stratosphere pierces the night sky, its top lost in low-hanging clouds. Out there, people are living their lives, celebrating, falling in love, getting in trouble, making mistakes.

My office still looks like I just moved in, despite the three years I've occupied this corner space. No photos, no plants, no personal touches. Just law books, my degrees from Yale, and stacks of folders arranged in piles. Everything has its place, and its place is exactly where I left it. The only concession to comfort is the cashmere throw draped over my chair—charcoal gray, like everything else in here.

The motion-sensing lights in the hallway flicker off, and I welcome the darkness. It makes the city lights sharper, more defined, like the edges I've honed around myself. In the dark, I can pretend I'm the only person left in the world. Sometimes, that doesn't feel far from the truth.

I check my watch—a Cartier Tank, Claire's gift. Her last gift. Time to head home. The thought of my big, empty house in The Ridges makes my chest tight, but I push it away. I've gotten good at pushing things away. Too good, my mother would say, if I ever answered her calls.

Standing, I smooth down my skirt and begin my nightly ritual. Files arranged by priority for tomorrow. Laptop sleeve zipped closed. Papers gathered into my Hermès briefcase. Each motion automatic like a dancer going through a well-worn choreography.

Movement catches my eye—a flash of light in the building across the street. Another late-night worker, another soul trading sleep for success. Through the glass, I see a desk lamp, a computer screen, a silhouette. We're all running from something, aren't we? The thought comes unbidden.

The security guard—Marcus? Mario?—looks up from his crossword puzzle as I cross the lobby. I should know his name by now. He's here almost every night.

"Good night, Ms. Walsh," he calls out.

I smile and nod, the closest thing to social interaction I've had all day.

My Tesla waits in its usual place, gleaming black and spotless. The navigation system automatically sets a course for home. Twenty-five minutes between me and another sleepless night.

As I pull onto the freeway, my phone lights up with a text from my mother. *Just checking in, sweetheart. We miss you.* The blue light illuminates the car's interior for a moment before fading to black. I let it sit there, unanswered. Like the last dozen. Like the dinner invitations from colleagues. Like the life that's waiting to be lived.

The Strip glows to my left, a neon rainbow against the desert night. Each casino charts its own peak: the Olympus rising like a modern Parthenon in white and gold; the Bellagio's fountains throwing liquid silver into the night; the Venetian's faux-Italian towers somehow less artificial in the darkness.

From this distance, you can't see the desperation, the quick-rich dreams, the wedding chapels and pawn shops. Instead, it's almost beautiful—a city's fever dream rendered in neon and ambition. During the day, it's gaudy, trying too hard, but at night...at night, it becomes something else entirely. Like all of us, it wears its best face in the dark.

The city thins out as I drive west, tourist traps giving way to local bars, then to quiet malls, then to nothing but desert and darkness. Red Rock Canyon looms ahead, and my headlights catch the eyes of a coyote watching from the scrubland. Out here, the air smells different—clean and sharp, with the lingering heat of sunbaked stone.

The entrance to The Ridges appears, marked by palms and meticulously maintained desert gardens. The guard waves me through without checking—I'm a regular fixture of these early morning hours. Houses grow larger and farther apart as I wind up into the foothills, each one a small kingdom unto itself.

I never wanted to live this far from the city. Our downtown penthouse suited me—close to the office, no yard and pool to maintain. But Claire fell in love with The Ridges the first time we drove through. She saw something here that I didn't. Possibility, maybe. Future. Now the house feels too big, too quiet, too full of plans that never happened. Some mornings, I wake up and think about calling a realtor, but I haven't found the courage yet. Maybe I never will.

The bass starts as I wait for my gate to open and turn into my driveway, a low throb coming from my neighbor's house—Ms. Stavros. I've never met her, only caught glimpses: dark hair, elegant silhouette, expensive cars. She owns the Olympus on the Strip. The noise started recently, a steady pulse that vibrates through my walls at night.

I should complain to the HOA. I should do a lot of things. Like answer my mother's texts. Like go to the firm's monthly dinners. Like finally clean out Claire's closet, still untouched after two years.

Instead, I park in my garage, take off my heels, and prepare for another hour of work until exhaustion claims me. It's easier this way. Safer. The contracts don't ask questions. They don't expect me to smile, to engage, to move on. They just need my attention and focus. I can give them that. It's all I have left to give.

TWO
ATHENA

The security feed from the club fills my phone screen, silent figures moving through the underground space. Below my home in The Ridges, twenty-seven women are letting go of their daytime personas. I watch a state senator shed her blazer, a tech CEO kick off her shoes and knock back a shot of tequila, a federal judge unpin her hair. My fingers trace the rim of my espresso cup as I observe, making mental notes of who's carrying too much tension, who might cause problems.

My office at the Olympus sits thirty-eight floors above the Las Vegas Strip, all glass and steel and intimidation. The casino floor spreads out below, a labyrinth of lights and sound designed to disorient. But up here, everything is peaceful.

A knock. "Ms. Stavros?"

I open the door, and Maria, my first assistant, is standing in the doorway, a file in hand. "The gaming commission numbers for last quarter just came in."

"Thank you." I take the file and practically close the door in her face. I'm not one for small talk; I don't see the point.

Returning to my phone, I see a new member is being introduced to the others. Software entrepreneur. She's nervous, fingers fidgeting with her necklace. They're always nervous at first.

The outdoor cameras show my neighbor's Tesla pulling into her garage. Right on schedule. Ruby Walsh, founding partner of Walsh & Associates, Las Vegas's most ruthless M&A firm. I've watched her come and go since I moved in, always alone, always late at night. There's something compelling about her solitude, the way she holds herself. Sharp. Fragile. Beautiful.

I should be watching the floor, monitoring the high-stakes tables. That's what an invested casino owner would do. But I've hired the best security team in Vegas—ex-military, ex-FBI, people who know what they're looking for and aren't afraid to handle it. Besides, the casino practically runs itself these days. My management team has been with me since I opened, and they know how to keep the money flowing. No. What happens in my underground club is far more interesting than watching rich men lose money.

My phone vibrates—Demetria, my younger sister, calling from Greece. I silence it, knowing she'll leave a message about missing me, about how I should visit more often. The usual guilt wrapped in love wrapped in obligation.

Another knock on my door. "Mrs. Chen is here," Maria says from behind the door in a raised voice.

"Okay." I close the security app and smooth the lines of my white silk jumpsuit. "Let her in."

The woman who enters is new money—her Gucci bag prominent, her jewelry bright. Her company's IPO numbers are solid, and more importantly, she knows how to keep secrets. I've vetted her thoroughly.

"Mrs. Chen." I don't offer my hand. "Please, sit."

She perches on the edge of the chair opposite my desk, trying not to look overwhelmed by the opulence of my office. Every piece was chosen with purpose—the massive black marble desk that dominates the room facing the floor-to-ceiling windows, the Greek antiquities displayed in subtle pools of light. A bronze Athena stands guard in one corner, her spear eternally ready, her owl watching over all who enter. The walls are dark-wood paneled, and a collection of rare first editions fills the built-in shelves—Sun Tzu, Machiavelli, books that most people only pretend to have read.

I built this. Everything imported from Greece—the hand-knotted silk rug, the leather chairs soft as butter, even the marble came from Athens. The room is designed to intimidate without trying, to whisper power rather than shout it.

"I've received your reference," I say, letting the words hang in the air. My club doesn't accept applications in the literal sense of the word. It doesn't even exist on paper. But power attracts power, and whispers travel in certain circles. "Have you read the NDA?"

"Yes."

"And you're willing to sign it?" When she nods, I continue. "Tell me why you're here."

She shifts, manicured fingers tightening on her purse. "I was told... That is, Sandra mentioned she might be able to introduce me and—"

"No," I cut her off. "Tell me why you're really here."

Mrs. Chen's shoulders drop slightly. "I'm tired," she finally says. "Of pretending. Of holding everything together all the time." Her voice cracks on the last word.

Now I lean forward. "And what would you do, if you could stop pretending? Just for a few hours?"

The blush that spreads across her cheeks tells me everything I need to know. I reach for a small black card and hand it across the desk. "Thursday. Midnight. The number on the back—call it and a driver will pick you up. Give him the password, it's Hedonism." I hold onto the card for a moment longer, catching her eyes. "What happens beyond those doors exists in a vacuum, Mrs. Chen. No names, no stories, no evidence. Consider this your only warning—discretion isn't just requested, it's required. Do you understand?"

"Yes, Ms. Stavros. Thank you." Her fingers close around the card like it's made of gold.

"Excellent." I lean back in my chair and shoot her a smile. A real smile, only reserved for few. "We'll take care of the NDA and payment on the night. I look forward to welcoming you into my circle of friends."

After she leaves, I turn my security app back on. The evening's energy is building, and I touch the control panel on my phone, adjusting the temperature up by two degrees. Clothes may come off soon and the slightest details matter.

There's movement in Ruby's house, still dark except for a single window. Through it, I can make out her silhouette, pacing. Working, always working. The camera was installed purely for security purposes, positioned to cover the perimeter of my property. The fact that it captures her top floor office is coincidental, yet I find myself watching that window more than I should, even though nothing interesting ever happens. She doesn't even give me the courtesy of a late-night show. At least, not with the lights on.

I gather my things—my purse, my phone, a set of keys that unlock doors most people don't know exist. The club needs my presence tonight. New members are always more comfortable when they see me there, making sure everyone feels safe. Seen. Protected.

My family back in Greece would have a collective heart attack if they knew that over eighty people have unrestricted access to my home—or at least the underground part of it. All it takes is a code at the gate and a whispered password at the door.

But it works because everyone has something to lose. It's a delicate balance of power and trust, of knowing just enough about each other to ensure silence. An ecosystem of secrets and safety.

The private elevator in my office opens directly into the underground garage where my Aston Martin waits, its dark-green paint almost black in the low light. A gift to myself when the Olympus's profits first hit nine figures. The engine purrs to life under my hands, and I take a moment to appreciate the sound.

Sometimes I still have to pinch myself. Sixteen years ago, I was fresh off a plane from Athens with an MBA from London Business School, a useful network of contacts through my late father, and a point to prove. Now I own a piece of the skyline.

THREE

RUBY

The bass pulses through the walls as I step out of the shower, the rhythm becoming impossible to ignore. God knows I've tried, but after two years of silence in this house, the nightly intrusion feels like sandpaper against raw nerves. When did this start? Two, three weeks ago? And only Thursday to Sunday. The consistency is maddening, like clockwork, like she's teaching midnight dance classes or something.

Water drips onto the cold marble floor. I keep forgetting to turn on the underfloor heating; it was one of the many luxuries Claire insisted on when she designed this bathroom. "You'll thank me in winter," she'd said, but now the control panel stays dark, along with the settings for the steam shower I use only for its basic function. I can't even bring myself to figure out how it works.

The walk-in closet still smells faintly of her perfume. Jo Malone London—Pomegranate Noir. I ordered a bottle after she passed, just to torture myself. It's hidden behind my row of dry cleaning and I spray it now and then. Her side remains untouched—an archeological record of the woman who used to share my life. Tailored blazers in jewel tones, the vintage band T-shirts she slept in, her favorite worn leather boots. The dress she was wearing when we met, emerald silk that matched my eyes. "It was a sign," she used to joke. "I had to talk to the gorgeous redhead in Valentino."

I dress—silk pajama pants, a thin cashmere sweater. The desert nights can get cold, even when the days are scorching. The sweater was a gift from her too—"Because you're always cold in your office, honey." She was always thinking ahead, planning for my comfort, our joint life, while I was planning mergers.

The house creaks and settles around me, five thousand square feet of empty space, of memories trapped in corners, of life interrupted. Each room holds a different version of the future we planned. The library upstairs, where Claire was going to write the novel she always talked about. The guest room we were going to turn into a nursery someday. The garden she started designing, desert-hardy plants that would bloom year-round.

The music from next door grows louder, pulling me from my thoughts. I head to my office that overlooks my neighbor's estate, and through the window, I watch an Aston Martin pull into the circular drive of the Stavros mansion. My gaze catches on the line of vehicles already parked there—four identical limousines. How had I never noticed them before? I suppose I'd never had a reason to concern myself with my neighbor's comings and goings until this incessant noise started.

Athena Stavros moved in about fifteen months ago, taking the last and by far the biggest mansion on this stretch of The Ridges where her property backs up against the desert. With no neighbors on her other side, she probably has no idea the sound carries this far. I vaguely remember some construction noise when she first moved in, but nothing since. Then again, what do I know about the daily rhythms of this neighborhood? I'm rarely home before midnight, and when I am, I'm locked in my office.

The owner herself steps out, and for a moment, I'm struck by the scene's cinematic quality. Ms. Stavros could have walked straight off a mob movie set—the white jump-suit with open back, dark hair falling in waves past her shoulders, even a white, wide-brimmed hat tilted at just the right angle to shadow her face. She moves with the kind of fluid confidence that comes from knowing you own not just the ground you walk on, but the whole damn block. Aren't all casino owners just glamorous crooks? There's something almost predatory about her movements, like a panther in silk, that makes my legal instincts prickle.

Before I can stop myself, I push open the window. "Ms. Stavros!" My voice carries across the lawn between our houses. "I'm sorry, but the music—"

She looks up, startled. "Ms. Walsh?" A pause, then understanding crosses her features. "Oh God, can you hear that? I'm so sorry. I recently had a new sound system installed. I had no idea you could hear that."

"I can only hear the bass, but it's rather...persistent," I say.

"I truly apologize. Just give me one moment." Athena pulls her phone from her purse and taps rapidly across the screen.

The bass cuts off mid-beat, leaving a sudden vacuum of sound. I hadn't realized how much the music had been pressing against my skull until it was gone. The night settles back into desert silence—crickets, a distant coyote, the whisper of palm fronds.

"Can you still hear it?" Athena calls up.

"No, it's quiet now, thank you." The tension in my shoulders starts to unwind.

She smiles. "I feel terrible about this. Please, let me make it up to you. Perhaps dinner?"

"That's not necessary," I say quickly, too quickly maybe. "Just the quiet is enough."

She nods, accepting my refusal. "Of course, Ms. Walsh. Have a good night."

As I'm about to close my window, the crunch of tires on gravel catches my attention. Another limousine glides up the circular drive, its black paint gleaming under the security lights. It's identical to the other three already parked there—same model, same tint. Not your typical Vegas limo company's garish fleet, but something far more exclusive.

I should turn away, go to bed—God knows I need the sleep—but something holds me in place. Maybe it's the way Athena's posture changes, becomes more alert, more focused, as she turns toward the vehicle.

She bends down to speak to someone in the back seat. The exchange takes longer than a simple greeting should, and I lean forward slightly, straining to catch a glimpse of the mysterious passenger. When the door finally opens, a figure emerges—definitely a woman, given the stilettos and the flash of bare legs below a cocktail dress, but she's holding a blazer over her head, the fabric obscuring her face from my view.

Athena's hand finds the small of the woman's back, guiding her toward the house. The woman's steps are hurried, and everything about the scene screams discretion, secrecy, the kind of midnight arrival that awakens something I thought I'd buried in work and grief—curiosity about another person's life. There's something intriguing about the choreography of it all, the way Athena shields the woman from view.

Just before they reach the door, Athena glances over her shoulder, her gaze sweeping upward toward my window. I step back quickly, heart suddenly racing, feeling like I've been caught prying into something I shouldn't have seen. My bare feet catch on the rug as I retreat, and I nearly stumble in my haste to get out of sight. By the time I've turned off the lights and dare another peek, they've disappeared inside, leaving only the line of luxury vehicles as evidence that anything unusual is happening.

I close my window, oddly unsettled. Not because I care about what's happening next door but because I was caught watching. That's not me. I don't peer through windows like some bored housewife seeking suburban drama. I don't spy on neighbors. I certainly don't stand in my office in pajamas gawking at midnight arrivals.

My hand lingers on the window latch, and I still feel it —that flutter of interest, of engagement with the world beyond my fortress. It's small, barely a ripple in the numbness I've cultivated, but it's there. Like a muscle twitching after too long in one position, almost painful in its awakening. I'm not sure if that's progress or trouble.

FOUR

ATHENA

The sunrise paints the desert mountains gold as I complete my daily swim. Fifty laps, no more, no less. Discipline is everything. The pool stretches along the eastern edge of my property, its infinity edge blending into the valley below. From here, I can see the top floor of my neighbor's house. She's up early for a Sunday. Ruby Walsh never sleeps, it seems, but then neither do I. A coffee cup sits on a table behind the railing of her sweeping balcony and the door is wide open. She comes out sometimes, in the darkest part of night, and just sits there.

Two weeks have passed since our exchange about the music, and she hasn't raised the issue again. I take that as confirmation that my sound engineer's adjustments have contained the bass to acceptable levels. Still, that brief interaction changed something. Ruby Walsh is no longer just the shadow next door. She's become real to me.

I've been drawn to the security feed more often than I should be. That precious half hour when I know she'll be home, perched behind her desk like a solitary queen in her tower. My underground club demands attention, but increasingly, I catch myself watching Ruby instead. There's nothing dramatic to see; she simply works, occasionally stands to pace. Yet something about her solitude calls to me. The way she holds herself, straight-backed and controlled, as if relaxing might let something dangerous slip through. Like someone who's forgotten how to exist without purpose.

Water streams down my skin as I rise from the pool, the desert air already warming despite the early hour. I catch my reflection in the glass walls of the pool house—olive skin wrapped in a white swimsuit, dark hair slicked back, the significant scar on my shoulder from a childhood fall in Santorini. Pappoús always said I was too wild, too determined to keep up with the boys diving from the cliffs.

Wrapping a fluffy white robe around my damp skin, I head barefoot across the travertine tiles toward the kitchen. The space is all clean lines, white marble countertops and professional-grade stainless steel appliances.

Zeus, my Savannah cat, follows me, his spotted coat gleaming as he winds around my legs, leaving a trail of muddy paw prints on the floor. I've lost count of how many times I've worried about him becoming prey to the desert's coyotes, but I couldn't bear to keep him confined indoors. Luckily, he's proven himself surprisingly content to stay within the estate's boundaries, spending his days hunting birds in the yard and lounging in sunny spots by the pool.

I scoop Zeus into my arms with a small grunt—all twenty pounds of him, solid muscle beneath that luxurious coat. He's far larger than a typical house cat and could easily be mistaken for a leopard. Despite his size, I cradle him like a kitten, ignoring his initial squirm of protest. He settles against my chest after a moment, a deep purr rumbling through his powerful body. Such a proud creature, refusing attention from anyone else—my staff have learned the hard way not to attempt to pet him. Even Asha, my housekeeper, who feeds him every morning, receives nothing more than an imperious stare when she sets down his bowl.

"You've been hunting again, haven't you?" I murmur, noticing a smudge of blood on his paw. His ears twitch at my voice, but his eyes remain half-closed in contentment. My arms start to tire, but I hold him anyway. Like me, he walks a line between civilization and wildness, and I see myself in his refusal to be tamed, his selective affections, his ruthless efficiency when hunting.

Zeus stretches in my arms, his considerable weight shifting as his claws extend briefly before retracting—a gentle reminder of the weapons he carries. Then he head-butts my chin, a rare display of affection that makes my heart swell.

"All right, little kitty-cat," I say, releasing him as he begins to squirm again. He lands gracefully on the floor despite his size, immediately restoring his dignity with a thorough grooming session. The moment of tenderness is over—we both have reputations to maintain, after all.

Asha looks up from the poached eggs she's placing atop artisanal sourdough toast. "Good morning, Ms. Stavros." The scent of freshly ground coffee fills the air as the espresso machine hisses. She's been with me since I moved in, arriving each morning like clockwork to prepare breakfast and maintain the upstairs portion of the house. She's efficient, professional, and most importantly, uninterested in anything beyond her designated domain. I watch as she slices an avocado, arranging it in a fan pattern beside the toast. The woman has an artist's eye for presentation.

"Good morning, Asha," I say, settling at the kitchen island. "How are you?"

"Very well, thank you. It's a beautiful day." Her reply, like every morning, is polite and minimal. Our exchanges rarely extend beyond these few pleasantries, and that suits us both.

I appreciate the simple luxury of a quiet Sunday morning. It's the one day I allow myself to move slower, to savor the ritual of breakfast rather than consuming it while in a meeting. A bowl of Greek yogurt sits beside my plate, topped with fresh berries and honey, and next to it is a newspaper.

Zeus jumps onto the counter, earning a disapproving look from Asha that he completely ignores. He's convinced that the rules of mere mortals don't apply to him. I scratch behind his ears as he investigates my breakfast, his tail twitching with interest at the eggs. "Not for you, little prince," I murmur in Greek, the endearment feeling more natural in my mother tongue.

My phone buzzes with the morning report—a simple summary from my "basement manager" as I call him. Thirty guests, no incidents, all departures completed by four a.m. I wasn't there to oversee things myself last night— a high roller at the Olympus had required my personal attention, dropping close to eight figures at the baccarat tables. These whales expect the owner to wine and dine them, to make them feel special. It's all part of the game.

I trust my basement team implicitly. The drivers, waiters, bartenders, fixers, and cleaning staff are handpicked not just for their skills but for their ability to be invisible, to see everything and remember nothing. I pay them a ridiculous fee, ensuring their loyalty.

I finish half of my breakfast, more interested in the coffee than the food. "Thank you, Asha," I say, standing. "I'll take my coffee outside."

Zeus follows me to the poolside and I see Ruby is now sitting on her balcony, coffee cup in hand. She quickly looks away when she notices me watching, pretending to be absorbed in something on her phone. A smile tugs at my lips.

"Good morning, neighbor!" I call out, raising my coffee cup in greeting. The formality of our last interaction has left a strange taste in my mouth, and something compels me to break it.

Ruby chuckles, lifting her own cup in response. "Good morning."

I'm not sure what possesses me to say the next words—perhaps it's simply curiosity about this woman, or perhaps it's the little voice in the back of my mind, reminding me to keep potential enemies close. "Care to join me for a coffee by the pool?"

Even from this distance, I can see how the invitation startles her. She shifts uncomfortably, gripping the balcony railing. "Oh, I actually have to head to the office..."

"On a Sunday?" I challenge. "Come on, it's just a coffee. Twenty minutes won't make a difference."

Ruby raises herself and stares down at me for a moment. Finally, her shoulders relax slightly. "Okay," she calls back, still with a hint of hesitation in her voice. "I could use another cup before I head out."

FIVE

RUBY

The guarded gates swing open at my approach, revealing a winding driveway bordered by date palms. Water dances in a travertine fountain, its soft music mingling with birdsong, while desert gardens bloom in defiance of the harsh climate —purple sage, golden lantana, and blood-red bougainvillea cascading over stone walls. The estate speaks of quiet wealth. It's not flashy, simply beautiful in every detail.

I sit in my Tesla for a moment and stare at the line of black limousines. My practical black car looks plebeian next to them, and the absurdity of driving here isn't lost on me. It can't be more than two hundred yards between our front doors, but walking in heels under the desert sun and arriving at my neighbor's disheveled before heading to the office sweaty is not an option.

Athena meets me at the door, and I'm struck by the casualness of her appearance up close—white robe, damp hair, bare feet. The robe gapes as she moves, revealing a white swimsuit underneath. The white's fitting—there's something almost mythological about her. It also makes me feel terribly overdressed.

"Thank you for the invitation, Ms. Stavros," I say. "That's very kind of you."

She laughs and steps back to let me in. "Please, call me Athena. And you're Ruby, right?"

The use of my first name gives me a bit of a jolt. I haven't heard anyone apart from my parents say it in a while. Ms. Walsh, sure. But Ruby?

"I looked you up," she admits, leading me through her house toward the pool. "I like to know who lives next door. Your firm's reputation precedes you."

The poolside setup is stunning—white loungers, gauzy curtains drifting in the breeze, the infinity edge of the pool overlooking the valley. Her housekeeper—Asha, I hear Athena call her—appears with a tray of coffee and dates. A massive cat, bigger than any house cat I've ever seen, jumps onto the chair next to Athena and fixes me with an imperious stare.

A laugh escapes me before I can stop it. "This feels a bit surreal," I say, shaking my head in amusement. "You're casually sitting here, flanked by a...what is it? It looks dangerous."

"This is Zeus," Athena says, scratching behind the cat's ears. "And yes, he can be tricky, so I wouldn't try to pet him if I were you. He's...selective with his affections."

"Noted." I'm happy to keep my distance. The cat's gaze is unnerving, too intelligent by half.

"Do you always work on Sundays?" she asks, leaning back in her chair. The robe slips slightly, revealing her cleavage. I force myself to look away.

"We're particularly busy right now—there's a major acquisition in process." I feel like I'm reading from a script. When was the last time I made small talk? Really talked to anyone outside of work? "But you must be busy too," I say. "I see you come home late most nights."

Athena waves a hand. "Yes, I work hard. I'm very disciplined, but the Olympus largely runs itself these days. I make appearances, charm the high rollers, play my part as the mysterious Greek owner." She chuckles and rolls her eyes. "It adds to the allure, apparently."

"Of course. That makes sense." I hesitate, coffee cup halfway to my lips. The question has been nagging at me for weeks. "Speaking of allure...those are some impressive vehicles in your driveway."

"The limousines?" Athena's smile doesn't waver. "They're for my guests. I like to entertain."

Something in her tone suggests that's all the answer I'm going to get, but it only feeds my curiosity. What kind of guests need identical black limousines and a protective detail?

"So you work hard," I venture, watching her stroke Zeus. "And play harder. Quite the social butterfly."

Athena tilts her head, regarding me over the rim of her coffee cup. Her dark eyes hold mine a beat too long. "And you're the opposite, aren't you?" Her voice drops lower. "All work and no play."

The way she says it startles me—not accusatory but weighted, almost flirtatious. That's when I see it. The careful tilt of her head, the measured fall of silk against skin, how she's positioned herself to command my full attention while maintaining just enough distance to make me lean in. She radiates a familiar energy I haven't let myself notice since Claire, that particular frequency of attraction. This woman is so gay.

"True. I don't have time to play." I set down my coffee cup.

My hand trembles slightly, and I catch Athena tracking the movement. Am I intimidated by her? That would be a first. In my line of work, I face down Fortune 500 CEOs and ruthless corporate raiders without blinking. But something about her steady gaze strips away my usual certainty. "So, you're Greek?" I ask, steering the conversation into safer waters.

"Yes. My family's originally from Athens, but my mother and sister live in Santorini these days." Her voice softens when she mentions her family, a rare crack in her polished veneer. "Greece is beautiful. Have you been?"

"No. I've traveled around Europe, but never made it to Greece." I study her deliberately, taking in the way she holds herself, how she seems to consider each word before speaking. If she's assessing me, I want her to know I'm equally observant. As a lawyer, reading people is my specialty, but I've rarely met someone who matches me at this game. "Do you go back often?"

"Once or twice a year. Not as often as I'd like." Athena pauses. "And where are you from? Everyone in Vegas seems to be imported."

"Something tells me you already know," I counter. "You said you like to know who lives next door."

"Touché." Athena shrugs like she's been caught but doesn't care. "Of course I know. You're originally from San Francisco, Berkeley Law. You moved to Vegas five years ago, your firm was founded here." She hesitates, her expression softening. "With your wife Claire Walsh, who tragically passed away two years ago in a car accident on the 215." She leans in a little. "I'm very sorry for your loss."

The facts of my life, laid out so precisely, leave me raw. Claire's name in a stranger's mouth feels wrong, and hearing it spoken aloud creates a strange ache—like pressing on a bruise to remember it's there.

"You're thorough," I manage, aiming for professional detachment. "I suppose everything's public record these days."

"Not everything," Athena says quietly. I glimpse something behind her eyes—a flicker of recognition, perhaps. Or understanding. Then it's gone, replaced by that enigmatic smile. "More coffee?"

I get to my feet, smoothing down my skirt. "No, I should head to the office. Thank you for the coffee."

"I hope I haven't made you uncomfortable by mentioning..." Athena trails off as she rises. "You know..."

"Not at all." The lie comes easily. "You should come over for coffee sometime. My turn to host." I don't mean it; it's social autopilot taking over. I'm already backing away, eager to escape. Maybe it's hearing Claire's name, or maybe it's the way Athena seems to read me like one of my contracts. Or perhaps it's Zeus, watching me retreat with those ancient, knowing eyes.

I make it to my car in record time, the morning heat already rising from the driveway in waves. In my rearview mirror, I catch a final glimpse of Athena standing in her doorway, one hand resting on Zeus's head, both of them watching me leave with the same inscrutable expression.

SIX
ATHENA

The slot machines sing their siren song through the vast expanse of the Olympus casino floor. I adjust my white wide-brimmed hat as I begin my nightly rounds. My white suit—Valentino—draws eyes as I move through the space. Mark, my head of operations, falls into step beside me, his tablet open to tonight's numbers.

He hasn't changed out of his usual black since he started working for me, as if he's permanently in mourning for fun. "Food and beverage revenue's up twelve percent from last week," he says, voice low. "The new Greek street food court is drawing crowds."

I pause to watch an elderly woman feed quarters into a Zeus-themed slot machine, her rhinestone-covered jacket catching the pulsing lights. The massive LED screen above shows the king of gods hurling animated lightning bolts with each spin. She doesn't notice me, too focused on her ritual—spin, sip of Diet Coke, cigarette, adjust her oxygen tank, repeat.

"Mrs. Ho is back," Mark notes, nodding toward the high-limit slots area. "Third time this week."

I see her, perched on a leather stool in front of a $500-minimum machine, immaculately coiffed. She catches my eye and gives a friendly nod. We've spoken several times in the high-limit lounge, usually about her grandchildren in Vancouver and her love of classical music.

We pass the Olympian Garden, where a thirty-foot sculpture of Athena rises from a cascading fountain. Her spear points toward the high-roller rooms, a subtle suggestion to the wandering masses. The water features create a constant white noise that helps mask the casino sounds, making conversation more intimate. Every detail is considered, down to the specific angle of the goddess's gaze.

"The Parthenon Restaurant is fully booked through next month," Mark continues as we climb the marble stairs to the mezzanine level. "That Michelin star really stirred things up. Chef Dimitris is asking for another sous chef."

I pause at the railing, surveying my domain. From here, the layout reveals itself—the flow of foot traffic, the strategic placement of bars and restaurants, the ways we guide players toward higher-stakes games, all paths eventually leading to more opportunities to spend money.

"Give him whatever he needs," I say. "The Parthenon is our crown jewel." The restaurant sits at the top of the hotel tower, its glass walls offering panoramic views of the Strip. The menu is a modern interpretation of Greek cuisine—items supposedly favored by gods and heroes, each dish coming with its own mythology. It's theatrical, certainly, but Vegas demands spectacle.

We pass through the Agora, our mid-level shopping arcade designed to mimic an ancient Greek marketplace. The spaces between luxury boutiques feature street performers—a woman painted gold poses as a living statue of Aphrodite, a fire-breather dressed as Prometheus entertains a crowd of tourists. The scent of souvlaki and fresh pita drifts from the street food court, where locals and tourists alike queue for authentic Greek food at reasonable prices. I insisted on keeping those prices low so everyone can have a small taste of real Greece amid the glamour.

"Security flagged a potential card counter at table twelve," Mark says as we approach the main gaming floor. "Robert's watching him."

I spot Robert, our head of security, lingering near the suspect's table. He catches my eye and gives an imperceptible nod. We don't rough up card counters—that's a myth. We simply make them uncomfortable enough to leave on their own, usually by offering them a free room upgrade and a personal escort to their new accommodations. Most get the message, especially if it's delivered by four beefy security guards.

A commotion draws my attention to the craps table, where a man in an expensive but rumpled suit is celebrating a winning streak. I recognize him—a tech CEO whose company is about to go public. He's been here three nights in a row, his bets getting progressively larger. The cocktail waitress hovers nearby, keeping his glass full with our best Scotch.

"Mark, make sure Mr. Harrison there gets an invitation to the Pantheon Room," I murmur. The Pantheon is our most exclusive gaming space, accessible only by personal invitation. The minimum bet is $100,000, but more importantly, it's where the real business happens. Many a merger has been negotiated over its tables. I've built my empire not just on games of chance, but on the whispered conversations and handshake deals that happen in that room—intelligence that proves invaluable for both my casino operations and my other, more discreet venture in my basement.

We take the private elevator to the Pantheon level, where the air is literally different—we pipe in a custom fragrance, a subtle blend of leather and cedar with notes of vanilla. The carpet is thick enough to swallow the sound of footsteps, and the lighting is specifically designed to flatter aging skin.

A Saudi prince looks up from his private blackjack table as we pass. "Ah, Ms. Stavros! Join us for a hand?"

I pause, letting my hand rest on the back of his chair. "Your Highness, you know better than to invite the house to play. But..." I lean in conspiratorially, "I hear the Poseidon Suite has an excellent view of tonight's fountain show. I'll make sure it's free should you choose to spend the night."

He laughs, appreciating the deflection. The Poseidon is the most popular suite in the house, with its private infinity pool overlooking the Strip. The art of running a casino is knowing when to press and when to retreat, when to comp a room and when to let them pay full price.

Mark and I complete our circuit through the high-limit areas and emerge into the hotel's grand lobby. The ceiling soars fifty feet overhead, covered in a mosaic depicting scenes from Greek mythology. During the day, natural light streams through skylights, making the gold tiles shimmer. At night, carefully placed spotlights create the same effect.

"The nightclub numbers are holding steady," Mark says, scrolling through his tablet. "Though the Margot is trying to poach our DJ."

"Double his contract," I reply automatically. "And give him a suite. The last thing we need is talent drain right before high season."

We head to the Elysian Pool, where private cabanas rent for thousands per day during peak season. Even at this hour, it looks to be full—beautiful people in expensive swimwear lounging on daybeds, ordering bottles of champagne, pretending the night will never end.

Two women catch my eye, and they lean in close to whisper when they spot me. *Club members.* They don't acknowledge me; we never acknowledge each other in public.

Mark and I end our rounds at my private elevator, which takes me back to my office. "One more thing," Mark says, hesitating. "The gaming commission is asking questions about our win rates. They're two percent higher than industry standard."

I remove my hat and ruffle a hand through my hair. "I suppose a dinner with Commissioner Jenkins will solve that problem. His wife still volunteers at that children's hospital we support, right? Perhaps it's time for another donation."

Mark nods, already typing. "I'll ask Maria to set it up." He knows how this works—we're not doing anything illegal, just operating more efficiently than our competitors. But efficiency makes people nervous, especially in Vegas.

"Oh, and Mark?" I add as the elevator doors open. "While you're there, will you ask Maria to send some of that street food up to my office? Souvlaki, extra tzatziki."

He smiles—a rare sight. "Sure. Extra tzatziki."

The elevator rises, and I watch the numbers climb. Below me, three thousand people are winning and losing, celebrating and despairing. Up there in my office, I feel like Zeus himself, watching the mortals at play. Though lately, my attention has been drawn to a different kind of observation—a single window in a mansion in The Ridges, where another woman sits alone.

SEVEN

RUBY

The clock on my laptop read 9:47 p.m. when I allowed myself to pack up at the office. Miranda, my paralegal, nearly choked on her coffee when I announced I was heading home "early." Her surprise was warranted—I haven't left this early in months, maybe years. The truth is, I've been distracted for weeks, my mind wandering to the strange parade of limousines outside Athena's house. They were there before, I suppose, but I never really noticed them until I complained about the music. Now it's all I can think about. The precision of it all fascinates me—same time, same vehicles, and for what purpose?

I sit in my home office, reviewing merger documents while stealing glances at the circular drive next door through my window. The papers are spread across my desk in a display of industriousness, Post-its marking key sections that need attention. A half-written brief sits abandoned on my second monitor, cursor blinking.

The first limousine arrived ten minutes ago and a woman emerged, her face obscured by an umbrella wielded by the driver, which he handed off to a security guard who appeared from the house. The angle of the umbrella, the fluid transition from car to doorway—it spoke of practice and purpose, and it felt shady.

I take a sip of freshly brewed coffee—Ethiopian blend, Claire's favorite. The familiar taste grounds me as I try to focus on the contract before me, its margins already bleeding red with my annotations. But then it happens. Another limousine, identical to the first, gliding up the drive.

"Seriously, Ruby?" I mutter to myself, but I get up to peer out the window anyway.

Four more vehicles arrive in quick succession, and each arrival follows the same routine—some women shield themselves with drivers' umbrellas, while others clutch blazers or pashminas over their heads. I catch glimpses of their attire: tailored suits and cocktail dresses. Why are these women trying so hard not to be seen?

That's when it hits me, the realization making me step back from the window, cheeks flushing with embarrassment. The property backs up against desert wilderness, a vast expanse of nothing. There's just my house. My window, positioned to overlook Athena's entrance like a theater box at the opera. The umbrellas aren't for general privacy—they're specifically blocking *my* view.

My stomach twists. How long has Athena known I've been watching? Is that why she invited me for coffee that morning? To assess the nosy neighbor, figure out if I was a threat to whatever's happening in that house? The thought makes me feel simultaneously foolish and increasingly intrigued.

Athena appears in her doorway, greeting another arrival. She's wearing one of her signature white suits, immaculate as always, her wide-brimmed white hat tilted.

Even from this distance, she emanates that particular energy—part mob boss, part Greek goddess. She turns, suddenly, and looks directly up at my window.

Fuck. My heart jumps into my throat, pounding against my ribs like it's trying to escape. Do I duck away like a guilty neighbor caught peeping? Wave casually as if I just happened to be standing here, admiring the sunset two hours after it disappeared? Neither option seems particularly dignified.

Before I can decide, Athena raises her hand in greeting. Then she takes a few steps into her driveway, still looking up at me while she slides her hands into her pockets. Her posture suggests she's waiting for something, expecting a response, and now I feel like I'm the one being watched.

I swallow hard and push open my window. The desert air rushes in, carrying the scent of the Mojave at night.

"Good evening, Ruby," she calls up. "How about that coffee you promised me?"

My mouth goes dry. "You have company," I call back, gesturing vaguely at her house.

She shakes her head. "They'll be fine without me for a while. Let's have a coffee." Her tone leaves no room for negotiation. A pause, then, "Though perhaps something stronger might be better at this hour? I have an excellent bottle of Assyrtiko."

I glance at my desk, at the pile of work. My coffee cup still steams, sending tendrils of aromatic mist into the air. "It's a bit late for—"

"For coffee, yes," she interrupts. "But not for a nightcap. And we should talk, don't you think?"

There it is. The conversation I've been dreading. The "mind your own business" talk that I absolutely deserve. Yet her tone doesn't match the rebuke I'm expecting. She sounds almost...amused. Playful, even.

"Give me ten minutes?" I reply, knowing I can't get out of this.

"Excellent." She smiles and it feels dangerous. She's invited herself over and I clearly have no say in the matter. "I'll bring a bottle."

I close the window and lean against the wall, my heart still pounding hard. What am I doing? I should definitely not be having late-night drinks with my mysteriously magnetic neighbor who gets up to God knows what kind of shady business next door.

Everyone in Vegas knows about casino bosses—they operate in that gray space between legitimate business and something darker. They have their own rules, their own ways of handling problems. And I've just agreed to drinks with one who's caught me spying on her business. The smart move would be to say I've changed my mind, cite work obligations. But there's something in the way she looked at me, something that suggests saying no isn't really an option anymore.

I swap my suit for black silk loungewear—still elegant but less formal. In the bathroom mirror, I pause to run a brush through my hair and touch up my lipstick. The woman staring back at me looks uncertain, and I don't like that.

The gate buzzes exactly ten minutes later. I have to admire her timing. Athena steps into my foyer like she owns it, her presence immediately filling the space.

"I brought reinforcements," she says, holding up two bottles, not one. A white leather carryall is slung over her arm. "Sometimes conversations require options."

I lead her to my living room, acutely aware that I

haven't entertained anyone here since...well... The space feels foreign, as I never come here, struggling to face the furniture and the abstract paintings Claire and I chose together, the photographs of us, and the grand piano I haven't touched in two years.

"Lovely home," Athena says, but she's not looking at the room. She's watching me, those dark eyes missing nothing.

"Thank you. Shall we sit?" I gesture to the sofa, and she settles onto it, crossing her legs at the ankles. She sets both bottles on the coffee table—the promised Assyrtiko and an expensive Scotch.

"Options," she says again. "Wine for pleasantries, Scotch for truth."

"And which are we having tonight?" I ask, dreading the answer.

She removes her hat, placing it beside the bottles. "That," she says, her lips curving into that enigmatic smile, "is entirely up to you."

EIGHT
ATHENA

Ruby sets down two crystal tumblers. She's changed into an elegant black two-piece and her auburn hair falls loose around her shoulders now, softening the sharp angles of her face. She's beautiful—all controlled grace and barely contained nerves, like a caged wildcat pacing behind glass.

"Scotch," she says, not quite meeting my eyes. I know she doesn't sleep much—the security feeds don't lie—so I don't feel guilty about forcing this late-night meeting. Some conversations require darkness to flourish. "I'll get some water too. Would you like ice with your Scotch?"

"No, thank you. I like it neat," I reply.

While she disappears into the kitchen, I take in the living room. Everything seems staged like a museum exhibit of a life no longer being lived. The grand piano's lid is closed, its surface unmarred by fingerprints. The cushions on the sofa are perfectly arranged, corners crisp as if they've never been disturbed. There are no magazines, no coffee table books, no signs of casual occupation. Even the remote control sits exactly parallel to the edge of the side table. The only personal touch is a photograph of

Ruby and a pretty blonde, presumably her late wife. My chest tightens with unexpected sympathy, but I push it aside.

Ruby returns, and I pour us each a generous measure of Macallan 25. "To neighbors," I say, raising my glass.

"To neighbors," she echoes, eyeing me warily. She takes a sip, then another, longer this time. *Dutch courage.* "I assume you're here about what I might or might not have noticed next door since my office overlooks your driveway." Her voice is steady despite her obvious discomfort. "I can assure you, I have no interest in your business affairs."

"Yet it's caught your attention, hasn't it?" I lean forward, resting my elbows on my knees. "You've been watching. Actively watching."

Ruby's shoulders straighten, her lawyer persona emerging. "Look. I don't know what you want from me. If you're asking for discretion, you have it. For all I know, you just like to party."

"But you know it's more than that." I study her while the Scotch burns pleasantly, loosening my tongue. "You're intrigued."

A flush creeps up her neck, but she doesn't deny it. *Interesting.*

"I could show you," I say, carefully watching her reaction. "I'd rather include you than have you wondering. That could become...problematic."

Her brow furrows. "Show me?"

Instead of answering, I reach into my bag and withdraw a folder. "But before we go there, you'll need to sign this."

Ruby takes the folder, her curiosity clearly piqued. Inside is my standard non-disclosure agreement—thirty pages of ironclad legal language that would make most corporate lawyers weep. It includes clauses about digital surveillance, social media blackouts, and financial penalties that could bankrupt a small nation.

She skims through it and frowns. "This is ridiculous. A hundred thousand dollars to sign up? The liability clauses alone are broader than anything I've seen in international merger agreements. And this section about 'activities witnessed or participated in' is deliberately vague to the point of absurdity." Her expression hardens as she continues reading. "These provisions—they're the kind you'd need if you were protecting something criminal. Something that could destroy lives if it came to light, or send you to prison." She sets the NDA down like it might bite her. "I want no part of this."

"I thought you might say that. After all, you are one of the top lawyers in this country," I say. "But I can assure you, nothing criminal happens on my turf. Pleasure? Yes, in many forms. Pain? Perhaps, but only when desired." I lean forward, holding her gaze. "What I offer is freedom, Ruby. The freedom to explore, to feel, to be someone else entirely for a few precious hours. We all need to escape sometimes. Even you. Especially you."

Ruby shakes her head and shoots me an incredulous look. Gone are the nerves; she's offended, angry. "You don't know what I need. And just because you 'assure' me of something doesn't mean I should take your word for it. Do you think I'm stupid? I don't know you," she counters. "I've seen enough criminal enterprises disguised as entertainment to last a lifetime."

"Very well." I take the folder and slide it back into my bag. I'd anticipated this reaction, and that's fine. The seed is planted. Curiosity will do the rest. "Then we'll leave it at that. Whatever happens on my property is my business, and you can keep watching from your window, wondering. But when you change your mind—and you will—you know where to find me."

Her eyes narrow at that, but I see the spark of interest there too. She's hooked, despite her better judgment. "You're clearly used to getting what you want," she says. "But I won't change my mind." She looks me over, then lets out a sharp laugh. "And a hundred thousand dollars? For a membership fee to something I know nothing about?" Another laugh escapes her, this one genuinely amused. "Oh, my God. This is absurd. You're asking me to pay a fortune and sign away my rights without even telling me what I'm getting into. I doubt your 'club' or whatever it is, is even registered."

"You're right," I say. "It's not registered. The NDA refers to my personal home only. And I'm not doing this for money. I don't even make a profit." It's the truth—the yearly membership fees barely cover expenses. The fleet of limousines, the vetted drivers, the security team that undergoes thorough background checks, the staff who maintain absolute discretion, the free food and exclusive beverages—it all adds up. But this was never about money. I have enough of that from the Olympus. This is about something else entirely, something I recognize in the women who come to me, something I see in Ruby's eyes even as she protests.

"Naturally," she says, her voice dripping with cynicism. "You're doing it for the greater good." She sets down her glass. "So now that we've established I'm not signing your NDA or giving you a hundred thousand dollars, what happens? Someone shows up to threaten me into silence? Are you going to have me shadowed? Intimidate me until I move home?"

Now it's my turn to laugh. "I'm not sure what kind of person you think I am, but as I said, I'm not a criminal." I take another sip of Scotch. "Nothing will happen. We'll finish our drinks, and you're always welcome to drop by for coffee or something stronger." I pause deliberately. "Monday to Wednesday."

I watch Ruby process this, her mind visibly churning behind those sharp green eyes. She's looking for the trap, the hidden threat, weighing my words against her instincts.

"So that's it, then?" she says finally.

I nod. "That's it. This conversation never happened." I study her face in the dim light, noting the shadows under her eyes, the tension in her jaw. "But I want to ask you something."

She tilts her head slightly, cautious. "What?"

"When was the last time you let yourself feel anything?" I suspect the question lands like a stone in still water because Ruby stares back at me while her fingers tighten around her glass until her knuckles turn white.

I down my whiskey and rise to my feet. "I'll see you around, neighbor."

"Wait," she calls as I reach the door, her voice carrying a note of uncertainty. "Your wine, your whiskey..." She gestures at the bottles, like she needs something tangible to focus on.

"Keep them." I turn in the doorway, offering her a smile that I know will haunt her thoughts. "I have plenty. Think of them as a standing invitation." I pause, letting my hand rest on the doorframe. "For whenever you're ready to stop watching and start living."

NINE
RUBY

The conference room on the fortieth floor feels like a pressure cooker. Eight lawyers, three CEOs, and enough coffee cups to build a fortress. Miranda, my lead paralegal, sits to my left while Tom Chen from our corporate team is on my right. The downtown lights glitter through the floor-to-ceiling windows, but none of us have looked outside in hours.

"The payment terms aren't clear enough," David Morton, opposing counsel, says for the third time. He's been nitpicking all afternoon, his tie askew, a coffee stain on his sleeve. Amateur hour. "My client needs—"

"Your client needs to stop wasting everyone's time," I cut in. "The terms are crystal clear. Full payment upon closing, with forty million held in reserve for three years. That's more than generous." I slide a document across the table. "Here's the breakdown in simple English, since the legal version seems to be giving you trouble."

Mark Reynolds, the selling CEO, stops drumming his fingers. He's been here since nine a.m., watching his one-hundred-eighty-million-dollar deal come down to these final hours. We all know his tech is worth almost twice that—it's why my client, James Wilson, wants this deal so badly.

"Ruby," Morton starts, using my first name like we're buddies. "If we could just—"

"We're done negotiating." I lean forward, palms flat on the table. "Your client wants to sell. My client wants to buy. The terms are fair, the protections are solid, and you've run out of reasons to stall. So either we sign now, or we walk." I hold Reynolds's gaze. "And we both know you don't want us to walk."

Miranda slides the signature pages across without being asked. We're a well-oiled machine, and she knows my moves before I make them.

The room goes quiet. Morton whispers to his client, who nods. I've won. Wilson has won.

The next hour dissolves into signatures and handshakes. I watch Reynolds sign away his company, and when the last page is initialed, champagne is brought in.

I should feel something. Smug satisfaction at least. Seven months of work, the kind of deal that makes careers. Any other lawyer would be preening right now, mentally composing their LinkedIn post. But I feel nothing. Just flat. Always flat.

"Congratulations, everyone," I say, standing. It's only seven p.m.—early for me. The clients are planning their celebration at the Olympus as I start gathering my files, thinking about the Morrison deal waiting on my desk.

Miranda touches my arm. "Don't even think about going back to your office," she says. "You've been running on empty for months. Go home."

"I can't. I just need to review—"

"The Morrison deal can wait." She starts packing my briefcase herself. "Everything's filed, the press release is ready, and you have seven days of mandatory vacation starting now."

I want to argue, but exhaustion hits me like a truck. When did I last sleep more than four hours? Going home is the last thing I want, but Miranda's right. I'm no good to anyone if I crash.

"Fine," I concede, letting her hand me my coat. "But I'm taking the Morrison files—"

"No, you're not." She physically blocks my path to my office. "Seven days, Ruby. Doctor's orders." She means her own orders. "The firm won't collapse without you for a week."

The elevator ride down feels surreal, as it's still light outside. Seven days stretch ahead. No meetings, no deadlines, no distractions. Just me and my thoughts in that too-big house. I haven't taken time off since right after I lost Claire. Her post still sits unopened in the kitchen. Her gardening magazines still arrive every month. I should cancel the subscriptions.

There are a million things I need to do. Her clothes still hang in the closet, gathering dust. Her jewelry box sits untouched on the dresser, including the sapphire ring from her grandmother that she wanted her niece to have. I never called her niece about that. Her phone line is still active—I keep paying the bill in case I ever want to listen to her voicemail, yet I never do because it's too painful.

The life insurance payout sits in a separate account I haven't looked at. The thank-you cards for the funeral flowers were never sent. Her BMW is in the garage, registration renewal notices piling up. Her laptop holds thousands of photos I haven't backed up, emails I haven't archived.

The meditation app she used still charges my credit

card monthly and her standing hair appointment shows up on my calendar every six weeks like a ghost.

Maybe I should hire someone to handle it all—a personal assistant who can cancel subscriptions, make calls, pack up clothes for donation. Someone who can touch her things without feeling like they're dismantling a life. Someone who won't break down at the sight of her hand-writing on Post-it notes, who won't recognize her scent still clinging to clothes, who won't remember the stories behind every piece of jewelry and book and photograph.

"Ruby?" Wilson's voice breaks through my spiral. We're in the lobby now, the security guard—whatever his name is —nodding goodnight. "Are you sure you don't want to join us at the Olympus?"

I should say no. I never socialize with clients. It's always been one of my rules, even before I became a recluse—keep business and pleasure separate. But the thought of going home to those tasks...

"Actually," I hear myself say, "one drink sounds good."

"Excellent!" Wilson claps his hands. He's glowing like the cat who got the cream, and I have no doubt he's planned a long night with copious amounts of champagne.

I step into the warm evening air, letting the desert breeze carry away thoughts of insurance policies, voicemail messages, and untouched clothes. For tonight at least, I'll pretend to be someone else—someone who celebrates wins, who drinks with clients.

"My car's here," Wilson adds. "I have a reservation at the Parthenon."

The Parthenon. Of course. The Michelin-starred restaurant in the Olympus. I haven't been since it opened, and I wonder if Athena will be there tonight. The thought sends an unexpected flutter through my stomach. Our last conversation keeps playing over and over in my mind. Part of me wants to talk to her, accept that standing invitation for coffee or something stronger. There's unfinished business between us, a door left ajar, and that bothers me.

But what would I even say? Or ask? It's not like I'll get answers unless I sign that joke of an NDA and give her a fortune.

No. Better to keep my distance.

I slide into the leather back seat of the SUV and close my eyes for a beat, letting the hum of the engine wash over me. Seven days of freedom has never felt so much like a prison sentence. I desperately need a stiff drink.

TEN

ATHENA

I pause at the entrance of the Parthenon, smoothing down my white palazzo pants—Valentino, fresh from Paris. The maître d' nods in deference—no reservation needed when you own the place. Behind him, the dining room hums with the particular energy of success and celebration over wagyu beef and hundred-dollar glasses of wine.

My dinner companion, a gaming commissioner, has just canceled. His text suggests traffic on the Strip, but I know he's probably at the Bellagio, trying to squeeze concessions out of my competitors. Let them have their little victories. I own the sky up here.

A familiar voice cuts through the ambient noise of clinking glasses and murmured conversations. I turn and have to do a double take. It's really her—Ruby Walsh, looking decidedly less controlled than last time I saw her. She's sitting with four men in suits, an impressive wine bottle on their table. Her cheeks are flushed, auburn hair slightly disheveled. The top buttons of her silk blouse are undone, her jacket draped over her lap rather than the back of her chair—small details that speak volumes about her state.

I drift closer, drawn by curiosity. Ruby's head is thrown back in laughter at something one of the men has said. I've never seen her laugh so freely and it transforms her face completely, erasing the perpetual furrow between her brows. Her green eyes sparkle in the golden light from the Swarovski chandeliers overhead, and for a moment, I glimpse the woman she might have been before grief carved its way into her soul.

Without thinking, I place my hand on her shoulder. She startles at the touch, twisting to look up at me. Recognition floods her face, followed quickly by something else. Embarrassment? Fear? The wine has stripped away some of her usual armor, leaving her emotions closer to the surface.

"Athena," she says, her voice slightly husky. "I didn't expect..." She trails off, clearly struggling to compose herself.

"Hey," I reply, squeezing her shoulder. I survey the table—plates scattered with the remains of Chef Dimitris's dessert specialties. "What are we celebrating?"

The man to Ruby's right straightens himself, adjusting his tie. "Ms. Stavros, right? I'm James Wilson." He flashes me a smile. "We closed the deal of a lifetime today, thanks to this brilliant woman right here." He gestures at Ruby with his wine glass, nearly sloshing the expensive vintage. "She absolutely destroyed the other side."

"Did she now?" Under my hand, I feel Ruby's muscles tense, coiled tight.

"You know each other?" Wilson asks, looking between us with poorly concealed curiosity. The other men at the table lean in, equally fascinated.

"We're neighbors," I explain, not removing my hand

from Ruby's shoulder. "Ruby and I share a fondness for late nights." I catch her eye, enjoying the way she flushes deeper at the reference. The wine has made her more transparent than usual.

I signal to the sommelier. "This calls for celebration. Send over a bottle of the Krug, Andreas. On the house." The 1988 vintage is a $2,000 gesture that will be repaid tenfold in gossip about my generosity.

"Oh, I should actually be going," Ruby says, starting to rise. Her movement is unsteady, one hand gripping the table for balance. "I have a lot to do tomorrow."

"Nonsense!" Wilson protests, reaching for her arm. She flinches almost imperceptibly at his touch. "One more drink! This is a big day, Ruby. Just one more."

I watch her falter, clearly torn between escape and social obligation. Her eyes dart around the room like a trapped animal seeking exit. Time to intervene.

"I'm heading home myself," I say smoothly. "I'd be happy to give you a lift."

She looks up at me, relief warring with suspicion in those striking green eyes. "I have my car..."

"Which you absolutely shouldn't be driving," I say firmly. "Come on, neighbor. Let me help."

After a moment's hesitation, she nods. The men protest, but I silence them with a smile and a promise of champagne. Ruby gathers her things—briefcase, phone, suit jacket.

I guide her to the private elevator, my hand on the small of her back. She's warm through the thin fabric of her silk blouse, and I can feel the slight tremor in her muscles—too much wine, too much pressure, too much of everything. The doors close and we descend in silence, the casino lights rising up around us through the glass walls.

"I'm sorry," Ruby says finally, staring straight ahead at our reflections in the polished doors. "I never drink this much. I just... I didn't want to go home."

"A casino is the worst place to be when you're feeling down," I reply, watching her in return. The elevator's soft lighting smooths the shadows under her eyes but can't hide the bone-deep exhaustion in her face. "It's designed to prey on that exact feeling. The lights, the music—it's all calibrated to keep you in a state of hopeful desperation."

She turns to me, eyes sharp despite the wine. A strand of auburn hair falls across her face, and her hand trembles as she tucks it back. "Your poison."

I shrug. "Everyone's got to make a living."

The elevator reaches the garage where my Aston Martin sits waiting, and Ruby runs her hand along its sleek body as I open the passenger door.

"Beautiful car."

"The real beauty is in its power." I press a button and the roof begins to retract. "You look like you could use some air."

"Yeah." She sinks into the leather seat with a small sigh of surrender and I get comfortable behind the wheel. Ruby tilts her head back, letting the night wash over her as we emerge from the garage.

I can't stop stealing glances at my passenger while I drive. There's something about Ruby Walsh that pulls at me, a recognition of kindred spirit perhaps. We're both women who've gone through immense heartbreak. I have learned to deal with mine; she hasn't.

The I-215 stretches before us like a ribbon of black silk, the desert wind whipping through the open roof. Ruby's hair dances in the breeze, strands of auburn catching the moonlight.

"Mmm, this is nice," she murmurs, her eyes heavy-lidded. "It's..."

I glance over as her words trail off. Her head lolls against the headrest, lips slightly parted, tension finally draining from her face as sleep claims her. The supposedly ruthless woman who secured a huge deal just hours ago now looks peaceful and sweet.

I remember what it was like, those first raw years after my loss, when sleep only came in snatched moments of exhaustion. That was a long time ago.

My car purrs as we climb into the foothills, the landscape opening up around us.

Ruby shifts in her sleep, a small sound escaping her throat. I resist the urge to touch her cheek. Instead, I focus on the road ahead, and let her rest. Some forms of escape don't require contracts or passwords. Sometimes all it takes is the night wind and an open road.

ELEVEN
RUBY

"Ruby? I need you to open the gate."

Athena's voice cuts through the fog of wine-induced sleep, and I jerk awake, momentarily disoriented. The Aston Martin idles in front of my driveway. Heat rushes to my face as I realize I've been sleeping—actually sleeping—in my neighbor's car. The last fragments of a dream slip away, leaving only the warmth of the leather seat against my skin.

"God, I'm sorry," I mumble, fumbling for the gate remote in my purse. My fingers feel clumsy, disconnected from my brain. "I can't believe I fell asleep." The admission feels like failure. I've been shamefully reduced to dozing like a child on the drive home.

"Don't be sorry. You clearly needed it," Athena says. The gates swing open, and she guides the car up my drive.

The house looms before us, dark except for the motion-sensing lights that flicker on as we approach. It looks forbidding at night—all sharp angles and empty windows, like a mausoleum dressed up as a home. Claire loved this house.

She saw past the stark modernity to its potential for warmth and life. Now it's just a shell.

"Thank you so much. I can manage from here," I say as Athena kills the engine. The words come out less confidently than I'd like. "Thank you."

I push open the door and stand, but the world tilts alarmingly. My hand shoots out to steady myself against the car, leaving a sweaty palm print on its flawless polish. The wine that made me brave at dinner now makes me weak and wobbly, and I could kick myself for having too much.

"Clearly," Athena says dryly. She's already out of the car and at my side, one hand on my elbow. "Let me help you inside."

"That's not necessary," I protest, but my feet betray me, stumbling on the flagstone path. Athena's arm slides around my waist, strong and sure, and something in me wants to lean into that strength, to let someone else be in control for once. The thought terrifies me but right now, I have no choice.

"Your keys?" she asks, and I surrender them without argument.

My heels echo in the emptiness as we enter the foyer, and Athena guides me toward the stairs.

"I really am fine," I murmur, but there's no conviction in my words. "Second door on the right."

My bedroom door swings open, and I become vaguely aware of what Athena must see—the untouched side of the king-size bed; Claire's reading glasses on her nightstand, gathering dust as my cleaner is not allowed to touch them; the framed photo of us in Tuscany that I can't bring myself to look at but can't bear to take down either.

Athena helps me sit on the edge of the bed and turns on the light, then stands there, uncertain. She fiddles with her emerald bracelet as she looks down at me. Gone is the powerful casino owner, the mysterious neighbor. In her place stands a woman who has no idea what to do.

"Can I get you some water?" she finally asks, and the simple kindness in her voice undoes me.

A sob rises in my throat, unexpected and unstoppable. I try to swallow it back, but it's like trying to hold back the tide. The dam I've built around my grief develops a crack, then another, then shatters completely.

"I'm sorry," I gasp, but the words dissolve into tears. Real tears, the kind I haven't allowed myself since those first raw days after the accident. My body curls in on itself, protection against a pain that is unbearable. "I'm so sorry."

The bed dips beside me, and then Athena's arms are around me, pulling me close. I should resist—this woman is practically a stranger, and definitely dangerous in ways I don't fully understand. But I'm so tired of being strong, of being alone.

"Let it out," she murmurs, one hand stroking my hair. "I've got you."

The tenderness in her touch only makes it worse, and two years' worth of contained grief comes pouring out in great, wracking sobs that shake my whole body. I cry for Claire, for the future we lost, for the woman I used to be. I cry for the empty house and the untouched piano and all the phone calls I never returned. I cry until my throat is raw and my eyes burn, until my blouse is stained with tears and mascara.

Athena holds me through it all. She doesn't try to shush me or tell me it will be okay. She just lets me fall apart, murmuring soft words in Greek.

"I don't know how to do this," I whisper when the sobs finally subside a little. "I don't know how to be alone. I'm on leave and the house is so quiet." My voice cracks on the last word. "Everyone says it gets easier, but it doesn't. It just gets...different."

"I know," Athena says softly, and something in her voice makes me believe she actually does know what I'm talking about. She shifts, spooning me, and strokes my shoulder. I'm embarrassed but too exhausted to care.

"Claire would hate what I've become," I say, the words slipping out before I can stop them. "She wanted us to travel more, to have adventures. To start a family. Instead, I hide in my office and pretend the world doesn't exist."

"Grief isn't linear," Athena says, now stroking my hair. The gesture feels intimate. "It's not something you can schedule or control, no matter how good you are at controlling everything else."

A hollow laugh escapes me. "Control? I just fell asleep in your car and I'm having a complete breakdown in your arms. I'd say my control is pretty much shot."

"Maybe that's not such a bad thing," she whispers. "Sometimes we need to lose control to find ourselves again."

I turn onto my back to look at her sideways, wiping at my face. I must look a mess—mascara streaked, lipstick smeared, eyes swollen. But when I meet Athena's gaze, there's no judgment there. Only understanding.

Exhaustion washes over me, the combination of wine, emotion, and release leaving me barely able to keep my eyes open. My body feels heavy, weighted down by the magnitude of everything I've been holding back. The sobs have subsided into occasional hiccups, but tears still leak silently from the corners of my eyes, tracing warm paths down my cheeks.

"You should rest," Athena says, her hand still in my hair. The kindness in her touch almost breaks me again—

how long has it been since anyone has shown me such tenderness? Since I've allowed myself to receive it?

I nod, unable to form words. My bed has never felt so inviting, the promise of sleep a blessed escape from the rawness of emotion.

Through half-closed lids, I watch Athena get up. She looks around the room and spots the cashmere throw draped over the reading chair in the corner—Claire's chair.

She takes it and returns to the bed, spreading it over me. The soft weight of the cashmere settles around my shoulders, and I curl deeper into its familiar comfort.

"Thank you," I whisper, though the words feel inadequate for what she's given me tonight—permission to break, to feel, to be human again, if only for a moment.

She pauses at the bedroom door. "Sleep, Ruby," she says, and I'm already drifting, caught in that hazy space between waking and dreams.

The last thing I register is the soft click of my bedroom door closing, followed by the distant sound of her shoes on the marble stairs. Then sleep claims me completely, pulling me under into blessed darkness where grief can't follow.

TWELVE
ATHENA

Seated at my outdoor dining table, I struggle to concentrate, my gaze repeatedly drawn to Ruby's house. No movement, no signs of life since I left her last night. The balcony where she usually takes her morning coffee remains empty, the French doors closed. I didn't feel comfortable going into work until I knew she was up, but it's almost midday now.

Zeus sits in the chair beside me, his massive frame upright, more like an Egyptian deity than a mere house cat. He follows my gaze toward Ruby's house, then turns to fix me with those knowing eyes. We've long since established our peculiar détente—he refuses to act like a normal cat, and I've given up trying to make him one. My bed is his bed, my chair is his chair, and any attempt to assert dominance is met with imperial disdain.

"What do you think, big boy?" I murmur, reaching out to scratch behind his ears. He allows it. "Should we be worried?"

My laptop screen shows a dozen urgent emails from the Olympus—questions about tonight's high-roller event, press requests about our latest expansion plans, and a marketing campaign for me to sign off on. Mark has already called twice, and even Maria, my ever-efficient assistant, has started marking her emails with red exclamation points. They're clearly worried because I'm not there, but the casino has survived without my decision making before.

Zeus's tail twitches as a bird lands on the table, but he makes no move to chase it. His attention returns to Ruby's house, ears pricked forward as if he senses something I can't.

"Maybe I should check on her," I say to him, glancing at my watch.

The memory of last night plays behind my eyes—Ruby curled up, pain pouring out in sobs. The vulnerability in her voice when she admitted how alone she feels. My stomach tightens with worry. I've seen that kind of despair before, the way it can swallow someone whole when they're left on their own with it. Especially now, with her leave stretching ahead of her. I suspect work is the only thing that keeps her going.

"Yeah... I think I should check in," I continue, though Zeus has turned his attention to grooming his massive paw. He pauses to give me a look that seems to say, "Then do something about it."

I close my laptop. Enough watching. Time to act.

The mounting heat of the day is harsh as I walk to Ruby's house, and I pull my white hat farther over my forehead to shield my face from the sun. In my white palazzo pants and silk sleeveless blouse, I'm overdressed for a wellness check perhaps, but old habits die hard. The intercom buzzes, and I wait, counting heartbeats until Ruby's voice comes through.

"Athena?"

I let out a long breath. "Hey. I thought you might like some company."

A pause, then the gate swings open and Ruby appears in her doorway. Her silk pajamas are wrinkled, auburn hair tangled around her shoulders. Dark circles shadow her eyes, making the green even more striking against her pale skin.

"Did I wake you?" I ask.

"No," she says, one hand clutching the doorframe like it's holding her up. "I've been awake for hours. I just..." She swallows hard. "I couldn't seem to get out of bed."

"You look like you could use a friend." I step closer, noting how she shrinks slightly. "Let me help."

Confusion clouds her face. "With what?"

"With anything." I vaguely gesture toward the back of the house. "For starters, we could fill that beautiful pool—if only for my own pleasure. It's rather depressing, seeing an empty pool from my window. It looks...abandoned."

It's a lie, of course. I rarely spare a glance out my bedroom window. Between running the Olympus and my other ventures, I have more pressing matters than neighborhood watch. But I've learned that sometimes people need an excuse to help themselves, a reason that doesn't hurt their pride. And right now, Ruby looks like she needs any reason at all to get going.

"I'm fine and I don't need help," she says automatically. "I don't even use the pool, but if the view bothers you, I'll ask the yard worker to fill it when he's in next week. And about last night..." A flush creeps up her neck. "I'm sorry for being drunk and falling apart like that. The wine, and the stress, and—"

"Please, never apologize for being human," I interrupt. "And you should know by now that I'm not someone who takes no for an answer."

A ghost of a smile tugs at her lips. "So I'm learning." She

hesitates, then steps back from the doorway. "Shouldn't you be at work?"

"I'm taking the day off." I move past her into the foyer. "I'll check in later."

"I don't want to be your charity case. Or your pity project."

"Trust me," I say. "I have no intention of taking on any new projects. I'm just here as a friend."

She frowns, tilting her head slightly. "A friend?"

"Yes, a friend. Or a friendly neighbor. Call it whatever makes you comfortable." I meet her eyes. "I'm not here because I feel like I have to be. I'm here because I want to be."

Ruby studies my face, then her expression softens slightly, though doubt still lingers in her eyes. "Well, you're here now, so I guess I'll get dressed," she says, retreating toward the stairs. "Give me a few minutes? I'll make us coffee."

The house feels different in daylight—even more empty. I head to the living room that opens onto the pool area through sliding glass doors. They glide silently on their tracks as I open them fully. Outside, the pool sits empty, its blue tiles dulled by a fine layer of desert dust. The surrounding space holds such potential—built-in planters waiting for greenery, covered seating areas begging for cushions, an outdoor kitchen that's never known fire.

I walk into the kitchen where everything gleams with the particular shine of disuse. The professional-grade appliances stand silent, their surfaces unmarred by cooking spills or coffee rings. A high stack of mail sits on the counter, and my heart catches when I see the name on the envelopes— Claire Walsh. Bills, magazines, credit card offers, all still arriving for a woman two years gone. Ruby hasn't even opened them.

I pull out my phone and dial Asha's number. "I need you next door today," I say when she answers. "There's no cleaning involved, just small chores. Oh, and bring Andreas. Tell him he's doing yard work here instead."

As I hang up, the La Marzocco espresso machine catches my eye—top of the line. I find the Ethiopian beans in a container next to it, noting it's a brand I've never tried before. I must admit, it's been a while since I've done this, but the routine of grinding beans and pulling shots is almost meditative.

Ruby appears as I'm finishing the second cup, her hair damp from the shower. She's wearing loose white linen pants and a navy tank top. Her fingers tug at the fabric of her pants, like she's forgotten how to dress for anything but the office. She stops short, staring at me behind her own kitchen counter. "How on earth... That machine took me two months to figure out."

"What?" I chuckle, adding a precise amount of hot water to the espresso. "You think I don't know how to make my own coffee?" I slide her cup across the counter with a smirk. "Please. I make a small fortune before breakfast. Making coffee isn't exactly quantum physics."

THIRTEEN
RUBY

I stand in my bedroom, watching Athena's staff transform my backyard. The house feels alive for the first time in two years, but the activity still makes my skin crawl with an unsettling mix of gratitude and resentment.

The pool, empty for so long, fills inch by inch with crystalline water. Andreas, Athena's gardener, moves between the planters, setting plants into fresh soil. The loungers from the pool house gleam in their new positions, freshly cleaned and topped with plush cushions in shades of blue and white. I think they're mine, but I'm not even sure. Maybe Athena asked Andreas to buy new ones.

In just a few hours, Athena and her efficient team have dismantled pieces of my past. Her housekeeper, Asha, made the phone calls I couldn't—canceling Claire's subscriptions, her phone, her credit cards. Each cancellation felt like another small death, another erasure of Claire's existence, yet there was also relief in watching someone else handle the tasks that have paralyzed me for so long.

Even Claire's BMW, still sitting in the garage collecting dust, will be sold. "You'll never drive it," Athena said matter-of-factly. "And cars aren't meant to sit idle." She's right, of course, and that bothers me almost as much as her inexplicable determination to help me.

I still can't figure out her angle. Maybe she wants leverage—an IOU from the city's most feared corporate lawyer. Or perhaps she's ensuring I won't dig too deeply into whatever happens in her house. But when I catch her watching me, I see something that looks like genuine concern.

Now she stands in my bedroom, waiting as I finally head for the walk-in closet. My hand trembles slightly on the handle.

"We don't need to do this today," I say quickly, dropping my hand. "I can hire someone to deal with it."

"Some things can be handled by others," Athena says softly. "But this isn't one of them. You need to do this yourself, Ruby. It's part of the process—one you've been avoiding by burying yourself in work."

I let out a long, shaky sigh, finally pushing open the door. "What do you want me to do?" My voice cracks. "Just throw everything away?"

"No, of course not." Athena moves to stand in the doorway but doesn't enter the closet. "You could donate them to charity? Correct me if I'm wrong, but I don't think you need the money from selling them. There are people out there who could really use her clothes. If you want, we can pack them together, and I'll go with you to drop them off." She pauses, then adds quietly, "You know you need to do this."

I stare at Claire's clothes, each piece holding a memory: the blue dress she bought in Paris; the worn leather jacket that still smells of her. Leather holds scents for longer, and sometimes I torture myself by burying my face in it.

Asha has already brought in cardboard boxes—where did she even find them so quickly?

"I'm not ready," I say. "It's not a good time."

Athena nods and gives me a sweet smile. "It's never a good time."

She's right again, so with trembling hands, I reach for the first garment. A Harvard Law T-shirt, soft from years of wear. Claire used to sleep in it, claimed it was more comfortable than any silk pajamas. My fingers curl into the fabric, and suddenly I'm back in our bed, Claire's laughter filling the room as she stole my side, claiming it was warmer.

One by one, I take down the clothes. A blue blazer she wore to court. The dress from our first anniversary dinner. Her running shoes, still caked with red desert dust from her last morning jog. Each piece feels like I'm packing away a part of her.

Athena works silently beside me, folding everything I hand her with respect, not rushing me when I pause over certain items, letting me set the pace. She doesn't comment when I set aside a few pieces—the Harvard shirt, her favorite sweater, the emerald dress she wore when we first met. Some things I'm not ready to let go of yet.

The closet empties gradually, the boxes filling with the physical remnants of Claire's life. Finally, we reach the last few items. As I take down her winter coat—barely used in Vegas—the empty rails on her side of the closet create a void I can't look away from. The space yawns like an open grave.

"Asha can move some of your clothes over," Athena says gently. "So it won't look so empty. Or we can do it together, if you prefer?"

I stare at the bare space, at the hangers that once held pieces of Claire's life. Everything feels too fast, too efficient, too final. In just a few hours, Athena has systematically dismantled the fortress around Claire's memory. Each phone call, each packed box, each decision has stripped away another layer of my protection. She makes it all seem so simple, so logical—as if grief can be packed away in neat boxes and donated to charity, as if memory can be reorganized like clothes in a closet. But nothing about this is simple. Nothing about losing Claire has ever made sense, and I'm not ready for it to start making sense now.

"Ruby?" Athena's voice pulls me from my thoughts.

Something inside me snaps. "Who do you think you are?" The words come out in a harsh whisper that builds to a shout. "You just barge in here and start erasing Claire like she never existed! Canceling her subscriptions, selling her car, packing away her clothes—what the fuck gives you the right?"

Athena stays perfectly still, her expression calm. "This isn't about erasing her, Ruby. It's about—"

"Moving on? Is that what you were going to say?" I'm shaking now, rage and grief mixing into something toxic in my chest. "You don't know anything about moving on! You've been here what, six hours? And suddenly you're an expert?"

I grab one of the boxes, upending it. Claire's clothes spill across the floor like colorful wounds. "You want to help? You want to fix the sad widow next door? Well, guess what—I don't need fixing! I don't need your help or your pity or your mysterious interest in my life!"

The silence that follows is deafening and it's so quiet I can even hear the pool filling outside. I can't live with Claire's things surrounding me, but I can't bear to let them go either.

"Get out," I say, my voice raw. "Take your people with you and just...leave me alone."

Athena doesn't argue. She doesn't try to defend herself or explain her actions. She simply nods once and turns to leave. At the bedroom door, she pauses but doesn't look back.

"When you're ready," she says softly, "you know where to find me."

Then she's gone. I hear her giving quiet instructions to her staff before the front door closes.

I sink to the floor among Claire's scattered clothes, drawing a sweatshirt to my chest. Tears come without warning, and this time there's no one here to witness them, no one to fold my pain into boxes or hold me. I already regret sending Athena away and I don't know how to face her again, after I've thrown her kindness back in her face. The loneliness crashes back in, even sharper than before. Now that I've started crying, I can't seem to stop, and all I can think is I don't know how to carry on from here.

FOURTEEN
ATHENA

I adjust the drape of my white jumpsuit in the mirror, running my hands over the dramatically flared sleeves that fall around my wrists. Tonight isn't about business. Tonight I need to lose myself, to shed the weight of the past few days in my underground sanctuary, not as a host but as a participant. The wide legs sway around me when I walk, swishing against my bare feet.

I haven't heard from Ruby since she threw me out, and her car remains in the driveway. I feel guilty for upsetting her. Even though I know what we did was necessary, I might have pushed too hard, too fast. Grief has its own timeline, and I of all people should know better than to force it.

Zeus sprawls across my bed and yawns, then watches through half-closed eyes as I prepare for the evening ahead. His tail twitches occasionally in what might be judgment or might be approval—it's hard to tell with him. Unlike most cats who demand attention, Zeus merely allows it, bestowing his affection like a monarch granting favors.

The white hat collection fills an entire wall of my closet —wide-brimmed hats, gambler hats, porkpie hats, fedoras, panamas in various materials, and even a few top hats, each one chosen to complete my image. I select a fedora, then open my jewelry drawers and choose a set of heavy gold bangles. Each piece tells a story—some from my grandmother's collection in Athens, others acquired in Vegas.

A light comes on in Ruby's office. She stands at her window, her hand rising in a tentative wave. It's an awkward gesture. Is she apologizing? She's wearing something black. A nightgown, maybe? It's hard to tell from here.

I wave back, our eyes meeting across the space between our houses. The moment stretches, loaded with unspoken words. Then she drops her hand, and I turn away from the window. I need to stop worrying about Ruby, stop trying to control what's beyond my control. If she wants my support, she'll come.

"How do I look, little prince?" I murmur to Zeus, fastening the bangles around my wrist. "Want to come downstairs tonight? Party with me?"

He blinks slowly, supremely uninterested in my human affairs. The club holds no attraction for him—he's seen it all before and found it wanting compared to the simple pleasure of claiming my entire king-size bed for himself. Sometimes I think he understands more than he lets on.

I make my final adjustments in the mirror, ensuring everything is right. In my world, details matter.

My phone buzzes—Robert, head of security. "Ms. Stavros? Your neighbor is at the gate. Ms. Walsh. She wants to come in."

I freeze. "Ruby?"

"Yes, ma'am. She seems...determined." There's a pause, and I can hear the uncertainty in his voice. We have strict protocols, and Ruby's appearance has thrown them into question. "How would you like us to handle this?"

Through the window, I can see Ruby's home is dark now, and my mind races through the possibilities, the implications. "Bring her to my home office," I decide. "Make sure she doesn't encounter any of tonight's arrivals."

"Understood."

I head downstairs to my rarely used study. Dark wood panels line the walls and Greek antiquities rest in lit alcoves between them. A massive desk dominates the space, its surface unmarred by the usual casino paperwork. I lean back in my chair and prop my feet on the desk, crossing them at the ankles. Tonight I'm off duty, so to hell with my manners.

Robert appears in the doorway with Ruby. She's wearing a simple black cocktail dress with a low cleavage, her auburn hair sleek and gleaming. Makeup accentuates those striking green eyes but can't quite hide the shadows beneath them or the slight redness that speaks of recent tears. She's beautiful and broken, like a Greek statue missing its arms, and the damage only makes her more compelling.

"Thank you, Robert," I say, dismissing him with a nod. "Please close the door."

Ruby stands, her fingers twisting around a bottle she's holding. She's nervous, yet there's determination in the set of her jaw, in the way she meets my gaze directly.

"Ruby, I feel terrible—" I begin, but she cuts me off by raising her hand.

"No," she says. "I'm the one who needs to apologize. I shouldn't have sent you away like that. I panicked, and I'm sorry." She takes a deep breath, moving farther into the room. "You were right about everything. I need to deal with Claire's ghost in the house, and I'm very, very grateful for your help."

I study her face. The past few days have clearly taken their toll—the kind of emotional exhaustion that comes from finally facing what you've been running from. "How do you feel?"

"Like I'm drowning in loss," she admits, sinking into the leather chair across from my desk. Her dress rides up slightly as she crosses her legs. "But I'm trying to embrace it. I haven't allowed myself to cry much since Claire died, but I've been crying nonstop for the past few days." One hand rises to her throat, fingers playing with a gold chain.

"That's normal," I say softly, watching her fingers against her collarbone. "It will get better from here. You're not holding it in anymore. You're letting it out."

"You sound like you know what you're talking about," Ruby says, tilting her head. Her eyes search my face with an intensity that makes me want to look away. There's something different about her tonight—a recklessness born of exhaustion and grief.

She holds up the Scotch I brought to her house. "Scotch for truth, right?" she says, a hint of challenge in her voice.

The flutter in my stomach surprises me. I've never had trouble admitting to myself that I find Ruby attractive—I'd have to be blind not to—but acting on it would be complicated. She's my neighbor, she's grieving, and she's clearly not in a stable place right now.

"I'm glad you're here," I say, carefully choosing my words, "and I would love to have a drink with you, but it's Saturday and I have guests—"

"I know," she interrupts, setting the bottle on my desk. "But we could have one while you show me what's going on here? I'll sign the NDA, and after that, I have a feeling I might need some liquid courage."

"What?" I drop my feet to the floor, and my bangles

chime as I fold my hands on the desk's surface. "Are you sure?"

"Yeah, I'll sign it. I have no choice." She lets out a hollow laugh. "I've been crying for days, and I can't stand being in that house anymore. I feel like I'm going mad, locked in the prison of my own mind." Her voice cracks. "You offered an escape, so I'll take it. I need... I need help. Anything to get me out of this..." She taps her temple.

"Okay. Whatever you want." I reach into my desk drawer, withdraw an NDA, and slide it across to her. "Tonight?" I ask, watching her carefully.

She nods, opens the last page of the file and signs without reading—an action that would no doubt normally horrify her. But this isn't a normal situation. As she passes it back, she pulls out her phone, fingers hovering over the screen. "I have permission from my bank to transfer the funds, so—"

"Forget about the money for now, there's no rush," I interrupt, standing. I don't want to give her time to change her mind because she needs this more than she knows.

Holding out my hand, I shoot her a warm smile. "Come with me. We'll have that drink downstairs."

FIFTEEN
RUBY

My hand feels clammy against Athena's as she leads me through her home. It's strange to hold a woman's hand again after Claire—the delicate bones, the smooth skin, so different from the clinical handshakes I exchange in boardrooms.

We enter what appears to be a library, walls lined with leather-bound volumes reaching to the ceiling. The space smells of old books and sandalwood, and it's illuminated by antique brass sconces. My legal mind kicks in—is this it? Is this what people sign those ridiculous NDAs for? A hundred thousand dollars to access a private library?

"Let me remind you," Athena says. "We're entering a circle of trust. You'll meet likeminded women. Some may be useful in your career, some may become close friends..." She pauses, dark eyes holding mine. "Some may become lovers."

"Lovers?" The word catches in my throat.

She winks and gestures to a security guard I hadn't noticed lurking in the shadows. He approaches a particular bookcase and reaches behind a row of books. The entire unit swings silently outward, revealing a staircase descending into warm light, pulsing with music.

"What is this place?" I whisper, dumbfounded.

"I refer to it as Hedonism," Athena says simply, tightening her grip on my hand. The stairs curve downward, each step bringing stronger beats of music and the murmur of voices.

The space that opens makes me pause. The lounge is vast, with high walls and ceilings painted a deep red. Plush velvet sofas and intimate seating areas are arranged throughout, occupied by perhaps thirty women.

Some are gathered around a bar, others recline on chaise longues, smoking cigars or what smells distinctly like high-grade marijuana. A few dance together, bodies moving sensuously to the music. On a small stage, a belly dancer performs, her costume a masterpiece of dark-blue silk and silver coins that catch the light with each undulation of her hips. Her bare midriff gleams with oil, muscles rippling as she moves in ways that make me blush.

"Is this a brothel?" I whisper. "An illegal gambling operation?"

Athena laughs. "No. There's no gambling and no paid sex here. In fact, there's no exchange of money whatsoever. Everything is free—you can help yourself behind the bar or ask the waiter." Her hand slips to my lower back, guiding me deeper into the room. "But if you want sex, you can indulge. There are also rooms where you can watch if you prefer." Her lips brush my ear as she adds, "You like to watch, don't you?"

Heat floods my face and I can't form a response.

Athena steers me toward the bar and orders two Scotch. "Wait," she says to the bartender, "she's new."

The bartender nods and slides over a small crystal dish that contains glistening ruby-red pomegranate seeds, jewel-like under the bar lights. "A little initiation ritual," she explains, lifting the dish. "In Greek mythology, Persephone ate six pomegranate seeds in the underworld, binding her to Hades for six months of every year." Her dark eyes hold mine as she offers me the dish. "Think of it as crossing a threshold. Once you taste the fruit of this world, you're connected to it."

I'm too disoriented by the sensory overload of this place to question anything, so I take a seed, then another. They burst between my teeth, sweet and tart.

Athena watches as I swallow. "Perfect," she murmurs. "Now you truly belong here."

She hands me my Scotch, and I take a long sip while I scan the room, trying to process everything I'm seeing. I gasp when my eyes land on a familiar face.

"Is that Justice Donovan?" I whisper to Athena. "I once argued a case before her." The woman in question is dancing while sipping a martini and laughing at something another woman is saying. She's wearing a slinky red dress instead of her usual judicial robes, her silver hair loose around her shoulders.

"You make it sound like she's doing something wrong," Athena says, amused. "But she's not. Donna—that's what we call her here—just wants to have a good time. She likes her martinis with a menthol cigarette, loves to dance..." Athena's smile widens. "And she particularly enjoys flirting with beautiful women."

"She's gay?" I glance between the dancing justice and Athena.

"All the women here are queer," Athena says. "Donna's not out, and I provide a safe space for her to be herself." She places a hand on the small of my back. "Come, I'll introduce you."

"Are you serious?"

But we're already moving. The justice smiles when she sees Athena. "There you are, honey!" She accepts Athena's kiss on the cheek, then turns to me. "And Ruby Walsh of Walsh & Associates, as I live and breathe."

I stammer something about being honored, and she waves it away. "No 'Your Honor' here, dear. I'm just Donna. We all use first names or nicknames." She looks between Athena and me, one eyebrow raised. "Are you two together?"

"We're neighbors," I say quickly, feeling my face heat again.

Donna laughs. "Ah! *You're* the neighbor? So you finally caved? You know you're the reason we all had to arrive shielding our faces from view."

I apologize, but she just winks and turns back to her companion.

Athena's still holding my hand, her thumb stroking me as if trying to put me at ease. "Ready to see more?" she asks.

We move through a heavy velvet curtain into another space, this one more intimate. The lighting is lower, the music softer. About a dozen women occupy the deep sofas, some simply talking, others... My eyes widen as I spot another familiar face. The CEO of a major tech company deeply engaged in kissing a woman. Her hand slides under the woman's top, caressing her breast. It's hard to tear my gaze away from them.

"So all these women here are..." I trail off, mesmerized by the scene.

"Queer?" Athena nods. "It's sexy, isn't it? Watching powerful women let go of their public personas." Her gaze drops to my mouth and lingers on my lips. For one terrifying heartbeat, I think she might kiss me, but she snaps out of it and straightens herself.

"There's more," she says, showing me to the next room. It contains a large bed with an armchair on either side. Two women occupy the bed, one's head buried between the other's thighs. A third woman watches from one of the armchairs, her skirt hiked up and one hand moving slowly between her own legs.

The woman who's pleasuring her looks up, grinning at me. "Hey there, newbie. Want to join?" She licks her lips. "Plenty of room."

"Don't stop!" The other woman pushes her head back down and spreads her legs farther. "She's right, you should join us," she says to me through hazy eyes. "She's very, very good at..." Her voice trails off as her head falls back and she shuts her eyes tight, moaning.

The scene before me is raw, primal, impossible to look away from. Heat spreads through my body, an ache I haven't felt in years. My breath comes faster, and I press my thighs together, trying to calm the sudden throb.

"I'm sorry, but this isn't my thing," I manage. My hands tremble as I clutch my drink. I feel exposed, stripped bare. Athena has ripped me out of my comfort zone in every way imaginable and I'm not sure how much more I can take.

The woman on the bed moans again, the sound going straight through me. I can't stop watching, even as I back toward the door. Every cell in my body feels awake, alive, hungry for something I've denied myself for too long. I'm aware of Athena's presence beside me—the warmth radiating from her body, the subtle scent of her perfume, the way her fingers still rest against my lower back.

I wish I had pockets to hide my trembling hands, a way to anchor myself in this storm of awakening sensation.

"Ruby is new, girls! Give her some time to adjust," Athena jokes, guiding me out of the room.

"Are you okay?" she asks and continues without waiting for an answer. "Want to see my favorite room?"

"Can I handle your favorite room?" I blow out my cheeks, and she chuckles.

"I guess we're about to find out."

Athena leads me down another corridor, this one darker than the other, lit only by sconces that cast flickering shadows on the bare brick walls. The music is different here —slower, deeper. I catch glimpses through a partially open door: bare skin, leather, flashes of metal.

My mouth goes dry. Things are clearly getting more... intense. A woman's moan echoes, followed by the sharp crack of leather against skin.

Athena pushes open the heavy black door and the scene stops me in my tracks. A woman stands with her arms above her head, wrists bound in leather cuffs attached to a ceiling ring. She wears nothing but a black lace thong, her naked breasts rising and falling with rapid breaths. Another woman circles her, dressed in leather hot pants and a matching bra, wielding a riding crop.

"It's beautiful, isn't it?" Athena stares at the scene, mesmerized as if she's admiring a work of art in a museum.

I don't answer; I have no idea what to say. Instead, I watch, transfixed, as the crop traces a line down the bound woman's spine. It strikes the woman's behind and she lets out a throaty moan. My skin tingles in response.

Athena's fingers tighten on my hip, and the look she gives me when our eyes meet is knowing, intense—like she can see into my mind. "Come," she says. "Enough for now. I don't want to scare you away on your first night. Let's go back to the main lounge and I'll introduce you to a few friends. A wealth of valuable connections is about to open up to you."

I nod but don't move until she nudges me. I seem to have forgotten how to walk because I nearly stumble over my own feet as we head back to the lounge.

"So that's your thing?" I ask. "You like to be spanked?"

"No," she says, her voice dropping lower. She gives me a flirty smile. "I like to dominate."

SIXTEEN

ATHENA

"Hey, neighbor." Ruby opens her door. She's wearing a black bikini, partially covered by an emerald silk robe. The contrast between the dark swimwear and her pale skin is striking. "Come in, I'll make coffee."

"I brought sweets." I follow her into the kitchen, trying not to focus on the way the silk clings to her curves, and set down a silver platter on her counter. "Fresh dates from my private supplier in Dubai, and melomakarona from Greece —they're honey cookies."

"Thank you. These look delicious."

I watch as she examines the walnut-studded sweets dusted with cinnamon. "You left rather abruptly last night." I'd walked her out, watching as she paused to collect herself before heading up the stairs to the library. She'd seemed dazed, overwhelmed perhaps, but not upset.

"Yeah... It was a lot so I told myself I was tired, but when I got home, I couldn't sleep." She moves to her espresso machine to make us coffee, and I'm enjoying this glimpse of domestic Ruby. "My mind kept..." She trails off, busying herself with the grinder.

"Replaying?" I supply, leaning against her kitchen island.

Her hands tremble as she tamps the grounds. "That's one way to put it." The machine hisses and steams. "All the naughty stuff aside, I never imagined..." She shakes her head in wonder. "A state supreme court justice, three Fortune 500 CEOs, that hedge fund manager everyone's terrified of..."

"Impressed by the guest list?" I can't help but smile at her obvious fascination.

"More like shocked. They were so...normal. Friendly. Nobody was trying to network or make deals. It felt genuine." She froths almond milk, pours it on top, and hands me a cappuccino.

"That's the point," I say. "No business allowed in the club. But if you ever need a favor from a certain judge or want to pitch to that hedge fund manager..." I shrug. "You know where to find them. Many lasting partnerships have started over shared secrets."

"It's brilliant, really." Ruby pours her own cappuccino. "A space where powerful women can just be. No agenda. And how did I not know they were queer?"

"Hence the NDA." I grin. "Well...there's that and the fact that some can't be seen tipsy or stoned or even just dancing in public."

Ruby studies me over the rim of her cup. "So how did it all start with the club?

"It actually started as something much smaller," I say. "When I still lived at the Olympus, I used to host these intimate gatherings in my suite—just a handful of queer women looking for connection. We talked about how nice it would be to have a real space where we could all come together without worrying about being seen or photographed or ending up in some tabloid. I thought about creating something within the Olympus itself, but that was too risky." I take a sip of my coffee. "When I was house hunting, one of the main selling points of this place was actually that underground space. It used to be a wine cellar."

"So you bought the house specifically for the cellar?" Ruby asks.

"It was a major factor. All I had to do was renovate the space and the rest is history."

Ruby chuckles. "And here was me thinking you were running an illegal gambling ring." She takes a bite of melomakarona, her eyes widening as she chews. "Mm...these are good."

"An illegal gambling ring?" I shoot her an amused look.

"Yeah. I had this whole narrative in my head—casino boss Athena, making shady deals in her underground lair, probably keeping someone's kneecaps in a trophy case somewhere."

I throw my head back and laugh. "Sorry to disappoint. No kneecaps, though I do have an impressive collection of designer hats."

"The hats!" Ruby exclaims, tapping the brim of my fedora. "I love them, by the way, but they slotted right into that dangerous stereotype. Meanwhile, you're just running a very exclusive...what do you even call it? A social club? A sanctuary?" She dips another cookie in her coffee.

"A sanctuary. I like that." I take a sip of my cappuccino. "Speaking of sanctuary, shall we move this outside?"

Andreas has truly transformed the poolside with white loungers arranged around the clear water and desert plants in terra-cotta pots. I have to give it to him; he's got a good eye for detail.

Ruby drops onto a lounger and her robe falls open. The

black bikini reveals more than it conceals, and I force myself to look away. I'm fully dressed, as I'm heading to the Olympus soon, but even if I wasn't, I'm not one for sunbathing.

"So," I say, taking the adjacent lounger that's shaded by a parasol. "Anything you want to talk about?" I need to address what she witnessed last night. Watching women together, seeing scenes of domination and submission—these aren't things one generally encounters on a Saturday night at their neighbor's house. "How did last night make you feel?"

A blush creeps onto Ruby's cheeks. "I felt alive," she admits. "For the first time in...God, I don't know how long. Watching those women together, so free, so uninhibited... It was incredibly sexy." She absently runs her finger around the rim of her coffee cup. "But I also felt guilty. Like I was betraying Claire by having those feelings again."

"But you know that's not true. Claire would want—"

"Want me to move on, yes." She gives me a small smile. "Everyone says that. And logically, I know it's true. Anyway, I was lying awake at three a.m., feeling guilty while I thought about..." She catches herself.

"About what?"

She stares into her coffee. "That room, with the bed. The women together. And then..." Her voice drops lower. "The other room. The one with the handcuffs."

She reaches for the sunscreen on the table between us and starts to apply it to her legs. Her movements are practical rather than seductive, but I can't tear my eyes away from her hands as they glide over her skin.

"You seemed particularly interested in that room," I observe carefully.

"I've never considered it to be something I might want

to try. But I can't stop thinking of it, and about..." She swallows hard. "Never mind."

I set my coffee down, my heart racing. "No. Tell me."

She bites her lip, now frantically working the lotion into her arms so she doesn't have to look me in the eyes. "It must be nice to be able to let go. To trust someone else to..." She doesn't finish the statement, but her meaning is clear.

Sensing it might be too soon for this conversation, I gesture to the sunscreen. "Can I help you with that? I don't want your back to burn."

She stares at the bottle like it might bite her, then at me. I can't help but laugh.

"Come on, Ruby. It's just sunscreen."

She hesitates, then hands me the bottle.

"Turn around," I say, letting a hint of command slip into my tone. Her reaction is immediate—a slight shiver, a quickening of breath.

Interesting.

I consider straddling her but decide against it. Instead, I perch on the edge of her lounger, warming the lotion between my palms before touching her skin. The first contact draws a soft gasp from her—whether from the coolness of the cream or my touch, I'm not sure.

What starts as a simple application becomes something more intimate. I knead the tension from her neck, trace the line of her spine, map the curves of her shoulder blades. Each stroke of my hands draws a deeper response—a sigh, a subtle arch, and finally a low moan.

The sound awakens something dangerously spontaneous, something I've kept dormant. In the club, intimacy is choreographed, controlled—a dance of power and submission. This is different. Raw. Unscripted. The simple act of touching her bare skin affects me more than any scene I've orchestrated underground.

Her skin is smooth and soft beneath my palms as I work the delicate knobs of her spine. I love the way her muscles jump when my fingers find a sensitive spot. I shouldn't be touching her like this—she's vulnerable, still processing her first night at the club, still grieving. But I can't seem to stop.

"You're beautiful," I murmur. Her muscles tense at my words. "Sorry," I add quickly, though I'm not. "Just objectively speaking. I'm not trying to—"

"You want me in those handcuffs, don't you?" She doesn't turn around, but I hear the tremor in her voice. It's not a joke.

"Yes." My hands move lower, skimming her sides, and she arches into the touch. Suddenly I'm acutely aware of how intimate this has become.

Last night, as Ruby moved through the club, I saw something awaken in her. The way she watched those women together, the flush in her cheeks, how her breath caught when we entered the playroom—it was like watching a flower slowly unfold. It was beautiful, and as much as she's been thinking of last night, I've been thinking of Ruby.

"I should go," I say, standing abruptly. *Not outside the club.* The loss of contact feels physical.

Ruby sits up quickly, adjusting her robe. "Wait, what? You're leaving?" She searches my face with concern. "Are you okay? Did I say something wrong?"

"No, of course not." I grab a towel from the lounger and dry my hands, trying to appear casual, though I'm a little flustered. "I just remembered I have a meeting at the Olympus in twenty minutes. I completely lost track of time." I toss the towel aside and try to slow my breathing. "Will you be at the club tonight?"

"I don't know..."

"You're one of us now," I remind her. "You can come and go as you please, even when I'm not there. You know my gate code and the password. It's your playground too."

She worries her bottom lip between her teeth, considering. "I need some time," she says finally. "To process everything. But maybe Friday, after work?"

I nod, gathering my composure. "Friday then." I pause at the foot of her lounger, allowing myself one last look at her. "And Ruby? When you're ready to explore those handcuffs..." I let the sentence hang unfinished, enjoying the way her pupils dilate. "I'll see you around, neighbor."

SEVENTEEN
RUBY

The donation center for the Safe Nest charity for women seeking refuge sits in a building off Eastern Avenue. I sit in my car for a while, eyeing the boxes in the back seat. Seven large cardboard boxes, neatly labeled, "Professional," "Casual," "Evening." Claire's clothes. She loved these pieces, wore them with such joy.

Marcus, the intake coordinator, meets me outside. His purple bow tie matches his glasses frames, and his smile is wide when he sees how much I've brought. "Ruby Walsh? We spoke on the phone. Here, let me help you with those."

The interior is bright and organized. Racks of clothing line the walls, sorted by type and size. A section for interview outfits commands pride of place near the front.

"Thank you so much for this. Many of our women are starting over completely," Marcus says as he leads me to a sorting table. "Sometimes all they have are the clothes on their backs, so we try to give them everything they need to build a new life."

I manage a smile despite the building discomfort in my stomach. "I'm glad they can be of use."

Marcus begins unpacking the first box. Each piece holds memories. Claire's Armani blazer emerges, classic black. She wore it to court, to client meetings, to charity galas.

"Oh my God," Marcus breathes, running his fingers over the lining. "This is exquisite. And in perfect condition!" He holds it up to the light, examining the stitching. "Honey, this must be worth a fortune. Not that I'm complaining, but why on earth would you want to get rid of all this? Someone in our shelter is going to be very, very happy to have an amazing blazer like this for their job interview."

I can't stop it. Tears spring to my eyes and Marcus looks at me properly for the first time, really sees me, and his hand flies to his mouth.

"Oh, honey, I'm so sorry. Did these belong to someone who..." He flinches. "I didn't mean to—"

"No, it's okay." I swallow away the lump in my throat. "My wife...she would have wanted them to come here. She always admired the work you do. She helped with fundraising sometimes. Claire Walsh."

Recognition dawns in his eyes. "Claire Walsh? Oh my God, of course. She organized that amazing auction three years ago." He pauses. "Oh, sweetheart... We heard about her passing. Would you like to help me unpack and sort them?"

I nod, not trusting my voice, and we work in silence for a while, Marcus handling each piece with care and respect. A coral Theory dress that Claire wore to summer parties. The cashmere sweater she lived in during winter weekends, soft gray with slightly worn elbows because she always pushed the sleeves up. A pair of Jimmy Choo pumps, barely worn. The dress she changed into after our wedding ceremony.

"She had incredible taste," Marcus says softly, arranging a DVF wrap dress on a hanger. "These pieces will help so many women feel confident."

"That's what she always said about clothes." I smooth my hand over a leather jacket. "That the right outfit is like armor. It helps you face the world."

When we reach the last dress—the one she wore the night we met—I hesitate.

"Why don't you keep it?" Marcus says.

I shake my head. "No. Someone else should wear it. Create new memories in it." Another stab in the heart, but I hand it over. *One foot in front of the other. Just move forward,* I remind myself.

Marcus wraps me in a sudden hug and squeezes me. "You're doing a beautiful thing," he whispers. "And you're right. Your Claire would want this."

I let myself lean into his embrace for just a moment. I didn't want to do this, but now I feel somewhat relieved that I got it over with, and it gives me strength to move on to my next task.

Back in my car, I pull out my phone and scroll to a number I should have called two years ago. If I don't do it now, I'll keep making excuses, and then I might never do it. My hands shake as I press dial.

"Hello?" a young woman's voice answers on the third ring.

"Sarah? It's...it's Ruby. Claire's Ruby."

Silence stretches for a beat. "Oh my God, Ruby? I can't believe... Are you okay? We've been so worried. When you stopped answering calls..."

"I'm sorry." The words feel inadequate. "I'm so sorry I

haven't called before now. I have something for you—your grandmother's sapphire ring. Claire would have wanted you to have it." I have to stop, take a breath.

"Ruby..." Sarah's voice softens. "I've been following your cases online—that huge merger last week made the business papers. At least I knew you were working, staying busy."

I laugh, but it comes out more like a sob. "Work is all I've been doing. It was easier than...everything else. Than calling family and dealing with the aftermath. But I'm finally getting to it."

"I understand." And maybe she does. She lost her aunt, after all.

"I could send it to you by courier or...we could meet up?" I suggest.

"Yeah. Next time I'm in Vegas, maybe we could get dinner? Catch up properly?"

"I'd like that. How are you, anyway? What's going on in your life?"

"A lot has changed," Sarah says with a small chuckle. "I met a guy. His name is Erik and he works in marketing. We recently moved in together. And I'm second-year associate at Gibson Dunn now—maybe you could give me some tips?"

"Of course. Well done on the job." I smile. "Why don't you bring your new man when you visit? You're both welcome to stay with me."

"Really?" Sarah pauses. "Thank you, that would be really nice. Erik has a job interview coming up in Vegas. I could tag along and we could come and see you?"

"I'm looking forward to it." I lean back in my seat and close my eyes. "Sarah...do you think I should call your mom and your grandparents? They must be so disappointed that I didn't stay in contact. Are they angry with me?"

"No, they'd love to hear from you," she says. "They worry about you, you know. Even after all this time. They lost a daughter and a sister, but they feel like they lost you too."

Guilt twists in my gut. Two years of unanswered calls and cards. Two years of running from the grief I saw reflected in their eyes. Two years of letting them worry. "I'll call them."

"Please do, that would make them so happy." I hear the smile in her voice. "And Ruby? I'm glad you called. Really glad."

We say goodbye, and I sit there, staring at Claire's parents' number in my phone. I feel like crying again, but I hold it in. Not yet. Later, when I get home. *Just press it, Walsh. One more step forward.*

I press dial.

EIGHTEEN
ATHENA

The security feed shows nothing but Ruby's empty balcony and office, yet I'm checking it every few minutes.

Mark has called three times already, wanting to discuss growth strategies. Maria keeps sending emails marked urgent again. The Olympus demands my attention, but all I can think about is the way Ruby's skin felt under my hands.

She hasn't been outside since Sunday and I'm acting like a lovesick teenager.

Life is beautifully uncomplicated right now. The Olympus runs smoothly, the club provides pleasure, and I answer to no one. Why would I risk that perfect equilibrium for someone who's clearly not ready for anything more than friendship? And even if she were, I know what loss can do to a person. I'm no less damaged goods than she is.

Everything in my life has a purpose, a reason. But this... this feeling that's taking root in my chest serves no purpose except to complicate things.

I don't catch feelings, and I don't pine over women. I take what I want, when I want it. That's been my way for almost two decades. If I desire something—or someone—I pursue it with single-minded focus until it's mine. But Ruby isn't some pleasure to be claimed. She's all raw nerve endings and healing wounds, fresh tears and tentative steps forward.

The truth is, I'm not used to feeling this uncertain. Desire, yes—that's familiar territory. But this constant awareness of her, this need to make sure she's okay, this urge to protect and possess her all at once...it's foreign and unsettling. Like a gambler who's forgotten the odds, I keep coming back to thoughts of her, hoping for a different outcome.

I don't even have her number. We exist in this strange dance of waves and impromptu visits, like we're playing at being neighbors in some quaint suburban fantasy. I shut down the feeds with more force than necessary. I'm driving myself mad and I need to get out of here.

Rushing to my car, I lower the roof and remove my hat —it's impractical for what I have in mind—and slide behind the wheel.

The contrast between the garage's climate-controlled darkness and the assault of Vegas heat is shocking as I emerge onto the Strip, tourist crowds squinting in the glare. I'm plotting my escape route—past the MSG Sphere, onto the 215, then out toward Red Rock Canyon where the real desert begins. My hands grip the wheel tighter than necessary. Some people drink or turn to drugs when they feel control slipping away. Some gamble. Some shop. I drive.

Vegas falls away in my rearview mirror as I push the car faster. The speedometer climbs past eighty, ninety. Heat ripples rise from the asphalt, making the road ahead shimmer. These escapes are rare—I can count on one hand the number of times I've felt this need since I moved to Vegas. Back in Greece, I would drive to the coast, find some deserted stretch of shoreline where the rhythm of waves would drown out my thoughts. Here, I've learned to let the combination of speed and desert serve the same purpose.

The mountains rise ahead, stark and magnificent in the brutal daylight. A red-tailed hawk circles overhead, riding thermal currents. Out here, the road stretches empty in both directions. That's the beauty of the desert—you can see other vehicles coming from miles away. There's no risk to anyone but myself. Just me and my beloved car testing our limits against the landscape.

I know these roads intimately—every curve, every rise, every place where civilization surrenders to wilderness. The Aston Martin responds to my touch like a thorough-bred horse, eager for more speed. We dance together along the empty road, pushing boundaries, seeking that edge where skill meets risk.

A sharp turn appears, and I take it fast, maybe too fast. The back end slides, tires losing their grip. For one heart-stopping moment, the car fishtails wildly. My hands move instinctively, correcting the slide, but it's closer than I like. The car skids to a stop, dust billowing around us.

I sit there, breathing fast, hands trembling on the wheel, heart hammering. The pulse in my temples is so loud it drowns out everything else. That was stupid. Reckless.

"Okay," I whisper to myself, letting out a long breath. "Enough." The adrenaline has done its job, cleared my head of thoughts I'd rather not examine too closely. The mountains loom silent and indifferent, unmoved by my small dramas. Their ancient faces have witnessed countless human struggles, and mine is just one more brief moment in their endless timeline.

I know a turnoff ahead, a viewpoint where the valley spreads out below. I downshift, feeling the car's power through my hands on the wheel, and take the dirt road carefully. The viewpoint is empty and beyond the windshield, heat waves distort the landscape while the sun sinks.

Nothing but wilderness stretches before me—layer upon layer of mountains fading into the distance, deep canyons carved by ancient waters, vast expanses of desert scrub. The harsh glare has softened, painting the rocks in shades of amber and rose. It's so still out here, not a hint of a breeze.

A family of quail scurries past, the babies following their mother in single file. They pause at the edge of a scrubby bush, the mother alert for danger while her chicks dart for cover. Nature's own little power dynamic—protect and control, lead and follow.

The sun touches the western mountains, and suddenly everything is gold. The light paints the rock faces, transforming the landscape into something almost otherworldly.

Does Ruby ever watch sunsets? I doubt it.

"Stop it," I tell myself. The desert swallows my words. This isn't why I came here. I didn't drive into the desert to think about Ruby Walsh. I came here to escape thoughts of her.

I'm alone by choice, by design, by necessity. The club provides everything I need—power, pleasure, the illusion of intimacy without its complications. I need to keep it that way.

The sun slips lower and violet shadows pool in the canyon depths while the peaks still flame with light. A raven calls somewhere below, its voice echoing off the cliff faces. This is the magic hour, when the desert reveals its secrets. When the line between earth and sky blurs, when anything seems possible. The time when decisions made in daylight's harsh reality might shift.

But I know better. Love can be dangerous—I learned that lesson well enough in another life. Better to trust in what you can control.

I watch until the last rays fade from the highest peaks, until the first stars appear in the deepening blue above. Time to head back and hold Mark's hand through Pankration Night in the Palestra. The massive arena, designed to echo the ancient Greek wrestling schools, has become the Olympus's main attraction on Tuesday nights. Mark gets nervous handling these events without my input. Our modern take on the combat sport draws a particular crowd—mostly MMA enthusiasts, all wanting to prove themselves in what they call "the purest form of fighting." The combination of ancient tradition and modern egos can be volatile, especially once the betting and drinking start. While our security team is excellent, some situations require a more diplomatic touch, making sure no one gets too creative with the wrestling rules.

The stars multiply across the sky as I get into my car. My mind isn't clear, but it's a little calmer. The desert's done its job.

NINETEEN
RUBY

The lights in the other offices have dimmed one by one, leaving our corner on the fortieth floor glowing like a beacon. Miranda is still at her desk outside my office, powered by what must be her tenth espresso of the day.

"That's the last of the Morrison paperwork," she says, adding another stack to my desk. "See? We've almost caught up on the backlog. You *can* take a vacation from time to time."

I glance at my watch—7:02 p.m. Usually at this hour, I'd just be hitting my stride, settling in for a long night of more work. But tonight, my mind keeps wandering to white suits and handcuffs.

"Earth to Ruby?" Miranda waves a hand in front of my face. "You okay?"

"Yeah. Thanks for this." I shuffle papers on my desk, trying to look busy. The truth is, I haven't accomplished nearly as much as I should have today. Every time I try to focus on work, I remember Athena's hands on my skin and fantasies flash before me.

Miranda perches on the edge of my desk—something she only does when we're alone.

"So..." she says carefully. "How was your week off? Did you actually relax for once?"

I consider my answer. "It was...interesting. Difficult at first." I pick up a random file, not meeting her eyes. "I finally dealt with some things I've been putting off. Claire's clothes, her subscriptions, calls I should have made ages ago."

"Oh..." Her voice softens. "That must have been hard."

"It was time. I'm ready to focus on work again."

That's not entirely true. While I've cleared some of the physical reminders of Claire from my house, my mind is caught between two worlds. Every memory of Claire that surfaces now tangles with new images—women giving themselves over to pleasure, leather against skin, power exchanged like currency. And through it all, Athena's dark eyes watching me. I'm suspended between grief and hunger, between letting go and holding on, between what was and what could be.

"Miranda?" I try to sound casual. "This is going to sound strange, but...where would you go lingerie shopping in Vegas? Somewhere high-end."

She nearly chokes on her coffee. "I'm sorry, what?"

"Lingerie. You know, nice stuff." I can feel my face heating.

Miranda sets down her cup and studies me. I've never asked her anything personal, let alone for shopping advice. "Okay, who are you and what have you done with my boss?"

"Never mind, forget I asked—"

"No, no!" She grins. "This is fantastic. There's an amazing boutique at the Wynn. Small, private brands. Very

sexy, very exclusive. Or La Perla at the Shops at Crystals."
She pauses. "Are you...seeing someone?"

"No!" I say too quickly. "I just need...I mean, I want..."

"You don't have to explain," Miranda says. "I'm just
glad you're thinking about...well, anything besides work."

I nod. "Yeah. I'm trying."

"Both shops are still open," Miranda continues,
checking her phone. "Want company?"

"No!" Again, too quick. "I mean, thank you, but this is
something I need to do alone."

"Of course." She slides off my desk, trying to hide her
smile. "Well, whoever they are, they're lucky."

If she only knew I'm not shopping for a date. I'm shopping for...what exactly? The chance to explore something
darker? Even if I never do, which is highly likely, I'd still like
to have something pretty to wear under my clothes. Just in
case...

"Go," Miranda says. "Before you change your mind."

I start packing up my things, then stop. "Miranda?
Thank you. For everything. These past two years...I know I
haven't been easy to work with. I pushed myself too hard,
but I'm aware I did the same to you."

"It's okay. I love my job," she assures me. "I'm just glad
you're ready to start living again."

I nod, resisting the urge to give her a hug. *Living again.*
Is that what this is? This electric feeling under my skin, this
constant awareness of possibility?

THE SHOPS at Crystals is quiet when I arrive. The luxury
mall's angular architecture soars overhead, glass and sharp
edges bathed in strategic lighting. I must have walked past

this store a hundred times without giving it a second glance. Now I stand outside, heart racing like I'm about to enter a courtroom.

The boutique is elegant, intimate. A sales associate approaches—tall, blonde—and gives me a polite nod as I enter. "Hi, I'm Sally. Can I help you find something?"

What am I looking for? Something that says *I think I want you to tie me up, but I'm not sure because I've never done this before?* Instead, I hear myself say, "Something black. Simple but..."

"Provocative?" she suggests.

"Yes." My voice comes out hoarse. "A little sexy."

She leads me through racks of beautiful lingerie. Everything is understated, expensive, designed to reveal and conceal in equal measure. I touch a black bodysuit, imagining Athena's reaction to seeing me in it.

Sally looks me up and down, taking in my proportions.

"I'm a 34B," I tell her, trying not to fidget under her assessment.

"I think you should try a 32C instead," she says decisively. "Trust me. Most women spend their whole lives wearing the wrong cup size. It's my job to get it right." She pulls out several pieces: a black lace balcony bra; a pair of matching Brazilian panties...

"Will you be wearing heels?" she asks.

My core flutters when I think about Athena's playroom. "Probably."

She nods. "Then you'll want stockings and a garter belt too." She selects a pair of sheer black silk stockings with wide lace tops. "These have a reinforced toe and heel— more comfortable for extended wear.

"The garter belt is essential," she continues, showing me a band of black lace designed to sit at the natural waist. Four satin straps dangle from it, each ending in a clip.

She lays everything out on the counter: bra, panties, garter belt, stockings. The ensemble looks elegant, sensual and decidedly wicked. "The fitting room is right this way. Would you like to try them on?"

I hesitate. Part of me wants to just buy everything and run, but I know fit matters. "Yes, please."

The fitting room is mercifully spacious, with warm lighting and an armchair in the corner. Sally hangs the pieces on hooks, and sensing I'm a little clueless, she demonstrates the proper way to attach the stockings to the garter belt.

Alone in the room, I strip down to my practical black underwear. The contrast between what I'm wearing and what's hanging on the hooks couldn't be starker. I've never worn anything like that. Never felt the need.

I slip on the bra and the fit is perfect, the lace soft rather than scratchy. Then the panties and stockings and the garter belt follow, sitting securely but comfortably at my waist. It takes some fumbling to get the stockings attached, but once they are, everything feels snug and comfortable.

Stepping back into my heels, I turn to face the mirror and a soft gasp escapes me. The woman staring back at me is a stranger. I look...powerful. Desirable. And fuck, I look hot.

My fingers trail over the lace at my hip, tracing where it meets skin. There's something magical about the way this lingerie transforms not just how I look, but how I feel—precious, like a gift waiting to be unwrapped. I feel like a woman who deserves to be looked at, to be touched, to be wanted.

"Can I come in?" Sally asks.

I hesitate, one hand instinctively moving to cover my stomach, the other to my chest. It seems too intimate to let anyone see me like this, even a professional. Then I remember where I might be wearing this outfit—what I might be doing while wearing it—and almost laugh at my modesty. A sales assistant should be the least of my worries.

"Yes, come in."

She enters and gives me a big smile. "See? I knew it. That's your size—32C." She adjusts one of the bra straps and steps back to inspect me. "Wow. You look stunning. Some lucky man is going to be very, very happy."

I chuckle. "Woman, actually."

"Ah!" Her smile doesn't falter. "Well, in that case, she's going to be one lucky woman." She winks. "Want to try on a few more pieces?"

TWENTY

ATHENA

"Jesus..." The word escapes me before I can stop it. Ruby stands in my foyer, and for a moment, I forget how to breathe.

"What?" she asks, arching a brow. There's a quiet confidence beneath her nervousness tonight, like she knows exactly what effect she has on me.

My mouth goes dry, and for once, I'm struggling to find words. "You look beautiful," I finally manage. And she does —devastating in an oversized black satin shirt dress, unbuttoned just low enough to reveal the edge of her lace bra. Her legs seem endless in elegant heels, and her skin glows like she's finally been sleeping.

The dress reveals more of her bra when she shifts her weight. I've seen countless women in various states of undress in my club, orchestrated scenes of exquisite submission, but something about Ruby fully clothed yet hinting at what lies beneath affects me more than any display of skin.

My eyes catch on the leather carryall at her feet. "What's that? Are you staying the night?" I joke.

She chuckles and hands me the bag. "No, it's the money. A hundred thousand dollars."

"Seriously?" I burst out laughing. The sound echoes off the marble floors, and Ruby looks startled by my reaction. "And you thought you'd just bring it over in cash?"

She grins goofily. It's endearing. "I changed my mind about the transaction. I was worried it might raise suspicion on my account. You know, if I ever got investigated or something."

"Investigated for what?" I can't stop laughing. She's so fucking innocent it hurts. Here she is, a high-powered corporate lawyer who can destroy companies, worried about a bank transfer. "And you think taking out the cash and carrying it in a leather carryall looks perfectly legit?"

"When you put it like that..." Ruby shrugs and laughs along. "Anyway, it's done, so just take it."

Every time I think I have her figured out she surprises me. The ruthless lawyer and the woman who watches from her window. The grieving widow and the curious observer.

I shake my head, still amused. "Actually, I was going to talk to you about that. I don't want your money."

Her brow furrows, creating that little line that I'm learning means she's about to argue. "What?"

"Consider it a gift. Living next door, you don't need the limo service, and you don't strike me as someone who will drink me dry of Crystal or ask my runner to find you fresh sea urchin at midnight." Used to their comforts, most members love the personal concierge service, but I suspect Ruby's less demanding.

She shakes her head. "No. Absolutely not. You may be my neighbor, and I'm grateful for everything you've done, but I'm still cautious. I don't want to feel like I owe you anything."

"Because I'm a big, scary casino boss?" I stare at her, enjoying how I'm making her blush.

"Something like that." But there's a flirty edge to her smile that makes my pulse quicken.

This is a new side of Ruby—playful, almost daring. The grieving widow is still there in the shadows behind her eyes, but something else is emerging. Something that makes me want to discover every facet of her.

"Please. Just take it," she says. "I don't normally splash out like this, but it's worth it. I can only begin to imagine what it costs to run that place." She holds up a hand when I'm about to protest. "Don't argue with me. Not over this."

"Very well." I signal to Robert, who materializes from the shadows like he always does. "Put this in the safe, please," I tell him, handing over the bag. He nods and disappears with it, leaving Ruby and me alone again.

"Are you heading downstairs?" she asks.

"Yes, I was just about to, but—" I'm interrupted by the arrival of two women. One of our newest members, Dr. Lily Chen, the pioneering neurosurgeon behind groundbreaking clinical trials, and Captain Mari Rodriguez, one of the few female commanders in the Air Force's elite test pilot program.

After I greet them and introduce them to Ruby, they turn toward the library, but Lily pauses at the door. "Join us for champagne later? We're celebrating my grant approval." She winks at Ruby. "I hear you're quite the force in the boardroom—would love to hear about your famous take-downs sometime."

"Nuh-uh," I say firmly, catching Ruby's intrigued expression. "No shop talk at the club or I might have to punish her for breaking the rules."

The word "punish" lands exactly as intended. Ruby's

breath catches, and for a moment, she forgets about Lily and Mari entirely. Her fingers curl against her thigh, and there's a subtle shift in her posture—a yielding that's almost imperceptible but speaks volumes. When she finally responds, her voice has dropped lower, taking on a husky quality that wasn't there before. "Is that a threat or a promise?"

"Both," I murmur, letting my voice drop to match hers.

Lily whistles low through her teeth. "And on that note, we'll leave you two to...discuss club policies." She winks at Mari. "Come on, let those sparks fly without an audience."

Ruby stays against the wall where she's backed up. She watches them disappear into the library, clearly trying to collect herself. "Those women...how do you find them?" She's changed the topic, which is interesting. "They're amazing."

"They find me," I say, purposely maintaining the distance between us, letting her recover her equilibrium. "No one outside the club talks about what happens here, but if they know someone who might want to become part of it, they discreetly send them my way." I step closer then, drawn by the lingering vulnerability in her pose. "And yes, they're amazing, though I have to say, none of them have made quite the entrance you did tonight."

Ruby's cheeks flush at the compliment. She moves to follow them downstairs, but I catch her hand and feel the jump in her pulse where my fingers rest against her wrist.

"Wait."

Her eyes meet mine, questioning.

"All jokes about scary casino bosses aside..." I pause, choosing my words carefully. "If you ever want to explore those handcuffs—if it's what you want—I need something from you." I'm deliberately *not* using words such as submission or BDSM, conscious it might scare her. "I'll need you to trust me. Completely."

"I just gave you a bag with enough money to buy a house without asking for a receipt," she says with a hint of sass, her eyes flicking to my mouth.

I smile, noting how she licks her lips without even realizing it. She wants to kiss me. The realization sends a rush of heat between my thighs, but I force myself to stay still. Kissing crosses a line that I'm not ready to cross. It goes beyond the controlled exchange of power, beyond the dance of dominance and submission. Kissing is messy, emotional— it leads to feelings that can't be contained within scene boundaries or safe words. But God, I want to kiss her too.

I could do it right now. She's close and her lips are slightly parted, plump and so inviting. But kissing Ruby Walsh would be like lighting a match in a room full of gunpowder.

"Athena?" Her voice pulls me back from my thoughts and I realize I've been staring at her mouth for too long. She squeezes my hand. "Yes," she says, her voice soft and without sarcasm now. "I trust you. I don't know how or why, but I do. And that says a lot. But..."

"But?"

Ruby shifts, her fingers tightening around mine. "I'm not sure I'm ready for..." She pauses, cheeks flushing. "You know."

"Hey." I cup her cheek and feel the heat radiating from her body. "You don't have to do anything you don't want to. Have a drink. Enjoy yourself. Let your hair down and hang out with a bunch of cool women. I'm just really happy to have you here."

TWENTY-ONE
RUBY

The whiskey burns pleasantly as I take another sip, letting the exclusive spirit linger on my tongue. From my position on one of the velvet sofas, I have a good view of the main lounge. It's busier than last time—at least forty women are scattered across the space, some dancing, others gathered around tables in intimate conversation.

Captain Rodriguez—"Call me Mari"—is telling me about flying an experimental aircraft, her hands animated as she describes breaking the sound barrier.

"Another round?" she asks, noticing my nearly empty glass.

I nod, watching as she signals one of the waitresses. The service here is impeccable—discreet staff who appear when needed and fade away just as smoothly, and no money changes hands. The rules are simple: no business talk, no gambling, no financial transactions, no illegal substances. It creates a sanctuary where powerful women can truly relax.

My eyes drift to Athena, who's across the room talking to a small group near the bar. She's shed her white hat, but otherwise looks immaculate in her signature white suit.

Even here, she maintains that aura of control. The way she commands attention without trying, how other women defer to her gestures—it's mesmerizing.

"See something you like?" A new voice joins our conversation. I turn to find Justice Donovan—Donna— settling onto the sofa beside me. She's traded her red dress for a black pantsuit tonight.

"I don't know what you mean," I say, but the heat in my cheeks betrays me.

Donna laughs. "Honey, I've been coming here for a while. I know that look." She accepts a fresh martini from the waitress. "Athena has that effect on people. Especially the ones who crave what she has to offer."

"And what's that?" I ask, though I already know the answer.

"Control," she says simply, lighting a skinny cigarette. "Or rather, the freedom that comes from giving it up." She studies me over the rim of her glass. "Some of us spend our whole lives maintaining iron control. Making decisions that affect hundreds, even thousands of lives. Never showing weakness." Her eyes drift to Athena. "Sometimes the greatest relief is in letting someone else take the reins."

The whiskey must be hitting me because I ask, "Do you do that with her?"

Donna's laugh rings out again. "God, no. That's not my thing. I just stay here, in the lounge. But Athena... She's a regular on that side of the club."

I watch as Athena moves through the room, stopping to chat with various groups. She touches women casually—a hand on a shoulder, fingers brushing an arm.

The belly dancer from last week is performing again, her hips moving in hypnotic circles. Two tipsy women have joined her on the small stage, matching her movements with varying degrees of success. Their laughter floats across the room, uninhibited and free.

"It's strange," I say. "I've spent two years building walls, and somehow she just...walked right through them."

"Walls don't work here," Mari says, gesturing around the room. "That's the whole point. Look at Angela over there—runs the biggest tech company in Silicon Valley. Going on what the tabloids write about her, she's a loner. A workaholic with no social life. Yet she's here every week, dancing badly and having fun."

"How did you start?" I ask Mari. "How did you end up here?"

She exchanges a look with Donna. "Someone recommended me. I was skeptical but also too curious not to meet with Athena." She grins. "I'm glad I did. The whiskey is excellent."

A burst of laughter draws my attention back to Athena. She's said something that has her group in stitches, and the sound of her laughter carries across the room. As if sensing my gaze, she looks up and our eyes meet. The intensity of her stare, even from a distance, makes me freeze. She excuses herself from her group and starts making her way toward us.

"And that's our cue to give you some privacy," Donna says, standing. She squeezes my shoulder. "I'll talk to you later."

Mari follows her, leaving me alone just as Athena reaches the sofa. She slides into the space they've vacated and places a hand on my thigh.

"Enjoying yourself?" she asks.

"Yes," I admit. "Very much." My gaze drifts to her hand on my leg. Her touch is deliberate, like she's creating excuses for contact rather than just finding a comfortable position. The chemistry between us is soaring—I'm not sure when it started, but I feel it in every look and touch.

"Good." She squeezes my leg and lifts my chin with her other hand, forcing me to meet her gaze. The gesture is pure dominance, and my body responds instinctively. There's no denying I'm physically drawn to her dominant side. "Tell me, Ruby, do I make you feel uncomfortable?"

I swallow hard, caught in her eyes. "No," I lie. "Well, maybe a little, but not in a bad way. It's more like..." I trail off, struggling to articulate the mix of attraction and nervousness she stirs in me.

She saves me from my fumbling attempt to explain by standing and extending her hand. "Dance with me?"

"I don't dance," I say, but she pulls me to my feet.

"Tonight, you do."

The music has shifted to something slower, more sensual. Athena guides me to a quiet corner of the dance floor, one hand settling on my waist while the other keeps hold of mine.

"Relax," she murmurs against my ear. "No one's watching. No one cares. Just feel. It's nice, isn't it?"

We move together, and suddenly dancing feels natural. I let her lead, my body gradually softening against hers. The whiskey has loosened my limbs, making it easier to follow her movements.

"See?" Her breath is warm against my neck. "You can dance after all."

I want to say something clever, but words fail me. I press closer, letting my head rest against her shoulder, and her hand tightens on my waist in response. She smells incredible.

"Do you dance with all the women here?" I ask.

"No. I don't usually dance at all." Her voice holds a hint of amusement. "Why do you ask? Are you jealous?"

"No," I say too quickly. "There's nothing to be jealous about."

"Hmm," she hums, the sound vibrating through her chest where I'm pressed against her. "If you say so."

I lift my head to look at her, finding her face inches from mine. The urge to kiss her is overwhelming. It would be so easy to close that small distance, to finally taste those lips. But something in her expression stops me—a mix of desire and restraint that mirrors my own confusion.

She pulls me closer and a soft moan escapes me. I can't help it; her thigh has slipped between mine, and the pressure is exquisite. My hand slides from her shoulder to the back of her neck, fingers threading through her hair. Her grip tightens on my hip, either steadying me or warning me —I'm not sure which.

"Careful," she whispers. "You're playing with fire."

"Maybe I want to burn." The words don't sound like my own—I blame the whiskey, the music, the way she makes me feel untethered from my usual self.

Her lips, those luscious lips, pull into a smile, and she tilts her head. She seems caught off guard by my reply, like she's the one struggling to find words now. It's satisfying to see her composure slip, even if just for a moment.

But then she recovers, nodding toward the red velvet curtains that lead to the rest of the club. "Very well. Would you like to watch a show with me?"

TWENTY-TWO
ATHENA

I open the door for Ruby, my heart racing as my control is slipping through my fingers. Tonight is about crossing boundaries, for both of us. I'm treading on dangerous ground, but isn't that what I created this sanctuary for? To explore desires without judgment? What I desire is to make Ruby mine.

Her reaction mirrors her first visit; her breath catches, pupils dilating in the dim light. On the bed, Alex and Morgan, two members who have been with me since the beginning, are lost in each other. Morgan's red lingerie stands out against her olive skin, while Alex's dark hair falls forward as they lean down to kiss Morgan's neck, their white shirt coming untucked from tailored slacks. Their soft moans fill the air, creating an intimate soundtrack to the scene unfolding.

There's no one else in the room with them tonight. The oversize armchair in the corner beckons, and I settle into it, then pat my lap in invitation. "Come here," I say to Ruby.

"Hi, ladies," Morgan purrs between kisses. "Athena, I didn't expect you here."

"I have a special guest tonight," I say, my eyes locked on Ruby. "And my special guest likes to watch."

Ruby opens her mouth as if to protest, then thinks better of it. Her gaze flicks between me and the couple on the bed, desire warring with hesitation. Finally, she moves toward me. When she sinks onto my lap, I pull her close, feeling the delicious tremor that runs through her body as my arms encircle her waist.

"Mm...in that case, enjoy the show," Morgan whispers as Alex's fingers find the clasp of her bra.

Ruby's weight on my lap is intoxicating, and I adjust her slightly, pulling her back against my chest. Her breath hitches as Alex slides Morgan's bra strap down, following the movement with their lips.

"Are you comfortable?" I whisper in Ruby's ear, one hand splayed across her stomach. She nods, unable to look away from the bed where Morgan arches into Alex's touch.

On the bed, Alex takes their time, slowly unbuttoning their shirt while Morgan watches with hooded eyes. There's something powerful in their dynamic—Morgan's feminine curves against Alex's lean angles, soft against hard, yield against take.

Alex finally shrugs off their shirt, revealing a toned chest bound in a simple black binder. Morgan reaches up, pulling them down for a deep kiss, and Ruby shifts in my lap, unconsciously seeking friction. Her reaction sends heat pooling low in my belly, and I tighten my grip on her waist, holding her still.

"Are they a couple?" she asks.

"No. They just like to fuck."

Morgan turns around and gets on her hands and knees, the silk sheets rustling beneath her. My hand trails along Ruby's thigh as she watches, inching the hem of her dress higher. She shivers at my touch but keeps her eyes fixed on the scene before us.

Morgan's long dark hair cascades down her back as she looks over her shoulder at Alex, her lips parted in a silent plea. Her heavy-lidded eyes are dark as Alex runs their hands along her sides, tracing the delicate lace of her lingerie before gripping her hips with controlled strength. They bend over Morgan to slide her hair to the side and kiss her neck.

My fingers trace patterns on Ruby's thigh and find the lace edge of her stockings. Fuck. She's wearing a garter belt. I'm such a sucker for garter belts. I pull at the elastic, stretching it taut before I let it snap back against her skin.

Ruby flinches, but she's shifting as if seeking more. I don't even think she knows she's doing it; she's so focused on the scene before her. Her breath hitches as Alex unbuttons their slacks, and even *I'm* pleasantly surprised when I see they're wearing a strap-on underneath. I don't normally watch, but this is going to be a treat.

"Fuck me," Morgan pleads when Alex slides her panties to the side. They stroke her, caress her until she's a moaning mess.

Ruby's breathing grows ragged as she watches Alex tease Morgan mercilessly, stroking her entrance with the tip of the toy.

"How do you feel?" I ask Ruby, my hand inching higher up her thigh.

"I'm so turned on," she whispers, unable to tear her eyes away as Alex finally pushes into Morgan with a slow thrust. Morgan's cries of pleasure fill the room, her fingers gripping the sheets. Ruby presses back against me and I trail kisses along her neck, reveling in the way she trembles at my touch.

"They're good together, aren't they?" I murmur, letting my fingers drift higher up her thigh before retreating again.

Ruby's reply is a moan, and I trace her earlobe with the tip of my tongue, drawing another, louder moan from her lips. She's putty in my hands, but I'm not going to give her release. She'll have to wait, beg, plead for as long as it takes. Days, weeks...

Morgan rocks back, taking Alex deeper with each thrust. It's intimate and beautiful—the kind of synchronicity that comes from knowing exactly how to please each other. Ruby squirms against me, seeking more friction, but I keep my caresses light.

Alex's grip tightens on Morgan's hips, leaving faint marks on her skin as they guide her movements and increase their pace. Morgan's other bra strap slips down her shoulder, revealing more of her breast, and Alex reaches around to cup it, rolling her nipple between their fingers. There's the sound of skin slapping against skin and Morgan's escalating cries of pleasure mixing with Alex's low growls of encouragement. It's primal watching them together—the way Alex's muscles flex with each thrust, the sheen of sweat on Morgan's back, how her body yields to their control. The building tension affects me.

Alex shifts their angle slightly, drawing a deep moan from Morgan that makes Ruby wiggle in my lap. Their movements become more urgent, more demanding, and Morgan responds beautifully. Her back arches deeper, head thrown back as Alex fists her hair, pulling just enough to make her gasp.

Alex's movements are relentless now, each thrust powerful, their free hand still teasing Morgan's breast while the other grips her hair. The tension in the room is charged, the air heavy with the scent of sex and desire. Morgan's limbs begin to shake, and Alex wraps an arm around her waist, holding her up as she starts to come apart beneath them. The sight of Morgan's complete surrender, combined with Alex's raw display of power, has Ruby practically vibrating in my lap.

I spread my legs, and intentionally in doing so, I spread Ruby's legs along with them, exposing her lingerie to the women on the bed. She gasps at the sudden move, her body tensing against mine, but she stays still. I can feel the heat radiating from her, her arousal evident even through her dress.

Ruby grabs my hand and guides it inside her shirtdress, pressing it firmly against her breast. Her breasts are full and delicious, her heart racing beneath my palm. She arches into my touch, a quiet whimper escaping her lips. Part of me wants to give in, to take her right here—but another part holds back, reminding me to be careful. To stick to my rules.

I squeeze her breast while my other hand firmly massages the inside of her thigh, higher and higher. She's writhing, grinding against me so restlessly I think she might climax from this alone.

On the bed, Morgan's cries reach a fever pitch as she climbs toward her peak. The sound seems to ignite something primal in Ruby as she lifts her arms and reaches behind her to caress my hair, arching her back in the most sensual way.

"Please," she whispers, her voice thick with need.

Morgan moans out as her orgasm crashes over her and Ruby presses herself harder against me. It's mesmerizing to watch, like she's in some sensuous trance, years of withholding spilling out.

Morgan and Alex collapse and lie tangled in each other's arms. It's my cue to withdraw my hand from Ruby's thigh, earning a sound of protest that makes me smile against her neck. She's wound tight from watching, from my relentless teasing, her skin flushed and warm. The truth is, I'm just as affected.

I'm about to suggest we have another drink to cool off a little when Ruby suddenly turns to look at me, then at Alex and Morgan on the bed. She brings a hand to her mouth and shakes her head. She looks like she's just snapped out of a moment. A moment she regrets.

"I'm sorry," she murmurs. "I have to go."

I kick off my heels and dive into the pool fully dressed. The shock of cold water hits like a slap, exactly what I need to snap out of whatever spell I was under tonight. I push deeper, letting the water muffle everything until there's nothing but the sound of my own heartbeat. My shirtdress tangles around my thighs, dragging me, but I push deeper until my fingers brush the tiles at the bottom.

Not until my lungs are about to burst do I surface, gasping for air as I cling onto the poolside. I glance at the steps, then decide I'm not ready to get out. I turn onto my back and float, facing the sky while my sleeves billow around me like dark wings. *What am I doing?* The question echoes in my head, impossible to silence.

For two years, I've wrapped myself in armor. Work became my shield, loneliness my constant companion. But tonight, watching those women together, feeling Athena's hands on me...I wanted things. Craved things. Physical things. The intensity of that desire terrifies me. Even now, floating in the cold water, my body is burning remembering her touch—the firm pressure of her fingers on my thigh, the heat of her breath against my neck, the way she held me still when I wanted to move against her.

"I'm sorry," I whisper to the night sky. My voice breaks. "I'm so sorry, Claire." The words dissolve into the desert breeze.

Tonight, I forgot about her. Claire wasn't on my mind for even a second while I was sitting on Athena's lap. For the first time since she died, I existed completely in a moment without her shadow over me. And that betrayal cuts deep—the fact that another woman could make me forget, even for a moment, the love of my life.

Guilt crashes over me. Not just because I wanted someone else—that seems almost secondary to the betrayal of wanting Athena more intensely than I ever wanted Claire, at least in the physical sense. My intimacy with Claire was sweet, tender, built on years of love and trust. What I felt tonight was something else entirely—raw, primal, overwhelming. The kind of desire that threatens to consume everything in its path. The kind of desire that makes people do stupid things.

I feel heavy with shame. In Athena's club, watching strangers find pleasure in each other's bodies, I forgot myself. Forgot my grief, my guilt, my walls. Worse, I didn't want to remember. For those moments in Athena's lap, I was someone else—someone who could feel desire without drowning in loss, someone who could watch two people fuck without blushing, someone who could spread her legs and beg to be touched.

I dive under again, hoping the cold will clear my head. It doesn't. The shame burns hotter than the desire now. God, what was I thinking? I so desperately wanted to be part of it.

Claire and I used to swim here together on summer

nights. She would joke about skinny dipping but never actually did it. She would talk about making love in the pool, but we always ended up in bed instead. The memory feels distant now, like it belongs to someone else —someone who didn't know that desire could feel like drowning.

"What would you think of me now?" I ask the stars. Claire had such faith in me, such trust, and she knew me inside out. Would she understand this version of me? Would she understand that I could want something so different from what we shared? That the tenderness we had, while beautiful, never made me burn like this?

What would she think of me sitting in dark rooms watching strangers fuck while trembling at another woman's touch, fantasizing about being tied up, controlled, made to beg?

We never talked about things like that. Sex was sweet between us, comfortable like everything else in our relationship. We made love on Sunday mornings, slow and gentle, and it was more about connection than passion. She never pushed for more, and I never knew I wanted more. Physical intimacy was just one part of our life together, not something that consumed our thoughts.

Crossing my arms over the pool's edge, I stare at my reflection in the glass doors. A stranger stares back at me; I barely recognize myself anymore. The controlled lawyer seems far away. In her place is this new creature, dripping and desperate, caught between desire and duty, between the safety of solitude and the dangerous promise of pleasure.

"Ruby?"

The voice startles me out of my reverie. Athena appears at the pool's edge.

"How did you get in?" My voice sounds rough, like I've been crying. Maybe I have; it's all a bit of a blur.

"I followed you. Slipped through before your gates closed." She doesn't apologize for the intrusion, just studies me with those dark eyes. Her gaze travels over my face, taking in what must be quite a sight—wet hair plastered to my neck, mascara streaking my cheeks. "May I join you?"

I hesitate, then nod. The surreal quality of this night deepens as I watch her kick off her shoes and remove her hat. Then she steps to the edge and dives in fully clothed.

She surfaces near me in a sweep of dark hair and white fabric, water streaming down her face. When she reaches me, she grips the edge of the pool beside me.

"You must think I'm crazy," I say. "The unstable woman next door who can't make up her mind."

"Not at all." A breeze stirs the palm fronds overhead. "If anything, I should apologize. I pushed too hard again." She meets my eyes. "Do you feel guilty?"

"Yes." The admission comes easier than I expected.

She nods. "I understand."

"I believe you do. I even feel like you understand everything I'm *not* saying." I frown as I study her. "You know so much about me and I know nothing about you."

"I don't like to talk about myself," she says.

"Why is that?"

She chuckles. "Answering that question would require me to talk about myself."

I'm not willing to give up. I've bared my soul to her, and as much as she wants me to trust her, I want the same in return. "Tell me why it is that I feel like you understand my grief," I whisper. "What happened to you?"

Athena's expression shifts, something vulnerable flickering across her features before disappearing like a ripple in still water. She seems uncertain, as if weighing how much of herself to reveal.

"Okay," she says finally, pushing away from the pool's edge. "Let's get dry and make coffee." She swims to the steps, water streaming from her suit as she rises. Turning back to me, she extends her hand. "And I'll tell you a story about a girl from Athens who used to be a hopeless romantic."

I take her offered hand, letting her pull me up.

"But I'm warning you," she adds. "It's not the happy kind. It's a tragedy."

TWENTY-FOUR

ATHENA

The temperature has dropped and I shiver as I sit on one of Ruby's sun loungers with a cappuccino, wrapped in one of her toweling robes. Ruby sits cross-legged on the adjacent lounger, wearing an oversize sweatshirt, her wet hair darkening the fabric where it touches her shoulders.

Her eyes hold mine, patient but expectant. I owe her this story, though every fiber of my being wants to deflect, to change the subject, to maintain the distance I've cultivated. But she's shared so much of herself with me. Perhaps it's time to open up in return.

"I studied international business in London," I begin, the words feeling strange in my mouth. I haven't spoken about this in years. "I could have gone anywhere—my father's influence opened doors worldwide. But I chose London because of what it represented. Freedom." I pause, watching the play of moonlight on the water. "The kind of freedom I couldn't find in Greece."

Ruby shifts, drawing her knees to her chest. "Freedom to be yourself?"

"Yes." I twist one of my gold bangles. "In Athens, I was

Alexandros Stavros's daughter, heir to one of the largest shipping empires in the Mediterranean. Being gay wasn't—still isn't—entirely accepted in those circles. I had this wild vision of what London would be like—clubs, dating, dancing until dawn, and finally being able to live openly without looking over my shoulder." A smile tugs at my lips. "None of that happened, though. Because during my first week at university, I met Elena."

It feels strange to say her name out loud, but I continue. "She was Greek too—studying international finance. The moment I saw her, everything else faded away. She had this way of moving, like she was dancing to music only she could hear. But whenever I tried to get close, she'd pull away."

"Playing hard to get?" Ruby asks.

"That's what I thought at first. We'd go on dates, but she never let it progress beyond the restaurant. She was... guarded. Secretive about herself. Canceled on me regularly. I was used to getting what I wanted, so her resistance only made me more determined."

Ruby makes a soft sound. "Tell me about it."

"Yes, I suppose you've experienced that side of me first-hand." I meet her eyes briefly before looking away. "Eventually, though, things happened. She started coming home with me and feelings grew between us. After a few months, I asked her to move in with me. That's when she finally told me the truth."

My throat tightens and the lounger creaks as I shift, trying to find comfort in a story that offers none. "Elena had systemic scleroderma—an autoimmune disease that was slowly hardening her tissues and organs. She'd been diagnosed two years before we met. The doctors gave her maybe five years. The only reason she studied was because she wanted the last years of her life to be normal and, like me, free."

Ruby brings a hand to her mouth. "Oh, Athena..."

"She told me we could never have a life together. We had no future." I stare at my hands, remembering how they felt wrapped around Elena's increasingly frail ones. "But I insisted. I loved her. And somewhere deep inside, I held onto this foolish hope that there would be a miracle. Some experimental treatment, some breakthrough that would save her."

Needing a moment, I blow on my coffee and take a careful sip. Ruby doesn't push, doesn't try to fill the silence with empty comfort. She just waits, giving me space to find my way back to the story.

"Still, I had these visions of our future," I continue. "The house we'd buy, the life we'd build. Even while I watched her body betray her, I kept planning. As if my determination alone could change what was happening. But you can't fight time. You can't negotiate with fate. No amount of money or influence could change what was coming."

I sit in silence for a while; I don't know how long. I've never told anyone but my therapist this story in full. Yet here I am, spilling my past to Ruby.

"You know the worst part?" I whisper. "The hope. It's cruel, how it lingers even when you know better. Every good day felt like a sign that maybe the doctors were wrong. Every time she smiled, every moment she seemed stronger, I'd think, 'This is it. This is the turning point.' But there was no turning point. Just a slow, relentless progression toward the inevitable."

I pause again, wrestling with memories I've kept locked away for so long. Ruby reaches across the space between us and takes my hand. Her touch anchors me, gives me strength. Perhaps this is why I feel drawn to her—she understands the specific weight of losing someone you love so much.

"Elena wasn't out to her family either," I say. "We were both living this double life—the perfect Greek daughters to our families back home, different women entirely in London." My coffee has gone cold now, but I take a sip anyway, needing something to do. "During our final year in university, she went home to Greece for what was supposed to be a short trip. Then she stopped answering her phone."

Ruby's fingers tighten around mine, keeping me tethered to the present as I navigate through these painful memories.

"I was worried sick. Elena had been getting weaker, but she insisted she was well enough to travel. After a week of silence, I managed to track down her parents' number." My throat constricts around the words. "That's when I learned she had passed away five days earlier. Just like that. No warning, no goodbye. Her parents had no idea who I was— just a concerned friend calling to check on their daughter. They didn't know about us, about how much we meant to each other.

"I missed her funeral," I continue, swallowing down the lump in my throat. "Can you imagine? The love of my life was buried, and I wasn't there."

Ruby shifts closer, and I realize I'm crying.

"The cruelest part was when a team of professional movers came to our flat in London to collect Elena's belongings. Her things were everywhere—half-empty teacups, books with corners folded down, a shopping list on the fridge in her handwriting. She'd left expecting to come back." I close my eyes, remembering. "Her sweater was still draped over the back of a chair, like she'd just stepped out for a moment. But she was gone, really gone, and I had no one to share the burden of that grief."

Ruby moves to my lounger and wraps her arms around me. I lean into her embrace, letting down my guard completely for the first time in years. Tears fall silently as she holds me, and I cling to her.

We sit like that for a long moment, my tears gradually subsiding as she strokes my hair. The intimacy of the gesture should unnerve me, but instead it's comforting.

"Thank you for sharing this with me," Ruby whispers against my hair. "I get you now. I understand."

I know she does. Ruby understands not just my words but the spaces between them, the grief that shaped me. In her eyes, I see not pity but recognition—that quiet knowledge that comes only from walking the same broken path.

"I learned something from losing her," I say. "I learned that losing love—real, deep love—it breaks you. So I've avoided relationships since. The club lets me control everything, keep my affairs surface-level, and I steer well away from emotions."

"And how's that working out for you?"

I don't answer. I let myself be held, let myself be vulnerable. It feels like the bravest thing I've ever done.

TWENTY-FIVE
RUBY

The sky lightens gradually and the desert dawn brings with it a particular kind of silence—not the dead quiet of midnight, but the expectant hush before the world wakes. I check my phone—5:17 a.m. We've been here for hours.

"What happened last night?" I ask, still nestled against Athena on the lounger. "None of this feels real."

"No," she agrees, her fingers tracing patterns on my arm. "It doesn't feel real at all."

We've been talking, really talking. The kind of raw, honest conversation that only seems possible in these liminal hours between night and day. About my parents in California, who I rarely see, who send text messages that I sometimes take days to answer. About Claire's family, who I've neglected but am finally reaching out to again—the awkward phone calls, the tentative plans to visit.

Athena tells me about her mother and sister in Santorini, who she visits when she can, though not as often as they'd like. About Sunday phone calls and guilt-laden text messages, about missing Greek Easter and namesake days. About her father, who passed away of a heart attack shortly after her graduation, putting her in charge of the family fortune. She was left with another black hole in her soul but enough money and contacts to start fresh anywhere she wanted.

"Why a casino?" I ask, tilting my head to look at her. Her features seem softer, more vulnerable. The sharp edges that make her so intimidating have mellowed, like watercolors bleeding into each other.

She chuckles. "Honestly? It just seemed cool at the time. I was young, grieving both Elena and my father, and I needed a distraction. Something to consume me twenty-four seven so I wouldn't have to be alone with my thoughts." Her eyes meet mine. "Much like you."

I nod, recognizing the truth in her words. We're more alike than I initially thought—both of us hiding behind work and success.

The mountains have turned rose gold now, and the desert awakens with sound. A family of Gambel's quail scurries through the yard, their distinctive topknots bobbing as they move. A pair of mourning doves lands near the pool, their cooing mixing with the cry of a red-tailed hawk circling overhead.

"We're in a weird space, aren't we?" I say. The words feel inadequate to describe whatever this is—this strange dance of attraction and understanding, of shared pain and tentative hope. "There's obviously chemistry..."

"Obviously," she agrees, her lips curving into a smile that makes my stomach flip.

"But I can't do more," I say. "I just...can't."

"Neither can I." Athena's hand stills on my arm. "So maybe we keep it purely physical. No dates, no commitment, no meetings outside the club."

"No coffee dates?"

"Hmm..." Athena considers that. "How about coffee is okay but Scotch is a nay?"

I laugh, feeling a strange sense of relief at the proposal. This way, we can indulge without the weight of expectations and emotions and guilt. "That sounds good. No complications, no promises we can't keep." The structure feels comforting—like a contract with clear terms and boundaries. Good. This is something I know how to navigate.

"Just pleasure," she agrees. "Nothing more, and certainly nothing less." She shifts then and moves to hover over me. Her weight settles half on top of me as her hand finds its way under my sweatshirt. "But fuck, Ruby. I really, really want to kiss you and I don't want to wait until we're back at the club."

My body responds before my mind can catch up—a forgotten language now remembered. I arch into her touch, heat flooding through me at the need in her voice. My pulse pounds in my throat as her fingers drift higher.

"You're already about to break the 'nothing physical outside the club' rule," I say, sliding my hands over her thighs. "How very hedonistic of you." The robe falls open under my touch and my fingers find bare skin.

She makes a sound low in her throat that sends heat pooling in my belly, and the last thread of restraint between us snaps. "Well, it is kind of my brand."

And then she claims me, because there's no other way to describe how she moves to straddle me fully, her knees pressing into the lounger on either side of my hips. Her hands find mine, fingers interlacing for just a moment before she guides them above my head, pinning my wrists against the cushion with one hand.

Her other hand cradles my jaw, thumb pressing lightly

against my chin, controlling the angle as she hovers just out of reach. I strain upward, seeking her mouth, but she holds me in place, the corner of her lips curving into a wicked smile that's equal parts tease and promise.

I want to retort, to challenge her, but then her mouth is on mine—soft, a contrast to the firm grip on my wrists. She alternates between brushing her lips over mine and pulling back just enough to leave me chasing her mouth. Each retreat makes me more desperate for her return.

How is she maintaining such control? I'm seconds from begging, from breaking completely under her touch while she plays me. The pressure of her body against mine, the slight rock of her hips—everything calculated to drive me to the edge without pushing me over.

When she finally releases my wrists, it's only to thread her fingers through my hair, tightening just enough to hold me firmly while she kisses me again, thoroughly this time. And fuck, this woman can kiss. Her mouth moves against mine with intensity, using her lips, teeth, and tongue, knowing exactly when to be soft and when to demand more. Her tongue sliding against mine in a rhythm that makes me think of other things, other places she might apply this same devastating attention.

When she catches my bottom lip between her teeth, the sting makes me gasp, and she soothes the spot with her tongue before deepening the kiss again, setting a pace that leaves me breathless. She takes what she wants, gives what I need. Athena embodies a want that is raw and palpable, a hunger that transcends the ordinary.

I slide my hands to her hips, but she catches my wrists again and pins them back above my head with a single fluid motion.

"Don't move," she whispers against my mouth, and I

squirm at the command in her voice. It's a negotiation of power and she's winning. And I'm surrendering willingly, melting against her mouth while she shows me exactly what I've been missing.

Athena kisses like she's savoring every taste, drinking me in like a rare vintage wine, tasting notes that only she can detect. When we finally break apart, her pupils are dilated, making her eyes look almost black in the light of dawn. I've never seen her look so undone, so human.

Her weight lifts suddenly as she pushes herself upright, standing beside the lounger. I feel the loss of her heat immediately, my body still craving her.

"I should go," she says, closing her robe. And then she just stands there looking down at me as if battling her decision. She shakes her head and lets out a soft laugh. "Fuck. What have you done to me?" Without waiting for an answer, she turns and leaves.

TWENTY-SIX
ATHENA

The espresso machine hisses as I watch the dark liquid stream into my favorite cup. I should be exhausted—I haven't slept at all—but instead, I'm buzzing, craving caffeine before I jump in the shower.

I forgot my shoes, hat, and clothes at Ruby's and I'm standing in my kitchen wearing nothing but her robe. I walked home barefoot, barely registering the discomfort. My mind was elsewhere, replaying every moment of that kiss in vivid detail.

Zeus watches me from the kitchen island, his tail swishing back and forth in judgment. He knows I'm not myself right now—animals always sense these things. I scratch behind his ears, and he allows it, though his golden eyes remain skeptical.

"Don't look at me like that," I tell him. "I know what I'm doing."

But I don't. For the first time in a very long time, I have absolutely no idea what I'm doing. I pride myself on always being three steps ahead, but now I'm completely adrift.

I did exactly what I swore I wouldn't do. I kissed Ruby Walsh.

No, strike that. I didn't just kiss her. I devoured her like the world was ending. I lost control and gave in to every primal instinct causing a current of desire I can't shut off.

And it was magnificent.

The robe smells like her. I bring the collar to my nose and inhale deeply, letting the scent of her wash over me. My body responds immediately, heat pooling low in my belly at the memory of her beneath me, of her lips parting at my command, of the soft sounds she made.

"Fuck," I whisper as I head outside with my coffee.

The kiss wasn't even the most reckless thing. I told Ruby everything. Everything. About Elena, about my father, about London, about grief and loss and survival—all the things I keep locked away.

Why? Why her? Why now, after all this time of careful distance?

I've known powerful women, brilliant women. I've had them in my club, in my bed, in my life. None of them have ever breached my defenses like this. I've mastered the art of keeping people at exactly the right distance—close enough to touch, but never close enough to wound. Until Ruby.

My phone vibrates against the table, and I glance at the screen. It's my mother. I almost let it go to voicemail, as I often do, but something stops me, some lingering effect of last night's confessions, and I answer instead.

"Mom?"

"Athena?" She sounds surprised, as if she didn't expect me to pick up. It's been weeks since we've spoken in real time, our relationship maintained through brief texts and missed calls. "Sweetie, are you all right?"

"I'm fine, Mom. Just watching the sunrise." I switch to

Greek automatically, the language of my childhood flowing effortlessly despite the years away. "How are you? How's your back? Are you still seeing that physical therapist I arranged?"

She makes a dismissive sound. "Stop fussing. That's my job, not yours. My back is fine. The doctor says I'm as healthy as someone twenty years younger."

"You'd say that even if you weren't," I counter.

"And you'd worry either way," she replies.

"True." I smile. "How's Demetria?"

"Your sister is your sister. She's driving me crazy with her new boyfriend—another artist, can you believe it? As if the last three weren't enough trouble."

I laugh. "Let me guess—tattoos? Motorcycle? Lives in his mother's basement?"

"Worse! He's French! And he's moving to New York and wants her to go with him." She clicks her tongue in disapproval, the sound so familiar it causes an unexpected pang of homesickness. "But that's not why I'm calling, sweetie."

"Oh?"

"We've decided to visit you. Next week."

I nearly choke on my espresso, the hot liquid burning my throat. "Next week? Both of you?"

"Yes, Demetria and me. It's been seven months, Athena. Seven months since you visited. If you won't come to us, we'll come to you."

A complex mix of emotions washes over me—joy at the prospect of seeing them, anxiety about the timing, and a mild panic at having them in my space. "That's...that would be wonderful," I say, trying to infuse my voice with enthusiasm. "I'll arrange the Presidential Suite at the Olympus for you."

"No." My mother's voice brooks no argument. "Absolutely not. When you lived at the Olympus, that was one thing. But now you have a home, so we're staying with you."

My mind races through implications, complications, objections. My club. The comings and goings at all hours. The security measures. The risk. The fact that below my beautiful home lies a secret that would shock my traditional Greek mother to her core. The fact that they simply cannot stay with me.

"Mom," I begin carefully, "the Olympus would be far more comfortable—"

"Don't you want us in your home?" She sounds hurt. For all her strength, my mother has always been sensitive about our relationship, about the distance—both physical and emotional—that I've put between us.

"No! No, of course that's not it," I say quickly. "You're always welcome in my home, always. I'm looking forward to it."

And I am, despite everything. It's been too long since I've seen them, hugged them, shared a meal with them. Video calls are a poor substitute for my mother's embrace. For the connection to my roots that I've neglected since I moved to Vegas.

"Good," she says, satisfied. "We arrive on Tuesday. I'll text you the charter details."

After we hang up, I sit very still, watching as shadows retreat across my lawn. Tuesday. Less than a week to figure out how to reconcile my two lives. Can I close the club? That wouldn't be right. The members contract states that they have access Thursday to Sunday, no exceptions. How many lies will I have to tell? How many truths can I afford to reveal?

An idea flashes through my mind, absurd and desperate

—I could buy or rent another property, stage it as my home— and I actually consider it for a moment. I have the resources, the connections. But the deception would be massive, unsustainable. I'm overthinking this. Or not thinking clearly at all. Too much has happened, too many emotions have been stirred up. Between Ruby and now this, I need to take a step back and clear my head.

Zeus jumps onto my lap—a rarity. His weight is warm and grounding as he settles himself against my chest, his purr reverberating through both of us as I whisper into his fur.

"What am I going to do, big boy?"

TWENTY-SEVEN
RUBY

My phone buzzes beside my laptop. It's after nine, and I don't usually get messages on a Saturday night. The Morrison contracts blur in front of me as I reach for my phone.

I can see you.

My lips curve into a smile as I read Athena's text. We exchanged numbers last night, but I've been restraining myself all day from reaching out. I didn't want to seem too eager after everything that happened between us, but I never expected her to break first.

I glance out my office window, scanning the premises for a glimpse of her.

Where are you? I type back.

After sleeping most of the day—my body finally surrendering to exhaustion after our all-night conversation and mind-blowing make-out session—I've only been up for a few hours. It's too early for the club, too early for Athena to normally be home from the Olympus. Perhaps she stayed home and slept as well. My phone buzzes again.

I'm in my car on the drive.

I peer through the darkness and notice her Aston Martin. The roof is up, windows tinted black so I can't see inside.

What are you doing there? I ask.

Her reply comes quickly: *I was about to go for a drive, then saw you. I decided I preferred this view to the desert.*

I chuckle and feel my cheeks flush. How long has she been there? I'm wearing a simple black nightdress, comfortable enough for working late but quite revealing.

So you like to watch too, huh? I type, feeling bold. *Like what you see?*

The three dots appear, disappear, then reappear as she composes her response, and I hold my breath.

I do. Now, take off that dress.

My breath hitches. It's not a request; it's a command. Even through the impersonal medium of text, I can feel the authority in her words, the same dominance that had me pinned beneath her at dawn.

My heart pounds against my ribs. The woman who kissed me senseless is sitting in her car, watching me and asking for a show. Everything in me screams that this is madness and so unlike me, and that's precisely why I stand and reach for the hem of my dress.

In one fluid motion, I pull it over my head and let it drop to the floor. I'm left standing in my black bra and matching panties —not the fancy new lingerie I purchased, just my everyday set. But Athena can't discern the details from that distance.

Positioning myself directly behind the French doors, I'm silhouetted by the light of my office. I've never done anything like this before, never felt this combination of vulnerability and power.

My phone buzzes in my hand. *You are exquisite.* Then,

another message follows: *Take off the rest. I want to see you naked.*

The directness of her demand catches me off guard and something shifts inside me. The disciplined attorney who calculates every risk dissolves, replaced by the version of myself I've only just met. Not the grieving widow. Not the corporate shark. Someone entirely new.

I set my phone down on the desk, face up, and a boldness overtakes me. I've never been the type to perform, to put on a show, but something about the anonymity of the distance between us, the darkness hiding her and the light exposing me, makes me want to play.

I turn my back to the window, giving her a view of my behind, my shoulders, the clasp of my bra. I glance over my shoulder, imagining her eyes on me, and slowly reach up to gather my hair, lifting it off my neck as if I'm about to tie it up.

I arch my back and hold this pose for a moment, then let my hair cascade back down. My hips begin to move in a slow, rhythmic sway. I'm channeling every dancer in every music video I've ever watched, every fantasy I've never acknowledged.

My fingers find the clasp of my bra, but I don't unhook it immediately. Instead, I trace the edge of the band, running my fingers along my back. I roll my shoulders, continuing the sway of my hips, feeling both ridiculous and incredibly powerful.

When I finally unclasp the bra, I hold it in place, keeping my back to the window. I look over my shoulder again, imagining Athena's face, the way her pupils would dilate, the way she'd grip the steering wheel tighter.

I let the straps fall from my shoulders but cross my arms

in front of me, holding the cups against my breasts as I slowly turn to face the window again.

My phone lights up with another message and I look down to check it while I continue my sensuous dance.

Jesus Christ, Ruby. You're killing me here.

Finally, I smile as I drop both arms and let the bra fall, catching it before it hits the floor. I dangle it from one finger, twirling it once, twice, before I toss it over my shoulder, where it lands somewhere in a corner of my office.

The cool air makes my nipples harden instantly, and I feel strangely powerful standing here, bared to the night and to her hidden gaze.

You're beautiful. Don't forget the rest. I want to imagine my mouth on your pussy.

Fuck. A flash of arousal shoots between my thighs as I read it, and now it's all I can think of. She really knows how to push my buttons, and I can almost hear the husky quality her voice would have if she were speaking the words. There's something thrilling about knowing she can see me while I can't see her. About knowing I'm affecting her, that she's sitting in her car, watching me, wanting me.

I hook my thumbs into the waistband of my panties and turn to the side, giving her a profile view as I slowly— torturously slowly—ease them down over my hips, past my thighs, letting them drop to my ankles. I step out of them and kick them away, turning to face the window again, completely naked now. I stand there, allowing her to look.

Good girl, she writes, making me chuckle. *Bring your chair to the French doors and sit down.* I pause, wondering if this is a test. Is she seeing how far I'll go for her? How much control I'm willing to surrender? I've spent my entire professional life being in charge, and here I am, naked and following orders. The strangest part is how much I'm enjoying it.

I wheel my leather office chair across the room and position it directly in front of the French doors, in full view of her car, and lower myself into it. Then I cross my legs, rest my forearms on the chair arms, and lean back with an outward show of composure that belies the chaos inside me.

Another message from her. *Spread your legs for me.*

I hesitate, my eyes fixed on her car.

Do it, her next message reads.

My heart races as I slowly uncross my legs. I pause, knees still pressed together, then gradually part them, feeling the cool air of the room against my most intimate places. This game is both absurdly uncomfortable and incredibly sexy. I'm wet and throbbing, wondering what she'll ask of me next. My phone remains silent for what feels like an eternity, leaving me suspended in this moment of exposure and anticipation. She's doing this on purpose; making me wait.

I realize I'm breathing faster now, my chest rising and falling in a rhythm that matches my racing pulse. I'm simultaneously powerless and in complete control, able to end this at any moment but unwilling to break the spell she's cast over me.

Good girl, she writes again, and the praise feels like a physical caress. *I can't wait to taste that pretty pussy.*

My eyes flutter closed for a beat as fantasies flash before me. Her tongue against my sex. Her face between my thighs. Is she even aware of the effect she has on me? How my body responds to her in ways I never imagined possible?

Breathless and in desperate need of release, I lower a hand between my legs, but immediately, my phone buzzes.

Don't. Don't touch yourself.

I frown. *What the fuck?* She can't bring me to this point then leave me hanging. I pick up my phone and reply. *Are you serious?*

Yes. Come to the club after midnight. I'll make it worth your wait.

Her headlights spring on, her gates open, and she drives off, leaving me frustrated and alone. I stand and stare after her while my body thrums with unresolved tension. This game of hers—command and denial, promise and retreat—is simultaneously infuriating and intoxicating. Am I really going to obey? It's not like she'd know, right? I glance at my watch: two and a half hours until midnight. Two and a half hours to decide if I'll follow her rules or break them. But even as I consider defiance, I know I'll obey. And I'll be at that club when the clock strikes twelve against every last shred of my better judgment.

TWENTY-EIGHT
ATHENA

The air thrums with a low, insistent beat as I pull Ruby through the heavy velvet curtains. She's dressed in a red cocktail dress that clings to her curves, accentuating the slender lines of her body. Her auburn hair is pulled back, sleek and gleaming, drawing attention to her striking eyes.

"That was quite the show you put on earlier," I say, holding her gaze as I hand her a tumbler of whiskey. "Thank you."

She blushes as she takes the drink.

Several women approach us as we move through the lounge—Donna with her signature martini, Dr. Chen with a diet Coke, and Mari with a Scotch in hand. We greet them politely, but talking to others is the last thing on our minds. My body hums with anticipation, with a need that I haven't felt in years. Our hands brush as we navigate the crowd, and even that slight contact sends sparks racing up my arm.

I've limited myself to a kiss on her cheek when she arrived, my lips lingering a beat too long against her skin, inhaling her scent. Not a real kiss yet. That comes later, when it's part of the game. It's safer that way—desire contained within boundaries, pleasure without the dangerous intimacy of natural affection.

I glance at her again as we enter the playroom. She knew exactly where we were going. No discussion was needed, no questions asked. An unspoken agreement formed between us the moment she walked through that door tonight, perhaps even earlier, during her window performance. We've been circling each other like planets caught in each other's gravity, and tonight our paths are finally aligned.

The walls in this room are lined with mirrors, reflecting endless repetitions of the space. I love watching my submissives see themselves come undone, forced to witness their own surrender as I guide them toward release. Handcuffs hang down from the ceiling and there's another set of cuffs attached to the back wall. The only furniture in here is a leather armchair and a chest of drawers filled with brand-new toys.

"Did you behave yourself?" I ask.

She hesitates for a fraction of a second, then nods. "Yes."

"Good girl." I look her over once more. The red dress, the way she's holding herself—all of it speaks volumes. She wants this. Needs this. Badly.

I lead her to the chair and she sits—legs crossed at the ankles, her head tilted slightly. She's tense; her hands grip the fabric of her dress, twisting it between her fingers.

I slip a hand under her dress to caress her thigh and feel the tremble in her muscles. Her breath hitches as my fingers trail up, lingering just before they slip back down to rest on her knee.

Bringing my mouth to her ear, I whisper, "Do you know what a safe word is?"

She nods. "Yes. Do I need one?"

"Always." I cup her chin, tilting her head up to look at me. "The safe word is *pause*. If you want to stop at any point—even if you're not sure if you want to stop—say the word and I'll immediately release you. Okay? Pause."

"Pause. Got it." She swallows hard, her eyes darting toward the open door.

"I'm sorry," I say. "The door stays open. House rules."

"I know." She pauses. "What are you going to do to me?"

"I'm going to find out what you like." I caress her cheek and her eyes flutter closed as she leans into my touch. "And then I'm going to make you feel really, really good. So fucking good that you won't even know what's happening to you."

Her breath catches in her throat and arousal stirs at the thought of having her at my mercy. I'm going to push her to her limits.

"Stand." I raise my voice slightly, shifting my tone to one that's teasing yet authoritative, and wait until she's back on her feet. "We're going to continue where we left off earlier. Well, not entirely. You can keep your lingerie on for now—I do appreciate a little lace."

Ruby's eyes darken with a mix of excitement and trepidation. She's picking at her fingernails as if she's not sure what to do with her hands. I guess that's one problem easily solved.

"Lift your arms," I command, and Ruby responds, her obedience igniting a spark of satisfaction within me. As her arms rise, I take hold of the hem of her dress and savor the power of the moment—how easy it is to strip away her layers, both literally and figuratively.

I tug at the fabric, lifting it higher while I inch closer,

my lips nearly brushing against hers. I can see the desire flickering in her eyes, and although I long to kiss her, I hold back, keeping our connection just out of reach. When she tilts her head, trying to close the distance for a kiss, I inch back slightly, teasingly allowing the tension to swell.

Guiding the dress over her head, I'm revealing her stunning figure adorned in red lace. The intricate patterns of the fabric cling to her curves and accentuate her femininity. I appreciate the way the lace contrasts with her skin, the bold color making her appear even paler.

"You look exquisite," I say, draping her dress over the back of the chair.

A shadow falls across the room, and Ruby's eyes dart toward the doorway. Morgan stands there, her silhouette framed by the hallway light behind her. She's leaning against the doorframe, arms crossed, a smile playing on her lips as she takes in the scene before her. Ruby tenses immediately, and she nervously bites her bottom lip. I place a hand on her arm, feeling goose bumps rising on her skin.

"Are you okay?" I whisper, searching her face. "We can stop right now if you want."

Ruby's eyes flicker between Morgan and me. She takes a deep breath, squares her shoulders slightly, and gives me a small but definite shake of her head. She's surrendering, even as apprehension still lingers in her gaze. The uncertainty is both beautiful and maddening.

Moving my lips to her ear again, I tease her earlobe with my hot breath and whisper, "What's the safe word again?"

A soft moan escapes her. It's a delicate sound, almost a plea. "Pause," she says in a whimper.

"Good girl." I hear a rustle, and two more women appear in the doorway.

One of them steps into the room while the other stays

back. Women love to watch when I'm in here, and tonight is no different.

The mirrors multiply our audience—three watchers become thirty, their silhouettes rippling across the reflective surfaces until they form a silent gallery of eyes. Ruby's breath quickens; I can feel her awareness of being witnessed from all angles, the sensory overload of exposure.

"Don't mind them," I tell her. "This is between us. Look at me instead." I cup her face to focus solely on my eyes. "I'm not here to break you. I'm here to help you break free."

TWENTY-NINE
RUBY

The cuffs close around my wrists, and I'm stripped down to my red lingerie. It's one of the sets I bought with this moment in mind, but I wasn't convinced I'd actually go through with it until now. More women have joined and six pairs of eyes watch from the shadows, their presence both thrilling and terrifying.

I'm standing in the center of the room where a chain hangs from the ceiling. My cuffed hands are raised above my head and secured to that chain, leaving me exposed and vulnerable. The position forces me up onto my toes and my back arches slightly, pushing my chest forward.

Athena circles me slowly. The click of her loafers on hardwood marks each rotation, building anticipation. Her fingers trail across my shoulders, down my spine, raising gooseflesh in their wake. Her touch is light but deliberate—she's marking her territory, showing everyone that I belong to her in this moment.

"Beautiful," she murmurs, and though the word is meant for me, it carries to our audience. My cheeks flush at the praise, at being displayed like this.

"This is your first time," she says, raising her voice so our observers can hear. "Are you scared?"

"Yes," I whisper truthfully. In my professional life, I never show weakness. But here, with Athena, honesty feels like its own kind of strength.

Her hand cups my face, thumb brushing my lower lip. "Don't be. Use your safe word if you want to stop. Otherwise..." She leans close, her lips brushing my ear as she gropes my behind and pulls me against her. "You're mine."

The possessiveness in her voice makes me shiver. This is what I've been craving—the freedom to let someone else take control. To surrender.

Athena steps back, and the loss of her touch is immediate. She retrieves something from a nearby table—a silk blindfold that she slides over my eyes, plunging me into darkness. My other senses heighten instantly. I hear the rustle of her suit as she moves, smell her subtle perfume, feel the air stir against my exposed skin.

Two women whisper an exchange. A reminder that I'm being watched.

"You're trembling," Athena observes, her voice carrying that hint of amusement I'm learning to recognize. Her fingers trace the edge of my garter belt. "You've been fantasizing about this, haven't you?" she asks, circling behind me again. "All those nights watching from your window. Imagining what happens here."

Something cold trails down my spine—silk or leather, I can't tell which. The sensation makes me arch, pulling against the restraints. Athena hums in approval, and the sound goes straight through me. Even blindfolded, I can picture her expression—that mix of desire and control that makes her so magnetic.

"Well, you're about to find out..." She pauses. "The

hard way." The thing now trails down between my breasts and I suspect it might be a riding crop. Without sight, I can only track her movements by sound and the anticipation builds with each passing second. It continues over my left breast and then it stops at the edge of my bra. Athena unclasps it, causing my breast to spill out underneath.

She drags the crop farther down, skimming my nipple. I gasp at the contact, then cry out as she suddenly strikes the side of my breast.

I gasp at the unexpected sting, my breath hitching in my throat. The pain pulses, forcing me to confront the rush of conflicting emotions spiraling inside me. Is this what I wanted? The answer is slow to form, tinged with uncertainty as I wrangle my reaction.

It's not so much the pain that overwhelms me, it's not knowing when it's coming. If only I could see, I'd be more in control, but isn't that the whole point? The sting lingers, sharp and electrifying, but she leaves me little time to process, striking me again, against my nipple this time, sending another wave of sensations crashing through me.

"Fuck!" I yell, sucking in a breath through clenched teeth.

"Remember, you have a safe word," she murmurs.

I hesitate for a beat, then shake my head.

"I can't hear you," she says, raising her voice.

"No," I answer. "I'm fine."

Another quick and harder strike against my nipple, and a rush of adrenaline leaves me dizzy. My skin is sore and glowing, but the pain is contradicted by other sensations. The line between pleasure and pain blurs when I realize I'm wet and throbbing. I mentally brace myself for what comes next, but before I can gather my thoughts, Athena wraps her arms around me, pulls me in and encloses her lips around my sore nipple. The soft, enveloping heat contrasts beautifully with the sting, soothing the ache and sending shards of pleasure through me. I let out an involuntary whimper, my body reacting instinctively to the sensation. Arching toward her, I'm tiptoed, practically hanging from my cuffs.

She swirls her tongue gently, a balm against the sharpness that lingers. I'm wholly responsive to her every move.

Forgetting about my audience, I let go of any hesitation and surrender completely to the moment. It's as though every rational thought has been stripped away, leaving behind only raw emotion and instinct. I drown in the sensations—each flicker of pain and pleasure serving to heighten my awareness of her, of myself, of the space we occupy together.

Athena pulls away and lets go of me, and just like that, I'm back to where I started. Uncertain, nervous, vulnerable, and trembling in anticipation of what will happen. It's an emotional roller coaster. I miss the certainty of the contact, of knowing where she was.

Clenching my teeth, I hold my breath and just when I think that maybe this is it and she'll stop as it's my first time, the crop lands on my behind with a hard smack. I think I groan or hiss or something, but it's all a blur, overshadowed by the throbbing pain on my right ass cheek.

She strikes me again and again, alternating between softer and harder, longer and shorter pauses until my breath comes in ragged gasps and I'm not sure how much more I can take.

I'm so wet; my body betrays my arousal. In the darkness behind the blindfold, every sensation is magnified. The tightness of the Velcro cuffs, the stretch in my shoulders, the way my legs tremble with the effort of staying tiptoed. But most of all, I feel Athena's presence—commanding, controlled, completely in charge of my pleasure.

"More?" she asks, as if sensing my inner turmoil.

When I don't answer immediately, she runs her hand over my behind, caressing my sore skin. Her touch feels grounding, soothing, and it calms the storm inside me. "Let's take a moment, shall we?" she whispers in my ear.

She moves around me until her breath is on my face and then she kisses me. I've been longing for this since her lips were last on mine, and I think I might climax from the kiss alone. Someone moans and I'm not sure if it's me or her, but I know she likes kissing me. This isn't just for show, and it isn't just for my pleasure. It's just as much for hers.

When Athena tilts her head, molding her lips against my own, I melt and lose myself in the moment, surrendering to the warmth of her embrace. Her hand slips between my thighs, cupping my sex in a possessive kind of way that draws a loud, throaty moan from my mouth.

Fuck. This is crazy. What's happening in my body? Is this normal? Are these sensations even human?

She squeezes my pussy, making me squirm against her hand. Being touched like this while others watch should horrify me, but instead, I moan louder. This is what Athena does—she takes my darkest desires and brings them into the light, makes them beautiful instead of shameful.

"You're soaked," she observes, loud enough for everyone to hear, then withdraws her hand, leaving me aching. Even without sight, I sense Athena is right in front of me as the silence stretches, broken only by my rapid breathing. She's making me wait, speculate, wondering what's next.

Her fingers trace my garter belt, following the straps down to where they connect to my stockings. "Did you buy this for me?" she asks, though she must know the answer. "Did you think about me while you were trying it on?"

"Yes," I admit in a shaky voice. The confession costs me nothing now—I'm beyond shame, beyond hesitation. "I thought about you seeing me in it."

"And now everyone sees you," she murmurs. "But only I get to touch." Her hands continue their exploration, unfastening the clips one by one. All the while, she keeps talking, her voice a silken thread of control. "Only I get to decide what happens next. Only I get to choose when you've earned your pleasure."

The word "pleasure" from her lips slays me. I pull against the restraints, and even this small movement draws a response—her hand presses firmly on my hip, holding me still. She hooks her fingers in my panties. "I'm going to take these off, Ruby."

It's not a request. It's an announcement, but she does pause for a beat, giving me a chance to use the safe word. When I don't, she slides them down my legs, leaving me exposed to the crowd. I have no idea how many women have joined since she put the blindfold on me, how many pairs of eyes are fixed on me now.

She wedges her foot between mine and spreads my legs apart. I'm struggling to hold my balance. The stretch of my arms is intense and all my instincts go against me standing like this. When I move one of my legs back to the middle, she smacks my behind hard with her hand.

I let out a yelp, but Athena shows no mercy.

"No," she says. "Keep your feet apart." She corrects my stance, spreading my legs again.

"I'm sorry."

"You're not." She smacks me again, hard enough to

leave marks on my ass cheek. "But you will be if you don't do as I say. Now, stay still and I promise you won't regret it."

THIRTY
ATHENA

Ruby is standing perfectly still, her chest rising and falling fast. I suspect it's strenuous to keep the position, but she will thank me soon enough. She's beautiful beyond belief, red marks on her pale skin, limbs trembling.

Taking a moment to breathe, I let the intensity of the scene wash over me as I lock my gaze on her. Each time there's a sound in the room she tilts her head as if trying to pick up clues as to what's happening.

There are more bystanders than usual, and I know why —they've noticed my special interest in Ruby. My infatuation must be painfully obvious to everyone. Is it the way I look at her? The tenderness that slips into my touch despite my attempts to maintain control? The longing in my eyes as I circle her—a desire that goes beyond the physical act we're engaged in?

I wonder if Ruby would recognize it too, if she could see me now. This yearning to take her in my arms, to hold her close in ways that have nothing to do with dominance or submission. It's dangerous territory I won't allow myself to enter. Not again.

Ruby is the center of attention tonight, but I'm orchestrating every moment. This is what I do best—read desire, shape experience, provide exactly what someone needs before they even know to ask for it.

I trace a finger down Ruby's spine, pleased at how she angles into my touch despite her restraints. Her body speaks volumes that her disciplined mind would never allow. My corporate lawyer with her guarded emotions falls away here, leaving only primal response.

"Safe word?" I ask again, picking up the crop.

She shakes her head, and I trail the tip of the crop up her inner thigh. The anticipation is palpable. I can see it in the way she shivers, how her breath catches when she realizes what's coming. This moment of suspension between desire and fulfillment is where true vulnerability lives, and Ruby is giving me her trust completely. It's intoxicating and terrifying in equal measure.

I retract the crop, watching her jaw clench as she waits for the blow. Her hands are balled into fists above her head, her face turned away from me. I hold off, building tension, and wait, and wait...

She bites her lower lip and I want to kiss her so badly but instead, I slam the crop against her pussy. She lets out a sharp cry that echoes through the room and her body jerks forward, straining against the cuffs as the sensation ripples through her. I'm captivated by the visible wave of pleasure-pain that follows—how her head falls back, exposing the elegant line of her throat, how her skin flushes pink from her chest upward. The women watching shift and murmur, their collective breath held in anticipation of what comes next.

"Fuck!" Ruby gasps, squeezing her legs together. Her voice is unfiltered in a way I've never heard from her before.

"I told you to stay in position, didn't I?" I spank her behind hard with the palm of my hand, over and over until she parts her legs again.

I strike once more, gentler this time, and her hips cant forward automatically, seeking more contact, more friction. I resist the urge to drop the crop and take her right there, to kiss her and slip my fingers inside her and feel her come apart.

Instead, I maintain the choreography of the scene, following the dance we've begun together. I move behind her, my body close enough that she can feel my presence but not quite touching. My breath falls against her neck as I bring my lips to her ear. "You like this, don't you?" I whisper. She responds with a small nod, her breathing ragged. I reach around and cup her breast, feeling the weight of it in my palm, the hardened peak of her nipple against my thumb. Her whimper is barely audible, but in it I hear everything—need, surrender, and a plea for release. "More?"

"Yes," she whispers.

"What was that? I can't hear you," I say, pinching her nipple. "And where are your manners?"

"Yes, please," she corrects herself, louder this time.

I lick my lips as I position myself in front of her and glance down at her pussy, striking her one last time. The riding crop lands hard enough for the onlookers to flinch and for Ruby to cry out, but I keep a straight face, pretending her reaction doesn't affect me one bit. She's shaking, whimpering, head tilted toward the ceiling. She's had enough and I'm going to reward her.

Normally I would use one of the many vibrators we have here but that's not good enough. Not for Ruby and not for me. I want more.

Kneeling before her, I'm eye-level with the apex of her thighs, almost in a position of worship. Can my onlookers see I want this just as much? Can they see my hunger to taste her? Ruby's glistening with arousal and I blow softly against her exposed flesh, watching her shudder in response.

"Please," she whispers, the word barely audible.

"Please what?" I ask, loud enough for our audience to hear. "Tell me what you want, Ruby."

Her cheeks flush deeper, the color spreading down her neck to her chest. She knows everyone is watching, listening, but desperation has overtaken her shame.

"Touch me," she manages. "Please touch me. I need to come."

Grabbing her behind, I pull her against my mouth and devour her pussy, moaning as I taste her. This isn't part of the game and part of me is afraid I'm taking it too far. But it's what I want and I don't like to deny myself.

Her sharp intake of breath cuts through the room's hushed atmosphere. I take my time exploring her with my tongue, learning what makes her tremble, what draws those delicious little sounds from her throat. She tastes divine, forbidden, delicious.

When I circle her clit with my tongue, her hips buck forward and she gasps, every muscle taut. I smile, though she can't see it. Her breath comes faster, and I know she's close already, wound tight from all the teasing. Her body is tensing, climbing toward release.

I increase the pressure and her response is a loud moan. Her pleasure is intoxicating—the way she yields to it, fights it, surrenders to it. I'm getting lost in her.

Her breathing becomes erratic as she approaches climax

and then she shatters beautifully, her entire body convulsing.

"Fuck! Athena!" My name tears from her throat, loud and unrestrained, and it affects me more deeply than I anticipated. I continue working her through the aftershocks, gentler now, drawing out every moment of her pleasure until she's hanging limp from her restraints, gasping for breath. Only then do I stand and signal to Morgan to help me release her from the cuffs.

As Ruby's arms come down, I support her weight, turning her to face me before removing the blindfold. Her eyes are dazed, pupils dilated, and she blinks rapidly as they adjust to the light. The vulnerability in her expression catches me off guard—it's not just physical satisfaction I see there, but something deeper, more complex.

I stroke her cheek and tuck a strand of auburn hair behind her ear. "How do you feel?"

"I don't know," she whispers, and I understand. The first time is overwhelming, a tidal wave of sensation and emotion that defies simple categorization. Tears well up in her eyes and then her arms wrap around my neck and she embraces me.

Our audience begins to disperse as I hold her in return. Morgan brings me a glass of water, then leaves us alone with a discreet nod.

"Drink," I instruct, stepping back and holding the glass to Ruby's lips. She obeys without hesitation, another sign of how deep her submission has taken her. I help her into her dress but don't zip it yet. Instead, I wrap my arms around her again, pulling her against me.

She sighs against my neck, her breath warm on my skin, and I tighten my hold. "I've got you," I murmur, surprising myself with the tenderness in my voice.

I told her earlier I wasn't here to break her. But as I feel her heart beating against mine, her body softening in my arms, I'm suddenly afraid that I might be the one in danger of breaking.

I've been staring at the same vase of roses for God knows how long, arranging and rearranging them like they hold the secrets of the universe. My hands fumble with the stems, and I prick my finger on a thorn. The small pain yanks me back to reality—my backyard, Sunday afternoon, lunch preparations.

Sarah, Claire's niece, is coming, and she's bringing Erik, her new boyfriend. I'd completely forgotten until the reminder popped up on my phone this morning. Since then, I've been in a frenzy—stripping the guest bed and remaking it with fresh linens, dusting off surfaces, and throwing windows open to air out rooms. If I'd remembered sooner, I would have asked my cleaner to do it, but my mind's been elsewhere and she only comes in three times a week.

I rushed to the grocery store in yoga pants and sweatshirt, hair piled in a messy bun, frantically pushing a cart down aisles while trying to remember what normal people serve for lunch.

Claire was always the one who organized these gatherings. She'd plan menus weeks in advance, create elaborate centerpieces, and charm everyone with her effortless hostess energy. I just tagged along, happy to be the sous-chef, the wine pourer. Claire could transform a simple lunch into an event people talked about for months. She remembered everyone's dietary restrictions, anniversaries, favorite wines. I never had to worry about any of it—she handled the details while I handled the bills. Now it's all on me, and I feel like I'm fumbling through a script written in a language I barely understand.

I've bought premade lasagna that I transferred to my own baking dish, made a salad I saw on Instagram, and found a tiramisu at the deli on my way back that looks homemade enough to pass inspection. It's not that Sarah would judge me for not cooking—she knows I'm hopeless in the kitchen—but I want to appear functional, put together. Like someone who didn't spend last night blindfolded and handcuffed in her neighbor's secret club.

Am I functioning? I can barely focus on anything today and desperately need some normalcy in my life. Part of me is grateful for Sarah and Erik's visit.

I put the store-bought lasagna in the oven. Perfect. It looks like it's something I've slaved over all morning.

Last night keeps flooding back in flashes—not visual memories, since I was blindfolded for most of it, but sensations. The restraints around my wrists. The sting of the crop against my skin. Athena's mouth on me. My body responds immediately to the memory, and I grip the kitchen counter to steady myself.

"Focus, Ruby," I mutter, carrying the bowl of salad out to the patio table.

The pool sparkles in the midday sun, the water so blue and inviting it almost hurts to look at.

I check my phone again. No messages from Athena. I'm

not sure what I expected—a "good morning" text? I want to talk to her, but Sarah and Erik will be here any minute, and then there's no chance of that happening.

The patio table still needs setting. I fetch placemats, napkins, silverware—all the trappings of a normal Sunday lunch. My hands shake slightly as I place each fork, each knife. I haven't slept. How could I? Every time I closed my eyes, I felt Athena all over me. My body still tingles in places, and there are marks—beautiful, secret marks— hidden beneath my linen dress.

The doorbell rings just as I'm putting out water glasses, and my heart leaps into my throat. I smooth down my dress, take a deep breath, and buzz them through.

Sarah stands on my doorstep, so much like Claire that for a split second, I can't breathe. The same blonde hair, though Sarah wears hers shorter. The same smile, though Sarah's doesn't have those crinkles at the corners of her eyes. Beside her stands a tall man with kind eyes and a nervous smile—Erik, I presume.

"Ruby!" Sarah throws her arms around me, and I hold her tight, breathing in the familiar scent of her shampoo— the same brand Claire used. It's a punch to the gut, but also strangely comforting.

"It's so good to see you," I say, meaning it more than she could possibly know. "Come in, come in. And you must be Erik."

Erik steps forward, extending his hand. "It's an honor to meet you, Ms. Walsh."

"Please, it's Ruby, and I'm so happy to have you both here," I assure them as I lead them inside.

"The house looks different," Sarah comments, running her hand along the back of the sofa. "But also the same."

"I know what you mean. I've made some changes lately." I don't mention that most of those changes happened because Athena pushed me to deal with Claire's things. "Come on, everything's set up outside. Can I get you both a glass of white wine?"

"Please," Sarah says, and Erik nods.

I busy myself opening a bottle of Gavi while Sarah and Erik wander out to the patio. Through the kitchen window, I watch them admire the pool, the garden. Erik has his arm around Sarah's waist, protective and loving. They look happy together.

My mind drifts back to Athena. To the complete surrender I experienced. I've never felt anything like it—the intensity of sensation when all I could do was feel. I want to do it again. The thought forms clearly, undeniable in its simplicity.

With three glasses of wine balanced in my hands, I head outside to join them. Sarah is telling Erik about the times she came to stay with us.

"It's such a gorgeous house," she says, turning to me as I set down the glasses. "But it's strange to be here again, without Aunt Claire." I can tell she's emotional, even though she hides it well. An undercurrent of sadness hits me, and if Erik wasn't here, we might have shed a few tears together.

"It's still strange for me too," I admit, settling into a chair across from them. "It's only just now starting to feel like somewhat of a home again, but I don't think I'll stay here long term."

Sarah looks surprised. "Really? But you and Aunt Claire loved this house."

"Claire loved this house," I correct her. "I just wanted her to be happy. But there are too many memories here now. Too much space for just me." I take a sip of wine. "Anyway, that's a conversation for another time. Tell me how you two met."

Erik launches into the story—a coffee shop meet-cute that sounds straight out of a romantic comedy. Sarah interjects occasionally, correcting details or adding context. I nod and smile in all the right places, but part of me is somewhere else entirely—in a mirrored room with Athena's voice in my ear, her hands on my body. Then another memory washes over me. Claire and Sarah laughing at this very table the last time we had lunch together. I grab my linen napkin and fan myself vigorously. It's like I'm going mad. Like I have no control over my jumbled thoughts anymore.

"And we've been together ever since." Sarah's voice pulls me back.

"How lovely. You look so happy together." A drop of sweat trickles down between my shoulder blades as I dab my forehead.

"Ruby? Are you okay?" Sarah leans forward. "You seem feverish all of a sudden."

"Sorry, yes," I say quickly, forcing visions of Athena from my mind. "Just remembered I need to check on lunch. Give me a second."

In the kitchen, I press my palms against the cool marble countertop and take a deep breath, then blow out my cheeks. What is wrong with me? I need to be present for this visit, no matter how much last night distracts me or how much the past hurts.

I return with the lasagna and set it down with a smile I hope looks more composed than I feel.

"So, Erik... You have a job interview tomorrow, right? Where was it again?"

"It's at The Paris Casino on the strip. For the role of marketing director. It's the final round and there are two other candidates." Erik glances at Sarah. "Sarah and I have talked about doing long distance if I get it. It's not ideal, but it's a big opportunity for me so we've decided we'll cross that bridge when we get there." He turns to me. "And Sarah tells me you're the top attorney in Vegas, one of the best in the country."

"Well, I wouldn't go that far," I say with a chuckle.

"Ruby's being modest," Sarah tells him. "She's a legend in corporate law. Her firm is the gold standard."

I feel a rush of pride at her words. "Speaking of which, Sarah, I may have an opening at Walsh and Associates if Erik gets the job in Vegas. We could always use talent like yours. I've been working too hard and it's not sustainable. If I'm going to hire help, I prefer to work with people I can trust implicitly."

Sarah's eyes widen. "Are you serious? That would be... Wow! That would be amazing. I mean, to work with you..."

"Think about it," I say. "No pressure and no rush." I reach into my pocket and pull out the small velvet pouch I've been carrying around all morning. "Before I forget, this is the ring Claire would have wanted you to have—your grandmother's sapphire ring."

Sarah takes the box, opening it. The sapphire catches the sunlight, sending blue reflections dancing across her face. "I remember this ring," she whispers.

"Claire wore it on special occasions," I say, my throat tightening unexpectedly. "She loved that ring."

"It's beautiful." Sarah slips it onto her finger. It fits as if it was meant for her all along, and she holds her hand up to the light, admiring it. Claire's ring has found its new home. It's another small step in the long journey of letting go.

THIRTY-TWO
ATHENA

I stand before Ruby's gate and press the intercom. I'm dropping by unannounced, with no real purpose except to see her before I head to The Olympus. Last night plays on loop in my mind: Ruby trembling beneath my touch, the way she surrendered so beautifully, how vulnerable she looked afterward. She left after a long hug, but something felt unfinished between us.

Sleep eluded me. I tossed and turned, replaying every moment, every sound she made until I finally dozed off in the early hours. Zeus abandoned my bed in protest of my restlessness. I need to see her, to make sure she's okay. First-timers can sometimes experience subdrop—that crash after the endorphin high—and I don't want her to go through that alone.

"Hello?" a young woman answers, catching me off guard. Not Ruby.

"Hi. I'm looking for Ruby," I say, keeping my tone neutral despite my surprise.

"Oh, come on in!" The electronic lock releases with a buzz, and the gates swing open.

I hesitate, confused by the easy admission. Ruby has company—that's a first.

Still, I'm already here, and the gates are open. I drive up to the house and park beside a car I don't recognize. As I approach the front door, it swings open before I can knock, revealing a pretty, young blonde.

"Hi!" She greets me with a bright smile, and I'm struck by a vague resemblance to someone I can't quite place. She looks beyond me and her eyes widen appreciatively. "Wow, cool car! Is that an Aston Martin?"

"Yes," I reply, extending my hand. "I'm Athena Stavros, Ruby's neighbor. I don't normally drive here, I was just dropping in on my way to work."

"I'm Sarah," she says, shaking my hand. "Claire's niece."

Claire's niece. Of course. Ruby told me she was coming during our long talk by the pool, but I forgot. I see the resemblance. She has Claire's smile—I recognize it from the pictures. I realize I'm intruding on something personal, something familial.

"I'm sorry," I say quickly, already backing away. "I didn't mean to interrupt. I'll come back another time."

"Don't be silly!" Sarah grabs my arm before I can retreat. "We're just having lunch—come join us."

I open my mouth to refuse again, but Sarah is already pulling me into the house. "Ruby made lasagna," she chatters. "I swear, I had no idea she could cook."

"Neither did I," I reply, trying to formulate an exit strategy as we approach the patio doors.

Ruby sits at a table with a tall man who must be Sarah's boyfriend. They're both laughing at something, wine glasses in hand, plates of half-eaten lasagna before them. Ruby looks relaxed, wearing a khaki linen shirtdress that reveals just enough skin to remind me of what lies beneath.

Her smile freezes when she spots me, eyes widening in surprise.

"I found your neighbor! The one with the cool car," Sarah announces. "She was at the gate when I answered the intercom on my way back from the restroom."

Ruby's composure returns quickly, though I catch the flash of panic in her eyes. "Athena," she says. "What a surprise."

"I'm sorry, I didn't mean to interrupt," I say again. "I just came to ehm..." I pause until an excuse hits me. "I actually came to see if I left my shoes here yesterday. I can't seem to find them anywhere at home."

Ruby's eyebrows rise slightly. "Yes, your shoes are in the hallway. I was going to bring them over later."

Sarah laughs, settling back into her chair beside Erik. "How on earth did you forget your shoes?"

I feel heat creeping up my neck. "I had a few drinks," I lie. "Ruby makes a mean Martini."

"More hidden talents?" Sarah remarks, her eyes twinkling with mischief. "Were you guys having a girls' night or something?"

"Just catching up," Ruby interjects before I can respond. Her fingers tap nervously against her wine glass. "Athena moved in about eighteen months ago, but we've only recently gotten to know each other." She smiles, but it feels a little forced. "Have a drink with us, Athena. Have you eaten? There's plenty of food."

The man across from Ruby stands and extends his hand. "Erik," he introduces himself. "Sarah's boyfriend. Nice to meet you."

I shake his hand. "Pleasure," I reply. "I'm not staying, and I've already had lunch, thank you. I was just dropping in on my way to work to pick up my shoes, that's all."

"Where do you work?" Sarah asks before I get the chance to escape.

"The Olympus. You know it? It's one of the casinos on the Strip."

Erik laughs. "Of course we know it! It's super famous. I went there with a few friends years ago—it was amazing." He leans forward, curious. "What do you do there?"

I'm mildly uncomfortable, not used to explaining my position in casual social settings. Most people in Vegas already know who I am. "I own it," I say, shifting from one foot to the other.

Erik and Sarah laugh in unison, then their expressions shift as they realize I'm not joking.

"That's...Fuck!" Erik exclaims, clearly impressed. "I had no idea we were in the presence of Vegas royalty."

Ruby sips her wine, watching our exchange with an unreadable expression. I notice her twirling the stem of her glass between her fingers—a nervous habit I've come to recognize.

"It's just a business," I say, downplaying it. "Like any other."

"So you two are friends?" Sarah asks, looking from me to Ruby and back. "That's nice. It must be wonderful to get on so well with your neighbor. Erik and I live next to this grumpy old lady who keeps bashing her walking stick against the wall if our TV is too loud."

I laugh, grateful for the change of subject. "Ruby's complained about noise, actually. I had some sound system issues that were disturbing her peace."

Ruby's eyes meet mine and finally her lips pull into a genuine smile. She looks amused as she shrugs. "It wasn't a big deal. Athena fixed it."

"You're quite the party animal, huh?" Erik asks.

I shake my head with a grin. "Far from, Erik. Anyway, I should go. I have a meeting."

"Shoot. I was just about to ask you if you could arrange a discount on a room at the Olympus," Sarah jokes.

"You're both welcome to have a room on the house," I say without hesitation. "I don't give out my number, but if you arrange it through Ruby, I'll make sure you're comfortable."

Sarah and Erik exchange excited glances.

"Are you serious?" Erik asks. "That would be incredible!"

"Thank you!" Sarah beams. "That's so generous."

I smile, enjoying their enthusiasm. "My pleasure. Enjoy your time in Vegas." Then I turn to Ruby. "Ruby, would you mind showing me where my shoes are?"

"Of course." Ruby rises immediately. "I'll be right back," she tells Sarah and Erik, who are now whispering to each other.

I follow Ruby through the house, careful not to walk too close. The moment we're out of sight, I notice her shoulders relax slightly. "How are you?" I ask.

"I'm fine," she says, then hesitates. "Though I feel...it's hard to describe. It feels surreal, I suppose. Like it never happened." She looks away, tucking a strand of hair behind her ear. "But I don't regret anything, if that's what you're worried about."

"We should probably talk about it," I say, relieved she has no regrets. "But my mother and sister are arriving in two days, so between your visitors, work, and me prepping for their arrival, there won't be much time. It might have to wait, if that's okay with you."

"Oh, your family's coming? That's wonderful!" Ruby's

eyes light up. "How long has it been since you've seen them? They must be thrilled to spend time with you."

"Yes, but I'm also panicking because they insist on staying at my house and that's not an option because of the club." I take off my hat and ruffle a hand through my hair. "I'm looking at one of the houses farther down the street later today. I'm thinking of buying it. They've never been to my house, but they know I live in The Ridges, so it could work if I can arrange furniture and styling in time. It's a lot to pull off in two days and it will be a nightmare with Zeus, but—"

"Seriously, Athena?" Ruby interrupts me. "Come on, that's ridiculous. Can't you just close the club?"

"No. It wouldn't be fair, and even if I did close it, not everyone reads their messages and emails. Some might show up anyway, and then I'd have an even bigger problem."

Ruby nods, but she's still looking at me like I've lost my mind. "But...buying a house? Even with a whole team, I doubt you could pull that off by Tuesday." She frowns. "They're here for a week, you said?" She continues when I nod. "How about we just swap?"

THIRTY-THREE
RUBY

Athena's movers shuffle between our houses. Sarah and Erik left this morning and I thought the team would be done by the time I got back from work but there's still a lot to do. I stand in my bedroom doorway, watching as two men transfer an armload of Athena's white clothes into my closet —right where Claire's things used to hang. The symbolism isn't lost on me. Out with the old, in with...whatever this is.

"Ma'am, where would you like these?" A young woman appears behind me, arms loaded with a collection of Athena's white hats.

"You can put those on the top shelf," I tell her, stepping aside to let her pass. "And any shoes can go on the rack by the window." I stuck to a large suitcase myself. Why does she need so many clothes? It's only for a week.

I watch as she arranges Athena's hats. This doesn't feel real—none of it does. When I suggested the house swap, it had seemed so simple. Athena needed a place to host her mother and sister, and I needed...well, I don't know what I needed. A change of scenery, perhaps. A break from a house filled with memories. Now...it's all turning a little more complicated. I didn't think about the details. Pictures are either hidden or swapped, and some of Athena's art that her mother gifted her is on display in my living room.

"Do you think it's going to work?" I ask when Athena walks in, hands on her hips while she supervises.

"It has to," she says, but the worry lines between her eyebrows betray her confidence. "My mother is impossible to fool under normal circumstances. But she hasn't been to Vegas since before I moved. As long as I act like it's my home and the personal items are in place, it should be fine."

"And what about the club?" I ask, lowering my voice though the movers are occupied with their tasks.

Athena steps closer, her voice dropping to match mine. "There's a team that handles everything—security, bartenders, cleaning. They know what to do."

I nod, but apprehension still gnaws at my stomach. It's not so much leaving my own home—I'm actually looking forward to that—but Athena's house comes with responsibilities.

"Zeus," I say, voicing my biggest concern. "What if he tries to kill me in my sleep?"

Athena laughs. "He's a cat, Ruby, not a lion. Though I'll admit he sometimes thinks he is."

"He's enormous."

"He's twenty pounds of muscle and attitude," she agrees with a fond smile. "But he's also a creature of routine. As long as you share your bed with him, he'll tolerate you. Might even warm up to you eventually."

"Sleeping with Zeus is not exactly what I had in mind when I pictured myself in your bed," I blurt out, then immediately feel heat rushing to my cheeks. Did I really just say that out loud? Here, now, with movers bustling around us?

Athena's eyes widen slightly, then darken with interest.

"Oh? And what exactly did you have in mind, Ruby?" she asks, her voice dropping to that low, velvety tone that makes my skin tingle.

"I...that's not..." I stammer, unable to find my footing. This inappropriate flirtation was definitely not part of our house-swap arrangement, yet I can't seem to help myself around her.

Athena chuckles as she looks me up and down. "It's not what, Counselor?"

I'm saved from responding by the doorbell. One of Athena's assistants—a young woman named Belle who's been coordinating the move—hurries to answer it.

"The Greek food delivery is here," she calls out.

I glance at my watch. "I'm surprised they're delivering at this time of night."

"They don't normally. The company owner is getting a complimentary suite at The Olympus this weekend, and the delivery driver's getting a generous tip." Athena chuckles. "Amazing how flexible schedules become when there's something in it for everyone."

"Of course," I say, rolling my eyes good-naturedly. "I should have known. Nothing is ever straightforward with you, is it?"

"Where's the fun in straightforward?" She winks before calling back, "I'm coming!"

I trail behind, curious, and burst out laughing as I enter the kitchen. Two delivery men are unloading crates of food —olives, lemons, feta cheese, yogurt, honey, oregano and what looks like enough filo pastry to line the driveway.

"Is your mother planning to open a taverna?" I ask as Belle begins directing the unpacking.

Athena looks over the haul with satisfaction. "My mother would never believe I'm living somewhere without proper Greek staples." She stops Belle when she's about to store the dry ingredients. "Just leave everything on the counter. I'll put it away myself so I can find it."

Another assistant appears with jars of olives and Athena arranges them neatly in my cupboard. "These are specially imported from Kalamata," she explains, handling them like precious artifacts. "At least we didn't have to empty your cupboards first. Coffee, tea, sugar, peanut butter, and—" she pulls out a package, examining the date "—pasta that expired eight months ago." She turns to me with a mix of amusement and concern. "It's sad, really. Don't you ever cook for yourself?"

"No." I shrug. "I order in. Or I eat at the office." The truth is, I haven't eaten a home-cooked meal since Claire died. She was the one who loved spending evenings in the kitchen, experimenting with recipes while I sat at the counter with case files, stealing bites between briefs. I turn to Athena. "Don't tell me *you* cook at home, though. I'd find that hard to believe."

"Touché, I don't. But my housekeeper cooks. She alternates between six Greek recipes I gave her. She's pretty good." Athena's face is suddenly serious. "I can't thank you enough, Ruby. I owe you. Big time. Like, big-big time."

"You've been there for me. I'm glad I can do something in return." I shoot her a flirtatious grin. "But if you feel like you owe me, I can think of a way or two you can thank me."

Athena licks her lips and steps closer. She reaches past me for an olive jar, her body pressing against mine for one deliberate moment. I feel her exhale against my neck. When she pulls back, her eyes hold mine with such raw intention that I have to grip the counter to steady myself.

"When all this family chaos is over," she murmurs, "I

have some new toys at the club that are just begging for a test run. And I think you'd make the perfect volunteer."

Before I can respond to that, a man appears with a clipboard. "Ms. Stavros, we need you to sign for the wine delivery."

Athena sighs, the spell broken. "Duty calls. I'll be right back."

As she follows him, I lean against the kitchen counter and blow out my cheeks. This constant state of arousal can't be healthy. Every time she flirts with me, every lingering look sends my body into overdrive.

Tomorrow, I'll be living in Athena's house while her family thinks my home is hers. It's madness, but I don't mind. I'm looking forward to stepping out of my normal life for a while and getting a break from this house full of memories. And sleeping in her bed.

THIRTY-FOUR
ATHENA

"Where do you keep the garlic press?" Mom's voice calls out from across Ruby's kitchen. She's elbow-deep in preparations for moussaka.

"Just a moment," I say, opening a drawer that I'm almost certain only contains silverware. I was right. "Let me check the next one."

I've spent the entire afternoon playing a bizarre game of culinary hide-and-seek while trying to maintain the façade that this is actually my home. Opening and closing cabinets I'd barely examined during the rushed move-in, desperately trying to locate cooking implements I'm not even sure Ruby owns.

"Athena, if you tell me again you don't know where your own kitchen tools are..." Mom shoots me a look over her shoulder. She's dressed in a navy linen two-piece, covered by a white apron tied neatly around her waist. Despite her doctor's explicit instructions about her back, she's wearing high heels that click authoritatively against the tile floor. Sophia Stavros has never believed comfort should come at the expense of style.

"I don't use it," I admit, which is at least honest. I finally locate the garlic press in a drawer filled with miscellaneous kitchen gadgets—most of which look unused.

Mom sighs as I hand it to her. "This is exactly why I worry about you. Living on takeout and restaurant food." She tests the press in her hand with a critical eye. "This hasn't been used once, has it? Look, it's still got the manufacturer's sticker!"

"I eat very well, Mom," I protest, leaning against the counter. "The Olympus has an excellent Greek restaurant. You've been there."

She scoffs, wielding an eggplant like it's evidence in a trial. "Restaurant food! Full of butter and salt to mask inferior ingredients." She begins slicing the eggplant with surgical precision. "When your father and I were first married, I cooked for him every night, even though we had three cooks on staff."

"Because you enjoyed it," I remind her.

"Because I loved him," she corrects, pointing the knife at me for emphasis. "And because I love you and your sister, I cook for you too. Someone has to make sure you eat properly."

She sets down the knife and reaches for a wooden spoon to stir the simmering sauce. Without warning, she playfully swats my behind as I pass too close to her workspace.

"Mama!" I protest, jumping.

"You're in my way," she says with a mischievous smile that takes years off her face. She's always done this—using wooden spoons or kitchen towels to playfully swat us when we'd sneak tastes before dinner or get underfoot while she cooked.

I wonder, not for the first time, if my particular proclivities in the bedroom might have their origins in these childhood kitchen dynamics. The thought nearly makes me laugh out loud.

"You're too skinny," she declares, looking me up and down with the critical eye only a Greek mother can possess. "What happened to your appetite? American food is ruining you. You're going to become malnourished eating their processed garbage."

I glance down at myself, amused. "I literally weigh exactly the same as I did when you saw me last Christmas."

She waves this fact away as if measurements are merely opinions. "Your face is thinner. I can tell."

The sound of another pair of heels announces my sister's arrival before she appears. Demetria sweeps into the kitchen like she's making an entrance at a gala rather than joining us for dinner preparations. She's twelve years younger than me and dresses with the bohemian flair of someone trying very hard to look like a starving artist.

Today, it's a flowing vintage maxi dress in vibrant peacock blues and greens, frayed at the edges, with dramatic side slits. She's adorned it with layered thrift-store necklaces made of wooden beads and semi-precious stones, and stacks of silver bangles. Her dark hair—the same shade as mine—is twisted into an artfully messy updo. Her makeup screams "I woke up like this" but definitely took an hour to perfect.

"Sorry, that was Julian again," she announces, placing her phone on the counter. "He's having a crisis about his gallery showing next month."

"Why didn't you just bring him?" I ask. "That's the fifth call today."

"He's busy." Demetria grins. "At least I *have* someone who calls me five times a day. When was the last time you had a date, workaholic?"

"Children," Mom warns without looking up from her chopping. "Behave yourselves or neither of you gets dessert."

Demetria laughs and kisses our Mom's cheek, somehow managing to do so without getting in her way—a skill I've never mastered. "What are you making, Mama? It smells amazing."

"Moussaka, galaktoboureko, and maybe horiatiki if your sister can tell me where she keeps her tomatoes."

I gesture toward the refrigerator. "Bottom drawer." Small victories. At least I know that one.

Demetria slides onto one of the kitchen stools, stealing a slice of cucumber from the cutting board despite Mom's warning swat. "So, Athena, tell us what's new in your life that isn't work-related."

"Well—" I begin, but Mom interrupts.

"Yes, tell us. Have you met someone yet? A nice man, perhaps?" Mom pauses in her preparation, fixing me with a hopeful stare. "You're not getting any younger, Athena. Your biological clock is ticking." She throws her hands up dramatically, a piece of eggplant flying from her knife. "Though at forty, your eggs are probably as dry as the Sahara Desert. I should have started lighting candles to Saint Anna years ago.

I suppress a sigh. I've had this conversation so many times. "I'm not dating and I'm certainly not getting married, Mom. I'm not interested in that life."

"But you're all alone," she presses, her voice softening with genuine concern. "Aren't you lonely in this big house by yourself?"

Demetria suddenly looks up and frowns. "Wait," she says, glancing around the kitchen. "Where is that cat of yours? I haven't seen him since we arrived."

I freeze momentarily, then recover quickly, crafting a lie that's close enough to the truth.

"Zeus actually prefers to live with my neighbor," I say with a casual wave of my hand. "He's been spending so much time over there that I finally just let him stay. He's happier there."

"Your neighbor?" Mom's eyebrows shoot up in surprise. "And she's okay with that? With taking care of your beast of a cat?"

"Yes," I reply, relieved she's accepting the explanation. "We're friends. Ruby doesn't mind at all."

"Ruby? This is the first time you've mentioned having a friend close by." Mom looks genuinely pleased, as if the existence of Ruby somehow proves I'm not the complete hermit she fears I've become.

"She's really nice," I say, trying to keep my tone neutral.

"And she takes care of your cat?" Demetria asks skeptically. "That's a pretty big favor. Zeus isn't exactly a goldfish."

I shrug. "She likes him. He likes her. It works out."

Mom wipes her hands on her apron. "Well, then you must invite her for dinner. I want to meet your friend, serve her a home-cooked meal."

"That's not necessary—" I begin, but Mom cuts me off.

"No, no. I insist." She gestures at the extensive spread of ingredients covering Ruby's counter. "Call her now. Invite her."

"She's at work," I say quickly. "She works late."

Mom returns from the stove, wooden spoon in hand. "Well, tell her to take a night off. It's not healthy to work so hard." She shoots me a pointed look. "You should understand that better than anyone, Athena."

Demetria grins, clearly enjoying my discomfort. "Yes, invite your cat-sitting friend."

I'm cornered, and I know it. With both my mother and sister looking at me expectantly, I have no choice but to pull out my phone. I compose the message carefully, trying to communicate more than just the invitation.

Emergency. Mom insists you join us for dinner tonight. Sorry. Can explain more later. Reminder: I'm not out to them. 8 p.m. Dress nice but not too nice. Bring a bottle of Greek wine from the basement.

THIRTY-FIVE

RUBY

I slide into the chair across from Athena, amused to be sitting in my own dining room as a guest. The table is set with my dishes but arranged in a way I would never think to display them—artfully mismatched plates and bowls, cloth napkins I didn't even know I owned folded into elegant triangles. The center of the table holds a stunning arrangement of fresh herbs, lemons, and greenery—nothing like the sad grocery store bouquets I occasionally remember to buy.

"Ruby! We're so delighted you could join us," Athena's mother exclaims in a thick Greek accent. She's stunning for her age—elegant and poised in a way that makes me immediately conscious of my posture.

"Thank you for inviting me," I reply, shooting Athena a quick glance. She looks tense—I recognize the slight tightness around her eyes that I've come to associate with her rare moments of uncertainty.

"I'm Sophia," her mother continues, "and this is Demetria, Athena's little sister."

Demetria, dressed like a boho hippie chick, gives me a smile that's equal parts warmth and assessment. The family resemblance is striking—all three women share the same dark eyes, high cheekbones, and full lips.

"I've heard so much about you," I lie smoothly.

"Really?" Demetria's eyebrows shoot up as she glances at Athena. "That's surprising. My sister is usually so private about her life here. She never tells us anything."

Athena clears her throat. "Ruby and I have seen a lot of each other since Zeus moved in with her. I go over there to see him a few times a week, so we talk a lot." She turns to me. "I told them you confiscated my cat."

I nearly choke on my water. "Yes, Zeus is...quite the character," I manage. "I do love the little furball."

Athena's eyes widen at my description, a smile tugging at the corners of her mouth as she takes a sip of wine to hide her amusement. The idea of anyone referring to her massive, regal cat as a "little furball" clearly strikes her as absurd.

I smile, remembering last night's battle for bed space. Zeus had planted himself squarely in the middle of Athena's king-size mattress, his huge body somehow expanding. Every time I shifted to get comfortable, he stretched, yawned, or simply rolled over, pushing me inexorably toward the edge until I was clinging to the last six inches of mattress while he purred contentedly in his sleep. By morning, I was practically hanging off the side while His Majesty sprawled diagonally across what should have been my sleeping space. I should have moved to one of the guest rooms, but I was too tired to think. I guess that's where I'll be sleeping tonight.

"He's very...territorial about the bed," I add with a hint of humor. "Other than that, he's adorable."

"That beast has never respected boundaries," Sophia says, placing a large dish of food in the center of the table.

The aroma is intoxicating. "I'm surprised you agreed to take him."

She begins serving what I recognize as moussaka—layers of eggplant, potatoes, and some kind of meat sauce topped with a creamy béchamel.

"So, Ruby," Sophia says as she places a generous portion on my plate, "Athena tells us you're an attorney?"

"Yes, I specialize in corporate law. Mergers and acquisitions, mostly." I take a bite of the moussaka and it's delicious. "This is incredible," I say sincerely.

Sophia beams. "Traditional recipe—my grandmother's. Athena could make it too, if she ever bothered to cook."

"Mom," Athena warns, but there's no real heat in her voice.

"It's true!" Sophia turns to me, leaning in conspiratorially. "I taught both my girls to cook properly, but neither of them ever do. This one—" she gestures to Athena with her fork "—she always has an excuse. Too busy, too tired. As if running a business means you can't feed yourself properly."

I glance at Athena, loving this glimpse into her family dynamic. She rolls her eyes but doesn't contradict her mother.

"And what firm do you work with?" Demetria asks, twirling her wine in her glass. There's something about her that reminds me of an exotic bird—colorful, wild, watching everything with keen intelligence.

"I have my own firm," I reply. "Walsh and Associates."

"Oh, cool. And what about outside of work?" Sophia asks. "Are you dating?"

I feel Athena tense beside me, her fork pausing midway to her mouth.

"No," I reply carefully. "I was married, but my wife passed away a few years ago."

"Your wife?" Sophia asks. A moment of silence falls over the table. I watch the information register on their faces and suspect she's more shocked about the fact that I'm gay than that I'm widowed.

But then she reaches across the table to briefly touch my hand. "I'm so sorry," she says. "That's a terrible loss."

"Thank you." I take another sip of wine, grateful for its steadying effect. "It's been a difficult journey, but I'm doing better now."

"And you're good friends with my daughter?" Something in her phrasing makes me wonder if she suspects more than she's letting on.

"We've been there for each other," I say honestly. "Athena has been...very supportive during a difficult time."

"That doesn't surprise me." Sophia's gaze shifts to her daughter with unmistakable pride. "She has always been empathic." Athena looks uncomfortable with this characterization and Sophia shakes her head. "There's no shame in having a caring heart, honey."

Demetria laughs. "Don't let her fool you, Ruby. Behind that heart is a will of steel. When Athena decides she wants something, she gets it—one way or another."

I blush, remembering Athena's voice in my ear, her hands on my body. *You're mine.*

"So, how is Julian's exhibition coming along?" Athena asks, clearly desperate to change the subject.

"Dramatically, as expected," Demetria replies, launching into a story that I soon figure out is about her artist boyfriend's latest creative crisis.

As Demetria talks, I observe Athena with her family. She's different with them—there's a softness I rarely see. When her mother laughs particularly hard at something Demetria says, Athena watches her with such undisguised love that it brings a lump to my throat. I'm not sure why I'm feeling emotional tonight. Maybe it's the aftermath of the club, or perhaps it's something about this rare glimpse into Athena's private world. Tonight feels special, intimate, as if I've been granted temporary passage through a doorway she keeps firmly closed to most. With each laugh shared between mother and daughter, each touch or knowing glance, I'm piecing together a different Athena than the one I thought I knew—a version of her that exists only within the orbit of those she truly loves.

The conversation flows around me, carrying stories and laughter. I'm drawn into their warmth, this family circle momentarily expanded to include me.

Sophia rises from her chair to collect our empty plates. "Now, who's ready for dessert?"

"I'll help," I offer, standing to gather dishes.

In the kitchen, Sophia pulls a baking dish from the oven. The smell is heavenly—butter, sugar, and something citrusy.

"It's galaktoboureko," she explains, noticing my appreciative sniff. "Semolina custard in filo dough, soaked in citrus syrup. Athena's favorite since she was small."

She begins cutting the dessert into squares. "You know," she says without looking up, "in all the years Athena has lived in America, she's never introduced us to a friend before. Not once."

I'm not sure how to respond to this, so I simply wait.

"My daughter is very private about her personal life," Sophia continues. "Always has been. Even as a child, she kept her hurts to herself. Her joys too." She glances toward the dining room where Athena and Demetria are still talking, then back to me. "It makes me happy to see she has someone here who understands her."

There's something in her tone that makes me wonder again how much she knows.

"Athena is..." I search for the right words. "She's remarkable. I'm lucky to know her."

Sophia studies me for a long moment, then nods, apparently satisfied with that.

"Yes, I think perhaps you are both lucky." She hands me two of the dessert plates. "Now, let's not keep them waiting."

I watch Asha wandering through Ruby's kitchen like a lost tourist, opening one cabinet after another in search of cleaning products. Her familiar routine has been disrupted by our temporary living arrangement, and the strain is starting to show. She opens the cabinet under the sink, finding nothing but an ancient bottle of dish soap and a stray sponge.

"Ms. Stavros," she says, her usual composure cracking slightly. "Where are the cleaning supplies? And the vacuum?"

"In the closet in the hallway," I reply, though I'm not entirely certain. Ruby showed me around in a hurried tour, pointing out essentials. Most of what she said has blurred together in my mind.

Asha nods and disappears, only to return moments later with a bewildered expression. "There's nothing there but towels and bed sheets."

I'm about to suggest another location when my mother steps into the kitchen, still in her robe, hair coiffed despite the early hour. She surveys the scene with a critical eye.

"Good morning. You must be the housekeeper," she says to Asha.

"Yes. Would you like a coffee?" Asha asks. "Or I could start breakfast?"

My mother waves a hand. "Don't worry, honey. I'll be making breakfast." She opens the refrigerator and begins pulling out eggs, feta cheese, and tomatoes. "You can clean later."

Asha's eyes flick to me in silent appeal. In my home, she has autonomy. But here, with my mother commandeering the kitchen, her world has been upended again.

"Actually, Asha," I say, making a quick decision, "why don't you take the day off?"

Relief floods her features, though she tries to hide it. "Are you sure, Ms. Stavros?"

"I'm sure. It's spotless in here and we're fine. Go home, rest. I'll see you tomorrow."

My mother fills the coffee machine with water. "That poor woman looked absolutely lost," she comments once Asha has departed. "Has she always been so disorganized?"

"We've reorganized some things," I reply, watching as my mother makes coffee. I notice with some amusement that she's using Ruby's Ethiopian beans. "It's been busy with the preparations for your visit."

"Hmm." My mother doesn't sound convinced. "Well, at least you have decent coffee. These beans smell delicious."

"Yeah? Guess what? They're not Greek beans," I say with a grin.

My mother's hand pauses mid-scoop. "Really?" She frowns. "I brought you those beans from Thessaloniki last Christmas. What happened to those?"

"I finished them, Mom." I move to stand beside her,

taking the coffee scoop from her hand. "And not everything Greek is automatically superior."

She looks at me as if I've just suggested the Acropolis is overrated. "Of course it is. Especially coffee."

"Look, I'm all about supporting my country," I say, filling the coffee maker, "but I'm not budging on these beans."

My mother sniffs. "Betrayal. My own daughter, turning her back on her heritage for foreign coffee."

"The horror," I deadpan, pressing the brew button.

"Next you'll tell me you prefer American yogurt over Greek."

"Now that would be true sacrilege."

The coffee maker gurgles to life and my mother pulls two mugs from the cabinet—somehow navigating Ruby's kitchen better than I've managed in the past twenty-four hours—and sets them on the counter.

"Oh!" she exclaims suddenly. "I forgot to tell you. I spoke with my friend Polina yesterday. Her grandson is getting married next summer in Santorini. Very handsome boy, studying medicine in London. You should come with us to the wedding."

I suppress a sigh. "Mother, please don't start."

"What?" She arranges her features into a mask of innocence that hasn't fooled me since I was seven. "I'm simply informing you of a family event."

"You're matchmaking."

"I'm doing no such thing. But if you happened to meet someone suitable while we're there..."

"I'm not interested in being set up."

"You're almost forty, Athena."

"And perfectly happy with my life as it is."

She purses her lips but says nothing more as she pours

the coffee. This is our dance—she hints, I deflect, neither of us addressing the chasm between what she wants for me and what I want for myself.

Demetria makes her entrance, yawning dramatically. Her hair is piled on top of her head, and she's wearing men's striped pajamas.

"Coffee," she moans, making grabby hands toward the machine. "I need coffee or I'll die."

"Good morning to you too, sunshine," I say, sliding my mug toward her before making another for myself.

Demetria takes a long sip, closes her eyes in momentary bliss, then opens them to fix me with a stare. "Your friend Ruby is nice."

Something in her tone puts me on alert. "Yes, she is."

"Beautiful too," she adds, watching me over the rim of her mug.

"I suppose she is."

My mother places a container of Greek yogurt on the counter, along with honey and walnuts. "She seemed quite comfortable here last night."

My heart stutters in my chest. "She comes here regularly."

"Mmm..." My mother's eyes linger on my face a beat too long.

Demetria divides the yogurt over three small bowls, drowns it in honey, and adds a few walnuts to each. "So," she says, setting them on the table. "Why didn't you tell us your neighbor was..." She pauses, glancing at our mother with a teasing smile.

"Was what?" my mother prompts.

"A lesbian," Demetria finishes, making the word sound both perfectly ordinary and slightly scandalous.

My mother clicks her tongue. "Demetria, please. There's no need to be so blunt."

Demetria laughs. "Mom, don't tell me you're shocked. It's not the fifties."

"Of course I'm not shocked," my mother replies with dignity. "She's a lovely woman, and I'm glad you two are friends." She turns to me. "I've never actually met a lesbian before. At least, not that I know of." She pauses, head tilted. "Do you have many gay friends, Athena?"

I feel heat creeping up my neck, and I take a sip of coffee to buy myself time. Demetria's gaze is suddenly laser-focused on me, as if she's seeing something she hadn't noticed before.

"I—" I clear my throat. "I live in Las Vegas, Mom. Of course I know queer people."

Non-answer. Safe ground. I've become an expert at this evasion, dancing around the truth without ever explicitly lying. It's not that I'm ashamed—far from it. I've been comfortable with my sexuality for decades, but my father, for all his love for me, would never have understood.

And my mother? The woman who still lights candles at church every Sunday, who crosses herself when we pass a cemetery, who believes marriage and children are the ultimate fulfillment of a woman's purpose? What would she think of me if she knew the truth? I've never been brave enough to find out.

THIRTY-SEVEN
RUBY

I stand in Athena's kitchen, locked in a standoff with twenty pounds of spotted feline attitude. Zeus sits on the countertop, his golden eyes narrowed to slits as he tracks my every movement.

"Listen," I say, pointing my chopsticks at him. "We've talked about this. The counter is off-limits."

Zeus blinks slowly, a gesture I've come to recognize as his way of saying he acknowledges my words but has absolutely no intention of obeying them.

I'm exhausted after a day of back-to-back client meetings, but I've been leaving the office earlier this week—worried that Zeus might be lonely despite his apparent disdain for my company. He tolerates my presence at best, but something about his regal solitude tugs at my heart.

"Don't give me that look," I mutter, arranging the sushi, sashimi, and miso soup from Nobu onto a plate. "You just had your dinner."

Zeus stretches languidly, extending one massive paw toward my plate.

"No. Absolutely not." I move the plate away. "You've

had premium cat food, which, may I remind you, is imported from Japan and costs a small fortune."

His tail swishes once, twice. I suspect it may be a warning sign.

As I reach for a piece of salmon, Zeus makes his move. With lightning speed, he swats at my chopsticks, knocking them from my grip. When I bend to retrieve them, he seizes the opportunity, snatching the salmon.

"Hey!" I yelp. "That's mine!"

Zeus doesn't even bother to retreat. He simply raises a paw while he chews, claws extended, and gives me a look that says, *Try me, human.*

"Are you even tasting that?" I ask. "Because that's top-quality salmon, and you're gulping it down like it's kibble."

A soft laugh from the doorway freezes me mid-lecture. Athena is leaning against the frame, arms crossed with an amused smirk. She's wearing white jeans and a simple white shirt, her hair loose under a white fedora.

My heart stutters at the sight of her. "How long have you been standing there?"

"Long enough to watch you lose an argument with my cat." She holds up a bag. "Lucky for you, Mom made me bring this over."

"Your mom?" I blink in surprise. "That's so thoughtful, but there's no need. I already have dinner." I gesture to my half-eaten takeout, now carefully guarded by Zeus.

"Trust me, refusing isn't an option. She insisted." Athena strides into the kitchen, placing the bag on the counter. "Apparently, you made quite the impression."

Zeus immediately abandons his sushi conquest and pads over to Athena, stretching up on his hind legs toward her. The transformation is startling—from fierce predator to needy house cat in seconds. He makes a small mewling sound I've never heard before.

"Hello, little prince," Athena coos, lifting him into her arms. Zeus settles against her chest, his purr rumbling loudly enough that I can hear it from where I stand. "Have you been terrorizing Ruby?"

"We've reached an understanding," I say dryly. "He gets whatever he wants, and I pretend I don't mind."

Athena laughs, scratching behind Zeus's ears. He closes his eyes in bliss, looking smug. "How's it been? Living here?"

"It's been nice," I admit. "Though the bed situation was a challenge."

"Let me guess—he takes up most of it?"

"All of it. I moved to one of your guest rooms." I begin unpacking the containers from the bag Athena brought. Inside, I find pastitsio, stuffed filo pastry, and salad. "This looks amazing. Please thank your mother for me."

"I will. How's work?" Athena asks, still cuddling Zeus, who has now draped himself across her shoulder like a fur stole.

"Busy. I've just signed a new major client." I glance at her. "What about you? How's it been with your family?"

Athena sighs, gently placing Zeus back on the floor. "It's great to see them, but also draining at times. I can't be entirely myself around them." She chuckles. "Plus, I can't find anything in your house."

"Same here." I laugh along. "They're lovely, by the way," I say. "Your mother and sister."

"They like you too." Athena meets my eyes. "Mom thinks you're sweet, smart, and polite."

"High praise from a Greek mother. I'll take it." The tension that's been simmering between us intensifies in the quiet kitchen. It's been days since we've been alone together, but now, with only Zeus as witness, the pretense feels impossible to maintain.

"I should put these away," I say, gesturing to the containers, but making no move to do so.

Athena nods, and when I reach for the containers, her hand covers mine. Her thumb traces the inside of my wrist, and I forget what I was about to do. She's standing close, her eyes holding mine with unmistakable intent.

Without warning, she steps forward, backing me against the refrigerator. Her hands find my waist, and then she's kissing me fiercely. My hands instinctively tangle in her hair, pulling her closer.

Her mouth moves against mine with a ferocity that leaves me gasping, and I lose myself in the sensation of her lips, her tongue, her hands that are everywhere at once. When we break apart, breathless, she keeps me pinned against the refrigerator, her forehead resting against mine.

"Fuck. I did it again," she whispers.

"I'm not complaining," I murmur, my hands still wound in her hair.

Zeus makes his presence known again, meowing loudly at our feet. He stretches up against Athena's leg, demanding attention.

"Someone's jealous," I say with a breathless laugh.

Athena reluctantly steps back. "Timing was never his strong suit, but it's probably for the best."

"Yeah..." I straighten my blouse that's become wrinkled, and we stand in silence for a moment, eyes locked, chests heaving.

Athena's gaze lowers to my lips again. She looks like she's fighting an internal battle. She takes a half-step forward before catching herself. "If I start again, I won't stop," she says. "And I don't think either of us wants that complication right now."

She's right, of course. But wisdom seems increasingly irrelevant when she looks at me like that. My body responds to her stare, a rush of heat between my thighs that makes me press them together.

"I'm sorry about that," she whispers. "I shouldn't have—"

"You're not sorry," I interrupt, feeling bold. "And neither am I."

Athena reaches out to trace the line of my jaw. "I'm so fucking hungry," she says, cupping my chin.

Behind us, Zeus knocks a container of pastitsio to the floor, as if reminding us that in this house, he decides when —and if—we feast.

I want her to take me, to rip my clothes off and do with me as she pleases, but she shakes her head and smiles. "I'd better head back before Mom comes looking for me. Don't be a stranger. She insists on seeing you again before they leave."

THIRTY-EIGHT
ATHENA

Two wineglasses catch the moonlight, nearly empty after my lengthy conversation with Demetria. We're on the loungers by the pool, lying down after Mom overfed us again.

"So, you're going to move to New York with Julian?" I ask.

Demetria stretches her legs out and yawns. "That's the plan. We'll see if it works out between us, but for now, yes."

"But what about Mom?"

She arches her eyebrows in challenge. "What *about* Mom? You moved away. Why should I be the one to stay behind?"

I wince, realizing how it sounded. "I didn't mean it that way."

"Didn't you?" Her tone softens slightly. "Look, Mom has plenty of friends and family back in Greece; she won't be short of company. If I'm not there anymore and she wants to be closer to us, she could move to New York. Or to Vegas." She gestures around us with her wineglass. "Be closer to you."

The thought makes me chuckle. "She would never move away from Greece."

"Exactly." Demetria reaches for the bottle to refill our glasses. "She complains about missing us, but do you think she'd actually leave Santorini? Her church? Her friends? Her sisters?"

"Not a chance," I agree, accepting the refill.

Crickets chirp somewhere in the desert beyond the property line. I love that sound at night.

Demetria shifts on her lounger, turning to face me fully. "I know this isn't your house," she says out of nowhere.

The wine turns sour in my mouth. "What?"

"You might be able to fool Mom, but you can't fool me." Her eyes are piercing, seeing right through me. My baby sister is clever. "This isn't your house, Athena."

I open my mouth to protest, but she raises her hand to stop me.

"First, there's no way that's your furniture. There's nothing wrong with it. In fact, it's quite nice, but it's not yours." She ticks off points on her fingers. "Second, you have no idea where anything is. Third, I went into your bedroom earlier when you were at your neighbor's, and there are clothes in there that are not yours. I haven't seen you wearing anything other than white since we were little, and you don't wear heels either. There were at least ten pairs of heels in there."

"You went into my room? That's not okay, Dem." My mind races for explanations, but Demetria isn't finished.

"It's not your room, so I'm not going to apologize," she says matter-of-factly. "And last but not least... when we got back the other night, you hesitated at the front door like you weren't sure which key to use." She leans forward. "Also, the bookshelf in the office upstairs? Half the books are legal textbooks. You run a casino, not a law firm."

Fuck. I should have been more thorough. Why did I think I could get away with this? I added books, convinced it all blended in and that neither my mother nor my sister would go into the office, let alone peruse the books in there.

I remain frozen, caught in my sister's keen gaze. I forgot how observant she can be.

"So whose house is this, really?" she asks. "Ruby's?"

There's no point in denying it. I nod, staring into my wine glass. "Yes."

"And your house is...?"

"Next door," I admit, gesturing vaguely toward my actual home.

She laughs, not unkindly. "Why the elaborate charade? Why all the lies?"

I take a long sip of wine, buying time. How much should I reveal? How much does she already suspect?

"Also...are you gay?" she asks directly.

I nearly drop my glass but manage to set it down on the table with trembling fingers. My heart pounds against my ribcage, blood rushing in my ears. I've imagined this moment for decades—one of my family members asking the question outright—but in my imagination, I was always prepared. I had calm responses, practical explanations. Now, faced with the reality, all those rehearsed words evaporate.

"Athena?" Demetria prompts gently. "It's okay. I've suspected it for years."

I stare at her, speechless. "How?"

"You're my sister." She laughs softly. "And you've literally never dated a man."

"Mom doesn't know," I whisper.

"No, she doesn't. Though I wonder if she suspects and just doesn't want to confront it."

"You won't tell her, right?" I don't remember the last time I put on a pleading tone toward anyone, but here I am, bowing down to Demetria.

"Of course I won't," she says. "That's up to you."

I rub my temples, trying to process what's happening. After decades of careful evasion, of half-truths and redirections, this is both terrifying and oddly liberating.

"Why didn't you ever say anything?" I ask.

Demetria shrugs, tucking her legs under her on the lounger. "I figured you'd tell me when you were ready. And then as the years passed, it just became this unspoken thing between us. I didn't want to force it out of you."

"But you just did."

"And it was about time, don't you think?" she replies dryly.

I chuckle and shake my head as I don't even know what to say to that.

"So this house swap..." Demetria continues. "Why? Is it because there's something in your house you didn't want Mom to see?"

I hesitate. "My house has certain...adaptations that would be difficult to explain," I say carefully.

Her eyebrows shoot up. "Like what? A secret sex dungeon?"

I choke on my wine, coughing violently and Demetria laughs, reaching over to pat my back.

"Oh my god, I was joking! Do you actually have a sex dungeon?" Her eyes widen.

"Something like that," I say, thinking on my feet. I can't tell her the truth, so I'll go with the sex dungeon.

I watch my sister's face cycle through shock, disbelief,

and finally morbid curiosity. Of all the ways I imagined coming out to my family, discussing fictitious sex dungeons by the pool wasn't on the list.

"So that's why you swapped houses?" Demetria asks, her lips twitching with suppressed laughter. "I've got to say, I'm impressed. Most people just hide their porn collection when family visits."

"I'm an overachiever," I deadpan. "Always have been."

Demetria bursts into laughter. "Oh my god, Athena! All these years I thought you were this boring workaholic, and meanwhile you're like the Christian Grey of Las Vegas."

"Please never say that again. I have standards."

"I bet you do." She settles back, watching me with newfound curiosity. "So can I see it?"

I grimace. "What? No, of course not. Absolutely not."

"Oh, come on! I won't judge," she presses. "Just a peek."

"Demetria, no. This conversation is making me nauseous."

She sighs and rolls her eyes. "Fine. I'll stop asking about your secret lair of debauchery on one condition."

I eye her suspiciously. "What's that?"

"You tell me what's going on between you and Ruby. You like her. I can tell."

"I do," I admit. "But it's not that simple."

"Because you're in the closet?"

"I'm not in the closet per se. Well, I am in Greece, I suppose. And here, I don't publicly flaunt it either, but my friends know."

"Then what's the problem? You're not in Greece." Demetria makes everything sound so simple. She's always had a different perspective than I do—more straightforward, less encumbered by the weight of expectations. But then, she wasn't the one growing up gay in a family where that identity could never be acknowledged, feeling the constant pressure to hide an essential part of herself just to maintain the peace.

"I'm fucked up," I say. "I'm broken inside and so is Ruby." I pause, chewing my bottom lip. "Besides, it's been so long since I've allowed myself to love, it...scares me."

Demetria regards me thoughtfully. "Two people who understand brokenness might actually fit together better than those who've never been shattered," she says. "Like those Japanese bowls repaired with gold—the cracks become part of the beauty."

I shake my head. "You don't understand. There are things that have happened... There's so much you don't know."

"Then tell me now," she says, taking my hand. "All these years, you've been this...enigma. My brilliant, successful sister who keeps everyone at arm's length. I want to know you, Athena. The real you, not the edited version you show the family."

My throat tightens as I look at her—really look at her—and see the sister who's always been there, waiting patiently for me to let her in. I take a deep breath, feeling something shift inside me, a door unlocking that I've kept bolted. I didn't think this would ever happen. I'm about to spill it all to someone who shares my blood.

THIRTY-NINE

RUBY

I cradle my whiskey, watching as women filter in and out of the lounge. Some I recognize, some I don't, but I'm no longer an outsider here.

They've witnessed me at my most vulnerable, and that creates intimacy. They've seen me laid bare, both literally and figuratively, and I've seen some of them the same way. It creates an unspoken bond.

I catch whispers, notice glances. I have no doubt they're speculating about my connection to Athena. In their world of power and discretion, relationships like ours become delicious puzzles to solve. But their curiosity doesn't bother me. In a strange way, I welcome it—this is perhaps the first time in years I've been interesting to anyone beyond my professional capacity. I'm not ashamed either. I'll do it again without hesitation.

Tonight, someone else will occupy that mirrored room; someone else will feel the sting of the crop, the rush of surrender. My experience here peeled away layers I didn't know existed, revealed hungers I'd spent years denying. It was revelation, not degradation—a key unlocking rooms inside myself I'd kept tightly sealed.

"Another?" Donna—Justice Donovan—slides onto the sofa beside me.

"I should pace myself," I say, though I hand her my glass when she reaches for it.

"One more won't hurt." She signals to a waitress, who appears almost instantly to take our order. "You look lost in thought."

"Just unwinding after a long day," I lie. The truth is more complicated—that I came here to see if the club still calls to me when Athena isn't present, if my desires are tied to her or to this space. The jury is still out.

Donna laughs. "If that's your unwinding face, I'd hate to see your stressed one." She accepts a fresh whiskey and a martini from the waitress who's materialized beside us. "But you've come to the right place."

She's right, of course. That's why we're all here—seeking release from the pressures of our very different lives. I'm blessed to be a part of this. Where else would I have the chance to connect with such special women? To make real connections?

Morgan catches my eye from across the bar where she's leaning against Alex, both of them watching me with undisguised interest. When I meet her gaze, she raises her glass in a toast, then whispers something to Alex, who smiles in my direction. I wave back and smile politely but quickly turn my attention to Donna when Morgan's stare becomes too inviting.

I know exactly what they're offering—a replay of the scene I witnessed my first night here, except this time with me as an active participant. Without Athena, I have no desire for any of it—that much I've learned tonight. She's the one who turns me on, makes me brave, opens me up to new experiences.

"They've been asking about you," Donna says.

"Oh. I—" I pause and shake my head. "I'm not looking for that tonight."

"Not without Athena?" She winks. "Where is she anyway?"

"Family obligations," I reply, taking a sip of my drink. "She'll be back next week."

Donna raises an eyebrow. "You're well-informed."

"We're neighbors," I say with a shrug, as if that explains everything. I don't mention that I'm currently living here, caring for her cat. That I've met her mother and sister, shared a meal and stories with them. That parts of my life are becoming intertwined with Athena's in ways neither of us anticipated.

"Neighbors," Donna repeats with a grin. "Seriously, are you two together?"

"Am I under oath?" I joke.

Donna laughs. "With me? Always." She shifts on the couch, crossing her legs. This woman has sentenced murderers and settled billion-dollar disputes, yet here she sits, genuinely interested in my complicated non-relationship. The world is a strange place.

"Well, in that case, I'm going to say the only thing I know is true right now, and that is that we're friends."

"Honey," she says, "Athena doesn't have 'friends'—at least not in the conventional sense. She has members, associates, allies, and she's fiercely loyal. I would even go as far as to say I trust her with my life, but friends? You'd be the first."

"I didn't have friends before I met Athena," I say. "But I

feel like I know her, and she knows me. All of me. Isn't that friendship?"

"Yes..." Donna tilts her head and regards me through narrowed eyes. "That certainly sounds like friendship. And maybe something more?"

I shrug. "We're floating in a strange space."

"Do you *want* more?" she asks, then raises a hand. "And tell me to back off and stay out of your business, by the way. I've been told I can be a nosey old witch."

I chuckle. I can't imagine who would dare say that to her face.

Do I want her to back off? Not really. It's nice to be able to talk to someone about my conflicted feelings.

"It's okay, I don't mind," I say. "And I don't know if I want more. Physically, I crave her. Emotionally, she's... she's good to me." I pause, measuring my words. "But there's a complexity to it. My wife died, and—"

"I know," Donna says gently. "I heard about that. I'm truly sorry." Her sympathy feels genuine.

"Thank you. It's been two years, but grief doesn't follow a timeline, does it? Some days, I wake up and it feels fresh. Other days, I can almost convince myself I'm moving on." I take another sip of my drink, letting the whiskey burn away the tightness in my throat. "Whenever I let myself get closer to Athena, there's this voice that whispers I'm erasing Claire. As if I'm retroactively diminishing what we had by wanting someone new."

Donna nods. "Opening yourself to new feelings doesn't invalidate what came before."

"I know that," I admit. "But emotions aren't rational. And these feelings for Athena—they don't even resemble what I had with Claire. It's so different that sometimes I wonder if I even understand what I'm experiencing."

"Sure," Donna says. "That makes sense. Each relationship we have changes us, becomes part of our foundation. Claire will always be part of yours, regardless of who else enters your life. Sometimes the most profound relationships don't mirror each other—they complement each other. One teaches you tenderness, another teaches you passion. Both are equally valid, and both can be built on love." She sets her glass down and turns toward me, resting her arm over the couch's backrest. "Let me tell you something. People have been talking."

"About Athena and me?" I frown. "What are they saying?"

Donna purses her lips and tilts her head from side to side. "Look, I'm not interested in going beyond that curtain, so I've never seen Athena in action so to speak," she says, making quote marks in the air. "But I heard she was different with you. She's never kissed anyone in that room, and she's certainly never gone on her knees for anyone, ever."

I stare at Donna, not sure if I should feel flattered or embarrassed. "I didn't realize that was unusual for her."

Donna nods. "Apparently so." Her gaze drifts over the room before returning to mine. "It's extraordinary, isn't it? That chaos inside when someone consumes your thoughts. That wildness? That delicious freefall? It's rare." She smiles wistfully. "I spent too many years believing the tumult meant something was wrong, when really, it was the surest sign something was deeply right. The anxiety, the obsession, the physical ache—they're all precious gifts. I've got decades on you, and if I could go back in time, I'd embrace them all."

FORTY

ATHENA

Ruby's bedroom ceiling has subtle imperfections in the paint—a tiny bubble here, a hairline crack there, barely visible in the dim light from the bedside lamp. I trace them with my eyes, creating constellations from the flaws. I tried to read but couldn't concentrate. Then I attempted meditation, streaming a guided session on my phone, but my mind wandered after a minute.

If I were at home, Zeus would be sprawled across the foot of my bed, his weight pinning down the covers. I'm not used to sleeping without him and his purring presence.

Ruby's bed is firmer than mine, the pillows fluffier. Even though I can't sleep, I like being here, surrounded by her things, sleeping where she sleeps. It makes me feel close to her.

The sheets are fresh, of course—Ruby had them changed before our swap—so they don't carry her scent. But her cashmere cardigan does. I found it earlier, hanging in her closet, and couldn't resist pressing it to my face. I felt ridiculous, but I did it anyway.

It's only one a.m., and I'm never in bed this early.

Never. But my mother is down the hall, sleeping in the nearest guestroom, and Demetria is on the other side of the house in another guestroom, presumably texting Julian.

I check my phone, then toss it aside on the bed with a frustrated sigh. No messages.

The club will be busy tonight. Is Ruby there? And if she is, what is she up to?

I grab my phone again, and opening our message thread, I stare at the blinking cursor. What would I even say? *Hey, just wondering what you're up to?* I type, delete. That makes me sound possessive, and God help me, I'm feeling possessive. Finally, I settle on something casual.

Having a good night? Such a simple phrase, yet loaded with everything feared and unsaid.

I press send before I can overthink it, then immediately regret it. What if she's busy? What if she's with someone? The images flood my mind before I can stop them—Ruby in one of the playrooms, but not with me. Morgan has been eyeing her since day one. Alex too. What if they've made their move now that I'm not there? What if Ruby's learning that she doesn't need me for the experiences she craves?

Five minutes pass. No response. An eternity compressed into three hundred seconds of anxiety.

Sorry, were you sleeping? I type. That makes no sense. If she's sleeping, she won't reply, but it's too late. I've already sent it and the message hangs—senseless, desperate, revealing everything about my weak state of mind.

I toss the phone aside again, disgusted with myself. I feel this...this churning in my gut at the thought of someone else touching her. What the fuck is happening to me?

The phone vibrates against the comforter just as I fling an arm over my eyes in frustration. I snatch it up, heart racing.

Hope I didn't wake you. Was in the shower, just saw your message.

Relief floods through me, so intense I almost laugh. In the shower. Not in the playroom with Morgan and Alex. Not in someone else's arms. Just...in the shower. *You didn't wake me. Can't sleep. How was your night?*

Her response comes quicker this time. *Good. Went to the club for a bit. Chatted with Donna most of the evening. How was yours?*

My fingers relax around the phone. Donna. The state supreme court justice. Not Morgan. Not Alex. I exhale slowly, unaware I'd been holding my breath. *It was nice. Just family time with lots of food. Donna's lovely. Do you like her?* I cringe as soon as I send it. Could I be more transparent?

Yeah, I do. She's good company. The three dots appear—Ruby's typing. Those familiar, agonizing ellipses that always seem to hold entire universes of potential meaning. They hover, promising something, then vanish. Gone. Then they return.

Wait. Are you jealous? Then a wink emoji.

I'm caught. Heat blooms in my cheeks, and I'm grateful she can't see me. I consider denying it, but what's the point? She's already seen through me. *Maybe a little. It's not a feeling I'm used to.*

I like it. It's cute.

I roll my eyes. *I am not cute.*

Yes, you are. And for the record, you have nothing to be jealous about. You're the only one who brings out a certain side of me...

My breath hitches, a sharp intake that draws the words into my skin. *What side might that be?*

The three dots dance. Tease. *My naughty side.* No

emoji this time. *Want me to tell you exactly what I was thinking about while I was in the shower?*

My mouth goes dry. The power has shifted. She's no longer just responding—she's orchestrating. Controlling. And it's sexy. My hand slides between my thighs, my fingers running through my slick heat. I'm so turned on I'm throbbing. Only Ruby can do that to me.

Go on, I type. Two words. A surrender.

I was fantasizing about you fucking me.

Tell me more, I type, my breath coming in short gasps.

From behind. Grabbing my hair, your arm around me, your mouth on my neck...

Circling my clit, I throw my head back and moan softly. I'm almost too aroused to type. *I can make that happen. How do you want me to fuck you? With my fingers?* I send it, then wait a few seconds. *With my strap-on?*

It takes a while for her to reply, and I suspect she, too, is trying to multitask.

I want you to fuck me with your strap-on, she types. *Hard.*

My fingers move faster, matching the rhythm of her words. *Are you touching yourself, Ruby?*

Yes.

I imagine her in bed, naked, like me, and I want to be there so badly it hurts. The Domme inside me is tempted to tell her to hold off, to wait until we're together.

How does it feel? I ask.

It feels amazing...but something is missing. You.

I bite my lower lip and swallow another moan, not wanting to wake my mother. I'm so close, trembling, bucking my hips. *Send me a picture.* It's a crazy demand, and I'm surprised when I receive an attachment.

There she is, in bed. Her bottom half is covered by

white sheets, her top half is bare, her breasts full, her nipples erect as she stares into the camera for the sexiest selfie I've ever seen. Her hair tousled and face free of makeup, her eyes heavy lidded, her hand reaching under the covers.

You're beautiful. I pause before I send another message. *I want you.* Intimacy is easier at a distance. A sexy exchange over messages, a striptease viewed from my car... It's almost like it doesn't count, like it's merely a fantasy that can never touch my heart. It's not the same though; I long to touch her.

I'm right here, she replies. *Now it's your turn.*

My turn? I hesitate for a beat before I make a split decision. *How about I come over instead? Stop what you're doing. I'll see you in my office.*

Descending the staircase, my silk robe whispers against my skin with each step. The club's bass pulses through the walls, vibrations matching the rhythm of my racing heart.

Robert, the security guard, gives me a polite nod as I pass. His expression remains professionally neutral, but I'm sure he's confused about the temporary living arrangements. I return his nod and continue toward Athena's office, my legs trembling as I let myself in.

I perch on the edge of her desk, bare legs dangling, and try to slow my breathing. The minutes stretch like hours as I wait, my body still thrumming with need from our text exchange.

Then the door handle finally turns, and Athena is there, wrapped in a white toweling robe, her hair tousled and curling against her shoulders.

She licks her lips and without hesitation, she crosses to me, her hands finding my waist with possessive certainty as she stands between my legs. She kisses me fiercely, her tongue sliding against mine with an urgency that makes me gasp. I lose myself in her taste, in the heat of her body, in the scent of her skin. When she grinds against me, I feel something hard under her robe.

"Fuck... is that..."

"Uh-huh." Athena shoots me a mischievous smile.

I want to take off her robe, but she stops me. "Turn around," she commands, her tone brooking no argument.

I turn, and she slides my robe off my shoulders until it falls to the ground. Her hand snakes around me, caressing my breasts while her mouth is on my neck, kissing me, grazing my skin as she whispers, "I'm wearing the best toy money can buy and I'm going to fuck your brains out."

Her words alone are enough to nearly make me come, and a whimper escapes my throat as she pinches my nipple. The sensation shoots straight between my legs, where I'm wet and throbbing. Her other hand slides down my stomach, tracing patterns that make my muscles jump beneath her touch.

"Bend over the desk," she murmurs, and I comply without hesitation, placing my palms flat on the cool surface.

I hear the soft rustle of her robe opening behind me. The silicone toy brushes against the back of my thigh, and I instinctively spread my legs wider. Her hand strokes my back, tracing my spine down to my ass. Then, suddenly, she slaps me, making me jump.

"Stay still," she murmurs, her voice husky with desire. Her fingertips trail between my legs, finding me slick and ready. I gasp when she slides two fingers inside me, my body clenching around her.

"Please," I breathe, pushing back against her hand. "Fuck me."

Athena chuckles, a low sound that sends shivers across my skin. "So impatient." She withdraws her fingers slowly, making me whimper at the loss. Then I feel the toy pressing against my entrance, the smooth head parting me gently.

She pushes forward in one fluid motion, filling me completely. My fingers scramble for purchase on the desk as she grips my hips, setting a steady rhythm that has me biting my lip to keep from crying out.

"Are you ready?" she asks.

I don't even have time to process the question because the toy starts to vibrate, taking away my ability to think. It feels so good that I don't even know what to do with myself, and I moan loudly, my movements almost erratic as I push back against her.

The base from the club reverberates through the walls, masking my sounds of pleasure while Athena increases her pace. Each thrust sends waves of pleasure through me, building toward something explosive. The vibrations must feel good to her too because she groans with each thrust and fucks me harder, almost like she's losing control herself. Her nails dig into my hip with one hand while the other reaches around to circle my clit.

"This feels so good," she murmurs, her breath coming in short pants that match my own. "Let me hear you."

I abandon any attempt at restraint, letting my cries fill her office. I'm teetering on the edge, but I don't want it to end.

"Athena," I gasp. "I'm so close."

"Come with me," she commands.

When the orgasm hits, it tears through me like lightning, my body clenching as waves of pleasure cascade outward. She doesn't stop, driving into me relentlessly, prolonging each pulse until I'm trembling, barely able to hold myself up.

"God, yes," she breathes. "That's it." Then she lets out a loud cry and I feel her shake against me.

My arms finally give out, and I collapse onto the desk, my cheek pressed against the surface as aftershocks ripple through me. Athena eases out slowly, then pulls out of me and lets out a long breath.

I turn just as she's closing her robe. "No..." I pout dramatically. "I want to see you."

"Next time." Athena bites her lip and grins, looking pleased with herself. Her cheeks are flushed and sweat glistens on her forehead. The sight of her undoes me completely.

"Where on earth did you get that from?" I ask breathlessly, my eyes lowering to whatever is under her robe. "Because you certainly didn't find it in my bedroom."

Athena chuckles and brushes her lips against mine. "I asked my staff to get it from the club. Perks of having a nice collection of the finest sex toys in the world." She runs a hand through my hair, cups my cheek and kisses me again. "I'd better head back before my mom and sister realize I'm gone."

I push myself up slowly from the desk, my limbs still quivering from the intensity of my release. My body feels both weightless and heavy at once, as if I've been unmade and reassembled in the span of minutes. The afterglow pulses through me, warm and golden, leaving me dizzy with satisfaction.

"Well," I manage, smoothing my hair back in an attempt to tame it, "that was certainly worth the trip downstairs." I have no idea what I really look like right now, but I suspect I'm a complete disaster—the kind of dishevelment that screams exactly what I've been doing. The thought makes me smile rather than cringe. There's something liberating about wearing the evidence of pleasure so openly, about being thoroughly undone.

Athena's eyes sparkle with mischief as she adjusts her robe. "I'd say it was mutually beneficial." She turns and blows me a kiss over her shoulder. "Goodnight, beautiful. Sweet dreams."

As the door closes behind her, I'm left leaning against the desk, wondering if my legs will ever regain enough strength to carry me back up the stairs.

FORTY-TWO
ATHENA

I close the front door with exquisite care, every muscle in my body focused on keeping the latch from clicking too loudly. Satisfaction hums through me, a pleasant warmth spreading from my core outward. Ruby's taste still lingers on my lips, and I can't help the smile that tugs at the corners of my mouth. Mission accomplished – and spectacularly so.

The hallway stretches before me, dimly lit and thankfully empty. If I can just make it upstairs quietly, this little midnight adventure will remain our delicious secret. I tighten my robe, hoping the strap-on is securely hidden as the shaft is poking against the fabric. Walking feels strange, the harness shifting against me with each step.

This has to be the most ridiculous predicament I've ever found myself in. If senior staff members could see me now, they'd probably die of shock. Or laughter. Definitely laughter.

I'm about to climb the staircase when I see movement and freeze in horror. There, on the landing, stands my mother.

Her hair is wrapped in pink foam curlers and she's

wearing a floral nightgown. In her outstretched hand is a brass candlestick, clutched like a weapon. The overall effect would be comical if it weren't so terrifying – not because she looks threatening, but because she caught me.

"Mom?" Damn it. I sound guilty.

She lets out a dramatic gasp, pressing her free hand to her chest. "Athena! You nearly gave me a heart attack!" I have to give her credit—she's not lacking in courage. Most women her age would hide in their bedrooms and call the police at the first hint of an intruder. Not Sophia Stavros. No, she arms herself with antique brassware and marches into the darkness ready for battle.

"What are you doing up?" I ask, desperately trying to maintain a casual stance while also ensuring that the bulge beneath my robe remains undetected. I shift my weight, crossing my arms low over my stomach in what I hope passes for a natural pose. I wonder briefly if this is what men feel like when they're trying to hide an inconvenient arousal. If so, I've gained a new appreciation for their struggle.

"What am I doing up?" She says loudly, her voice rising with each word until she's practically shouting. "What are YOU doing sneaking around at this ungodly hour? I heard noises! I thought we were being robbed!"

"Mom, please, lower your voice—"

"Lower my voice?" She waves the candlestick for emphasis. "I wake up to strange sounds, find my daughter creeping around in the middle of the night, and you want me to lower my voice?"

I take a tentative step forward, trying to shift my awkward stance. "I thought I heard something outside, so I went to check. That's all."

She stares at me in disbelief and gestures at my robe.

"Like that? Without a weapon? Are you completely insane, Athena?"

"I wasn't thinking," I mutter. "It was probably just a coyote."

"And you went to confront it in your bathrobe?" Mom plants her free hand on her hip, the candlestick now waving dangerously close to an antique vase. "Where is your common sense?"

"Mom, please be quiet, you'll wake—"

"What's going on?" Demetria's sleep-laden voice drifts down the hallway before she appears next to Mom, wearing an oversized t-shirt. "Why is everyone yelling at two in the morning?" she asks, rubbing her eyes.

Great. Now my entire family is gathered for this mortifying moment. Just my luck that my normally heavy-sleeping sister chooses tonight to wake at the slightest disturbance.

"Your sister has lost her mind," my mother announces, gesturing toward me with the candlestick again. "There's a potential burglar—or a wild animal, apparently—and she just waltzes outside to say hello to it."

Demetria blinks sleepily, then focuses on me. Her eyebrows arch as she takes in my rigid posture, my crossed arms, the flush I can feel warming my cheeks.

"Why doesn't this place have proper security?" My mother continues, oblivious to the silent communication happening between her daughters. "Your neighbor Ruby has a security guard at her gate. Why don't you?"

"The Ridges has security at the entrance," I explain. "It's really very safe here." If only she knew I employ an entire security team next door with protocols that would impress the Pentagon.

"Safe is not relying on some guard half a mile away!"

Mom huffs, the curlers bobbing indignantly. "And safe is not wandering outside in the middle of the night!"

"I'm sorry. I should have been more careful," I say, awkwardly shuffling on the spot.

Demetria's eyes narrow as she observes my strange shuffling. "Why are you standing like that?" she asks. "With your hands all..." She mimics my posture, exaggerating it grotesquely.

My heart stutters. "Like what?"

"I don't know. Like a chimp or something."

"I have to pee," I blurt out, the first excuse that comes to mind. "Desperately. Can we please continue this in the morning?"

Demetria's not buying it for a second. She's known me too long, has an uncanny ability to sense when I'm hiding something. Since our talk by the pool, she's been watching me with a newfound awareness and I can practically see the wheels turning behind her eyes as she takes me in once more. Her lips twitch almost imperceptibly. She knows I snuck out to see Ruby. Let's hope she keeps that to herself.

I silently plead with her not to push further, not to make this moment any more excruciating than it already is.

Demetria finally takes pity on me and her intervention saves me. "Come on, Mom," she says, taking the candlestick from our mother's hand. "Let's go back to bed. I'm sure whatever she heard was nothing."

"Fine," my mother concedes, allowing Demetria to guide her back toward her room. "But tomorrow we're discussing security measures."

As they turn away, I exhale slowly, my shoulders slumping with relief. That was too close. I head upstairs and shuffle toward Ruby's bedroom, mentally cursing the cumbersome equipment still strapped to me. The things I do for pleasure.

Once safely inside, I lean against the closed door, letting my head fall back with a soft thud. Tonight was reckless but it felt good to surrender to impulse for once. To want something, someone, badly enough to take risks.

I slide the harness under the bed and sink into the sheets. My mother armed with antique brassware, my sister's thinly veiled amusement, and me—frozen in place with incriminating evidence literally strapped to my body. Tomorrow I'll face Demetria's knowing glances and Mom's security lecture, but tonight I'm simply too exhausted to care.

FORTY-THREE
RUBY

I arrive early at the Parthenon restaurant, fidgeting with the sleeve of my green dress as the host leads me to a table by the windows with views of the Strip below.

I've spent an embarrassing amount of time choosing my outfit tonight—the dress that brings out my eyes, paired with black stilettos and minimal jewelry. I've spent an equally embarrassing amount of time staring at the picture she sent me last night.

"Ms. Walsh?" A young waiter approaches with a bottle of champagne. "Ms. Stavros asked that this be ready when you arrived. She'll be here shortly." He fills a flute and places it before me.

I sip the champagne while scanning the restaurant I dined at just under a month ago after celebrating the merger. That night feels like it belongs to another lifetime—to another Ruby entirely.

A month ago, I was sleepwalking through life, buried in work to avoid confronting my grief. My house was a museum to Claire's memory, her possessions untouched, her ghost lingering in every room. I was existing, not living —a distinction I couldn't even see then.

Now, I'm wearing makeup I took time to apply and a beautiful dress, with my pulse quickening at the thought of seeing Athena again. I've slept in her bed, cared for her cat, and met her family—crossing boundaries I never imagined breaching. I've felt desire again, surrendered control in ways that both terrify and exhilarate me. I've cleared out Claire's things, made those difficult calls, and begun to imagine a future that isn't defined solely by loss.

All because of one enigmatic woman in white who caught me watching from my window.

The irony isn't lost on me that we're meeting here, where this strange journey began—when Athena found me half-drunk and escorted me home, when she held me while I broke down. Before the confessions, before the club, before everything changed. We've come full circle, but nothing is the same.

I spot them—Athena is guiding her mother and sister through the restaurant. They look refreshed and relaxed, Sophia's hair arranged in an elegant updo, Demetria's wild curls tamed into something artful. Athena's gaze finds mine across the room, and her face breaks into a smile that makes my heart jump.

"Ruby!" Sophia exclaims as they reach the table. She takes my hands in hers, kissing both my cheeks. "You look beautiful, darling."

"Thank you," I reply, surprised by the warmth of her greeting. "You all look wonderful too."

"We've been thoroughly pampered," Sophia says, sliding into the chair across from me. "Athena treated us to the full spa experience here at the Olympus. Massages, facials, the works."

"The treatments here are exceptional," Demetria adds, settling into her seat with a contented sigh. "I'd love to bring that massage therapist back to Greece."

Athena laughs as she takes the seat beside me. "Don't even think about poaching my staff," she warns her sister. "My team spent months finding the right people."

"Always so territorial," Demetria teases.

"I insisted Mom take a night off from cooking," Athena says, smoothly changing the subject. "She's practically been in the kitchen since she arrived."

"I wanted to invite you over for dinner again before we leave," Sophia says to me, "but my daughter insisted we come here instead."

The first course of mezze arrives; platters with an array of small vegetarian dishes: dolmades, tzatziki, hummus, and salads. Sophia immediately begins arranging portions onto my plate.

"How has your time in Vegas been?" I ask.

"Oh, it's been wonderful having both my girls to myself for a whole week. As I said, Demetria is always out with her friends or Julian in Greece." She reaches across to pat her younger daughter's hand affectionately. "It's been nice to have this quality time together."

"Athena arranged the most magical hot air balloon ride over the desert at sunrise yesterday," Demetria adds with genuine enthusiasm. "The light was incredible."

"Yes, it was beautiful," Sophia agrees. She turns to Athena with a warm smile. "Now it's your turn to come to me, honey. Don't you miss Greece? The sunsets in Santorini? The smell of the sea?"

"Of course I do," Athena says softly. "And I miss you too, Mom. I'll come very soon, I promise."

"And you must come visit us as well, Ruby," Sophia adds warmly. "You're always welcome in our home."

I swallow against the sudden tightness in my throat, genuinely touched by her kindness. "That's very generous of you. Thank you."

I wonder if Sophia would be so welcoming if she knew the truth about what's developing between her daughter and me.

As we eat, Demetria continues her gentle interrogation, asking about my childhood, my education, my hobbies. I share stories I haven't told in years and even include one about Claire.

"What about your parents, Ruby?" Sophia asks. "Do you see them often?"

The question catches me off guard. I set down my fork, suddenly aware of the weight of truth I've been avoiding. "Not as much as I should," I admit. "They live in San Francisco."

"That's not so far, right? Is it the distance?"

I shake my head. "After Claire died, I struggled to face anything outside work, including my parents. It was that look in their eyes, the pity, the concern..." I take a sip of wine, steadying myself. "I started making excuses. Work emergencies, scheduling conflicts. Eventually, they stopped asking as often."

I never discuss my parents, certainly not the complicated tangle of guilt and avoidance that characterizes our relationship these days. Yet I'm revealing these private failures to Sophia, a woman I've met only twice.

Sophia reaches across the table and squeezes my hand. "Parents never stop missing their children, no matter how old they get."

"I miss them too," I confess. "And I'm facing things

head-on now. I think I'm ready to let them back into my life fully."

Athena shoots me an encouraging smile. "You could invite them over. I'd love to meet them."

I study Athena across the rim of my wine glass. Her mixed messages confuse me—the woman who insists on strict boundaries while constantly breaking her own rules. She introduced me to her family and now asks to meet mine. Perhaps the most dangerous game isn't the one we play behind closed doors, but this undefined territory we've wandered into—where rules blur, walls crumble, and hearts become collateral damage.

Yet in this beautiful contradiction, I find an unexpected haven—a place where grief loosens its grip and possibility breathes again.

FORTY-FOUR

ATHENA

The headlights of the limousine disappear around the bend as I stand in the driveway, hand raised in a final goodbye. A strange emptiness settles over me as their taillights fade into the darkness. For all the anxiety their visit caused initially, I'm surprised by how much I already miss them. My mother's final embrace still lingers, the scent of her perfume—Chanel No. 5, unchanged since I was a child—clinging to my clothes.

As I walk across to my property, I see lights around the pool area are turned on. It's only eight—Ruby is usually at the office much later.

Kicking off my shoes, I pad through the quiet house. The sliding terrace doors are open, and I stop at the threshold, smiling at the scene before me.

Ruby sits on one of the loungers, laptop balanced precariously on her knees. Her hair is pulled back in a ponytail, and she's wearing jersey shorts and an oversize sweatshirt. I've never seen her this casual, this relaxed.

Zeus prowls around her, occasionally batting at the corner of her laptop with obvious intent.

"For the last time, Zeus, leave it alone," Ruby says, her voice a blend of exasperation and affection. "I don't need your assistance."

Zeus makes a chirping sound, pawing at the keyboard more insistently.

"What do you want?" Ruby sighs, pushing her laptop aside to address the cat directly. "You've had dinner. I've given you everything, including my own food." She gestures to an empty plate where I can see the remnants of what appears to be grilled chicken. "What else could you possibly want? Do you want to write an email to Mommy? Because you don't need to worry, she'll be back soon."

"I know this might sound crazy," I interject, stepping onto the patio, "but I think he just wants you to pet him."

Ruby startles, her head snapping up. "Athena! Will you stop sneaking up on us like that?" Despite her complaint, her face brightens.

"Sorry," I say, though I'm not sorry at all. I love catching her in these unguarded moments. "How long have you been home?"

"A couple of hours. I left early to work here instead, but Zeus has been driving me insane—knocking over my coffee, swiping at my keyboard..." She shrugs, closing her laptop. "It's fine. I was about to call it a day anyway."

I settle onto the lounger next to hers, reaching for Zeus, who immediately leaps onto my lap. "You're becoming quite attached to him, aren't you?"

"Don't be ridiculous," Ruby scoffs, though her expression is fond as she watches Zeus kneading my thigh. "He's a terrorist."

"Try petting him," I suggest, running my fingers through his fur. "He likes to be scratched right behind the ears."

Ruby looks cautious but reaches out a hand anyway. To my surprise, he abandons my lap to settle on Ruby's lounger, presenting the top of his head for attention.

With visible hesitation, Ruby strokes the spot I indicated. Zeus closes his eyes, tilting his head into her touch. A deep, rumbling purr emanates from his chest—the sound he usually reserves exclusively for me.

"What the fuck?" Ruby's eyes widen in disbelief, her hand freezing mid-stroke.

I'm equally stunned. "That's...unusual. Asha's been feeding him since I got him and he's never done that with her." I watch in amazement as Zeus butts his head against Ruby's hand, demanding more attention. "You've been chosen."

"Chosen?" Ruby laughs, but she resumes petting him, a look of wonder crossing her face when Zeus stretches out beside her, his purr intensifying. "I thought he hated me."

"Zeus doesn't hate anyone," I say, meeting her eyes. "He's just very selective."

"Like his owner," Ruby observes with a smile.

I laugh. "Touché."

She keeps her gaze locked on me, and something flutters in my stomach. Fuck. I have actual butterflies, like a teenager with a crush, because this woman is smiling at me while petting my cat.

The sexual tension between us is back, soaring like never before.

"So," Ruby says finally, looking flustered. "They're gone. Was it hard, saying goodbye?"

"Harder than I expected," I admit. "Demetria and I talked. Really talked, and it's brought us a lot closer."

"That's good, right?"

"Yeah. She figured out we switched houses and confronted me about it."

"Really?" Ruby frowns. "I thought we'd gotten away with it. What did you tell her?"

"The truth. Or most of the truth, anyway. She also asked me if I'm gay." I shrug. "I didn't have to answer. She already knew."

Ruby's hand stills on Zeus's fur. "And how do you feel about that?"

"Relieved," I say. "Terrified. Liberated. All of it at once. I told her everything I never could. About teenage crushes, about Elena..."

"Athena..." Ruby takes my hand. "Did you tell your mother?"

I shake my head. "No. And Demetria promised not to tell her either."

Ruby nods. "I'm so glad you were able to talk to your sister. It's a big deal." Her fingers trace the back of my hand, and I watch the movement, mesmerized by this simple intimacy. It terrifies me how much I want little gestures like this.

Zeus stands, stretching one final time before leaping off the lounger and stalking into the house.

"And there he goes," I say, breaking the tension. "Back to claiming the entire bed."

I run a hand through my hair and sigh, feeling the weight of the past week lifting. "God, I could use a drink. Or several. Coming out to Demetria was...intense. Good, but intense."

The poolside lights reflect in Ruby's eyes as she watches me, a mixture of concern and something deeper crossing her face. "I should probably head home," she says softly. "You have a lot to process. You must need some space."

"Actually," I reply, holding her gaze, "The other night... I haven't been able to stop thinking about it." What I really want to say is, *"You.* I haven't been able to stop thinking about *you,* Ruby." We've been dancing around each other all week, both aware that something fundamental has shifted between us.

"Yeah...the shower..." Ruby's face turns pink as she's reminded of her own fantasy. She shakes her head and blows out her cheeks. I see the slight tightening of her jaw, the way her fingers clench around the lounger's armrest. "If I stay," she finally says, "this might get very, very complicated."

"I know," I agree. "My life was so blissfully simple before I met you." The words escape before I can censor them. "You're messy, Ruby."

Ruby hesitates. "Are you saying you *want* complications?"

"Yes. I think I'm ready for that," I say. "I have feelings for you."

I didn't mean to say it. It just tumbled out, and I feel stripped bare. For someone who's built an entire life around control, those five words are nothing short of revolutionary. The sensation is foreign, almost forgotten—this willingness to place power in someone else's hands and surrender emotionally.

I wait, watching Ruby's face, searching for a reaction. I've revealed too much, and now I can only brace for the consequences.

Ruby's expression shifts almost imperceptibly—a momentary widening of her eyes, a subtle tensing of her shoulders. For a fleeting moment, she leans forward slightly, as if drawn to me. Her lips part, and I think she might kiss me. Then something shifts in her expression—a flicker of uncertainty, a shadow of hesitation—and she pulls back.

"Athena, I..." She stops, swallows. "I need some time to process this." Her fingers tap nervously against her laptop. "I think we both need to figure out what we want." She tucks a strand of hair behind her ear, not quite meeting my eyes. "Let's meet at the club. Maybe we can get some of this tension out of our system."

The cable cars clatter in the distance as we make our way up one of San Francisco's iconic hills, my mother walking beside me at a pace slower than I remember—or maybe I'm the one who's slowed down. We navigate Russian Hill together, our shoulders occasionally brushing—a physical reminder of the space I've kept between us these past years.

"I'm sorry I haven't been home sooner," I say, adjusting my sunglasses against the glare. "And for not inviting you and Dad to Vegas."

Mom reaches up to smooth back her hair—auburn like mine but with elegant streaks of silver threading through it —as the breeze from the bay catches it.

"Sweetheart, you don't need to apologize." Her voice catches. "We just missed you."

"I know, but—"

"No," she says, stopping on the sidewalk to face me. "When you lose someone you love, there's no manual for grief. We understood that you needed space."

I swallow against the tightness in my throat. "It wasn't fair to shut you out."

She gives me a sad smile. "It was hard to know you were suffering and didn't want our help. Every time I called and you rushed off the phone, every invitation you declined...I felt like I was losing you too when all I wanted was to take you in my arms and hold you. But I don't blame you, Ruby. You handled it the only way you were able to handle it."

The weight of my selfishness settles on my shoulders. I've been so consumed by my own pain that I never fully considered theirs.

"But I shouldn't have shut you out," I whisper.

She squeezes my hand. "You're here now. That's what matters." She pauses, studying my face. "Though I'm still surprised by this spontaneous visit. When you called from the airport yesterday, your father and I could hardly believe it."

I smile ruefully, thinking of my abrupt departure from Vegas—tossing clothes into a bag, canceling meetings, barely stopping to think. Athena's words by the pool had left me reeling.

"I missed you and Dad," I say, and it's not even a lie. "I just...needed to be home."

We continue down to North Beach, and the neighborhood pulses with summer energy—tourists in shorts with city maps, sidewalk cafés filled with people seeking shade, ice cream parlors with lines snaking down the block.

My heart stutters when we turn onto Columbus Avenue and I spot Café Trieste. The small coffee house with its faded awning and cramped interior hasn't changed at all. Claire and I used to come here almost every Saturday when we first started dating—law students gorging on caffeine and stolen moments between study sessions.

I stop, staring at the entrance.

"Ruby?" Mom follows my gaze, understanding dawning on her face. "Is this..."

"Where Claire and I used to come," I finish. "Do you mind if we go in?"

The bell above the door jingles as we enter, and the blast of air conditioning is a welcome relief from the summer heat. Inside, it's just as I remember—worn wooden tables crowded too close together, vintage photos of San Francisco on the walls, the ancient espresso machine hissing behind the counter.

We order and find a small table near the window. Mom removes her sunglasses, laying them neatly beside her purse.

"Your father was disappointed he couldn't join us today," she says with a small sigh. "That board meeting couldn't be moved."

"I should have given you more notice."

She waves this away. "An unexpected visit from our daughter? We'll take it any way we can get it." She studies my face. "What really prompted this sudden trip home?"

I stare into my iced coffee, watching condensation gather on the glass. "Things have changed," I say simply. "For the better. But I couldn't think straight anymore, and I needed perspective."

"Something with work?"

"No. Something personal."

A cautious smile spreads across her face. "I can see it. There's color in your cheeks. Your eyes are brighter." She reaches across the table to place her hand over mine. "You look more like my Ruby again."

The wooden chair creaks as I lean back, gathering my thoughts. "I've met someone," I say. "My neighbor. She's been...very helpful."

Mom's expression remains carefully neutral, though I catch the momentary widening of her eyes.

"It's complicated," I continue. "Her name is Athena. She owns the Olympus casino."

"That's quite a neighbor." Mom takes a sip of her iced tea, watching me over the rim. "And she's been helpful how?"

"She lost someone too, years ago, and she understands grief." I pause. "She pushed me to move on and stop drowning myself in work."

"She sounds wonderful."

"She is."

Mom tilts her head, studying me with the perceptiveness that used to drive me crazy as a teenager. "And is she the reason you suddenly needed to come home? Did something happen?"

I look down at my hands, at the condensation from my glass making a small puddle on the table. "She told me she has feelings for me, and I panicked. I couldn't work, couldn't think. So I got on a plane."

"You ran," Mom says gently.

"I guess I did."

"Do you have feelings for her too?"

The directness of the question startles me, but it's why I came home—to hear the questions I've been avoiding asking myself.

"Yes," I admit. "And it terrifies me. I feel like I'm being unfaithful to Claire."

Mom frowns. "But you're not. You're moving on, and that's good, Ruby. That's really good."

"I know. It just feels that way."

The café has filled with the summer afternoon crowd—tourists seeking respite from the heat, students with laptops, locals reading newspapers. A barista calls out orders over the din of conversation and the hiss of steam.

"The last time we were here," I say, "Claire was working on her pro bono case for the environmental coalition. She had papers spread all over the table, completely oblivious to everything around her."

Mom smiles. "She was passionate about her work."

"She was." I feel a familiar ache, but it's gentler now. "We stayed until closing. The owner had to kick us out."

"I wish we'd spent more time with her," Mom says. "I always thought there would be more holidays, more visits."

"She loved you both," I assure her. "She used to say Dad's Christmas morning waffles were worth the entire flight from Vegas."

We both laugh at the thought of Dad standing proudly at the waffle maker in his ridiculous Santa apron, insisting that everyone needed at least three waffles to properly celebrate the holiday. I miss those days.

"We hoped you might move back after..." Mom hesitates. "After you lost her. Not just because we wanted to support you, though we did. But because this was home for you both."

"I thought about it," I admit. "But home stopped being a place after Claire died. It became more about where I could function, where I could keep moving forward without collapsing. And that was work. In Vegas."

"And now?"

I consider this. "Now I'm starting to feel like I might be able to build something new. Not replace what I had with Claire but create a different kind of life."

Mom's eyes fill with tears. "That's all we've wanted for you, sweetheart. To see you living again." She squeezes my hand. "And if this woman has helped with that, then I'm grateful to her."

"She's made me feel things I didn't think I was capable of anymore," I admit, replaying Athena's words by the pool. *I have feelings for you.* The vulnerability in her eyes as she said it shook me to my core, and I fled, claiming I needed time—which was true—but also because I was terrified of saying it back. Of speaking the truth.

"Claire would want you to be happy," Mom says. "You know that, don't you?"

"I do." I take a deep breath. Outside, the summer sun still blazes, heat radiating off the bustling street. "I've missed this city. The energy, the hills—even the summer fog this morning."

Mom smiles. "Your father and I walked past your old apartment one day when we were feeling nostalgic."

"On Green Street? The one with the terrible plumbing and the cranky downstairs neighbor?"

"That's the one. We stood outside like sentimental fools and remembered you and Claire inviting us there for dinner, so proud of your first place together even though it was tiny." Mom glances at her phone when it lights up. "We should probably head back. Your father is messaging me—he'll be home soon and anxious to see you." She stands, gathering her purse. "And while we walk, I want you to tell me all about your neighbor."

FORTY-SIX

ATHENA

Zara Nova sits across from me in a private corner, commanding attention without even trying. Everyone in the Pantheon is focused on her, waitstaff lingering a beat too long when they approach our table, the manager repeatedly finding excuses to walk past. Even I feel the pull of her gravity—that rare magnetism that can't be manufactured or bought.

Three Grammys, two world tours, and a cultural impact that transcends music have made her one of the most recognizable faces on the planet. And now she's here, in my casino, discussing her upcoming residency.

"Thanks for agreeing to meet one-on-one," she says, taking a sip of her champagne. "My manager wanted to tag along, but these conversations get so bogged down in details when the suits are involved. I told him to sit this one out— he can come next time when we're finalizing everything."

"I prefer it this way too," I reply, appreciating her directness. "It's easier to discuss your vision without being interrupted every other sentence." I refill her champagne flute. "We've gone through your checklist, and I don't see a problem with any of the points. The Palestra can be transformed however you wish, and we have state-of-the-art sound and lighting systems. Do you have any concerns from your side?"

Zara nods. "I do, but my concerns are on a personal level," she says, picking at the salad she's barely touched. "I need to know what I'm actually getting myself into. Twelve months in Vegas is..." She trails off, twirling a lock of curly dark hair around her finger. I'm getting a certain energy from her. Her stare when she meets my eyes is intense, and if I didn't know better, I'd think she was flirting with me. She wasn't like this when we met for the initial negotiations with her manager present.

"A long commitment," I finish for her. "Especially if you're not used to desert living."

"Exactly. I've done the weekend performances, the awards shows, but living here? I'm not sure I can handle the constant noise, the tourists, the artificial everything. And I like being outdoors, so I'm afraid I'll get cabin fever."

"Well, if you decide to live at the Olympus during your residency, you will have your own private entrance," I explain. "We have an excellent penthouse suite with a spacious terrace and a small private pool."

"That sounds good," she admits. "But what about when I need to escape? I'm used to having options."

"The desert is beautiful if you need to get away," I say. "Most people who visit never see beyond the casinos, but there's something almost spiritual about the landscape once you leave the city behind." I smile and add, "I'm happy to show you around. I love driving."

"Oh? You want to be my tour guide?" Something shifts in her expression—a subtle change in the tilt of her head, the curve of her smile. She leans forward slightly, her voice dropping to a more intimate register. "I'll take you up on that."

Wait. Is she...?

I freeze, replaying my words in my head, searching for anything that might have been misinterpreted. The invitation was purely professional, a courtesy I've extended to other performers.

But the look she's giving me now is unmistakable, and I'm thrown completely off balance. I had no idea Zara was queer.

"And do you live here too? I bet you have a bad-ass suite," she says and leans in even closer. "I'd love to see it some time, if we're going to be neighbors."

"I..." I hesitate, unsure how to navigate this sudden shift. Most people assume I still live at the Olympus, and for privacy reasons, I like to keep it that way.

Zara studies me for a moment, then her eyes widen in realization. "Oh God, I completely misread that, didn't I?" She laughs, though a flush creeps up her neck. "I'm so sorry. I thought you were—" She stops herself and brings a hand to her forehead.

"No need to apologize," I say quickly. "It's just that there's...someone special in my life. I'm not sure where it's heading. In fact, it may be going nowhere, but..."

"Say no more." She holds up a hand, composure returning. "Professional boundaries restored. And can we please keep this awkward exchange between us? I think the champagne has gone to my head, and no one knows I'm...well, you know what I mean."

"Of course. Don't worry about it." I'm grateful for her graceful recovery. "But if you'd like to explore things other than the desert while you're here, I can help you with that. Discretion is my middle name, and I have a lot of successful and attractive single female friends who are equally discreet."

Zara's eyebrows shoot up, and for a moment she looks genuinely surprised. Then she leans back in her chair, regarding me with newfound interest.

"Wow," she says. "The mysterious Athena Stavros runs an underground queer dating service too?" There's no malice in her tone, just amused curiosity.

"Not exactly, but I have connections," I say with a chuckle. I pull a business card from my jacket pocket and write a number on the back before sliding it across the table. "Anyway, the offer stands. That's my personal number. Please don't share it—I'm very private."

Zara takes the card, examining it before tucking it into her purse with a laugh. "That's usually my line." She pretends to look around for hidden cameras. "Am I being punked? I'm supposed to be the one giving out my closely guarded personal number with warnings about privacy."

I laugh along, and with the tension broken, I steer the conversation back to safer territory. "About the residency— we'd also arrange private transportation for you, of course. And the contract includes use of the Olympus jet for personal national travel during your off weeks."

We discuss scheduling details, performance frequency, and rehearsal space requirements, but I'm finding it increasingly difficult to concentrate. My thoughts keep drifting to Ruby. Her car has been missing from the driveway since yesterday, and I've sent her three texts today, receiving nothing in return. I don't even know if she's in Vegas, if I've ruined everything by admitting how I feel.

"What about the rehearsal schedule?" Zara asks, pulling me back to the present. "I'll need at least three weeks of setup time before opening night."

"Not a problem," I assure her. "We can close the Palestra during the day for a full month before your premiere if needed. The space will be completely yours from nine to five." I force myself to focus. This deal is important—potentially transformative for the Olympus. I need to be present.

My phone vibrates against the table, and I fight the urge to check it immediately. Another minute passes as Zara outlines her lighting preferences, and the phone vibrates again.

"I'm sorry," I say, unable to resist any longer. "Would you mind if I quickly check this? It might be important."

She waves a hand in permission, and I pick up the phone, my heart racing when I see Ruby's name on the screen.

Sorry for the late reply. I'm in San Francisco with my parents. A second message follows: *I'm thinking of you.*

Relief floods through me. She's safe. She's with her parents.

"I take it that's good news?" Zara asks. "You're smiling."

"Yes," I say, typing a quick response just to let her know she's on my mind too, not pushing for more. "Apologies for the interruption. I'm all yours."

When I look up, Zara is studying me. "Is that her? The special someone?"

I hesitate, then nod. There's no point in denying it. "Yes."

"She's a lucky woman." Zara traces the rim of her flute, her gaze drifting momentarily to the panoramic view of the Strip beyond our window. "I've always wondered what it would be like."

"What do you mean?" I ask, though I suspect I know where this is headed.

"To explore that side of myself." She smiles ruefully. "My whole life is decided for me down to who I'm allowed to be seen with."

"Have you had these feelings for a while?"

"Always." Zara hesitates. "I fooled around with girls in college sometimes, but that was a long time ago. And then fame came knocking on my door. I'm grateful for that, but it also meant my days of experimenting were over, and I fantasize about dating women all the time." She studies me for a moment before adding, "I wish I could be you for a day."

"Me?" The comment almost makes me laugh. Zara Nova has millions of adoring fans and chart-topping hits. "I'm not sure I understand where you're coming from."

"There's this sexual confidence radiating from you," she says. "I picked up the vibe immediately—that you're queer and completely comfortable with it. You just own who you are."

I frown and shake my head. "Between you and me? I'm not as out and proud as you might think." The confession slips out before I can consider it. "I don't hide exactly, but I don't date in public either. The business pages feature me occasionally, and word travels. I've spent my life making sure my family in Greece doesn't find out, so I'm careful."

I wonder why I'm sharing this with her. This meeting is supposed to be about her residency, not trading personal secrets.

"You're not out to your family?"

"My sister knows now. Found out recently, actually. She's supportive. But my mother is traditional Greek Orthodox, so it's complicated." I take a sip of champagne. "Sometimes I wonder what it would be like too. To walk through my casino with a woman on my arm."

"Huh." Zara tilts her head as she looks me over. "Who would have thought?"

"We all have our blind spots," I say. "Areas where courage fails us, despite how strong we appear elsewhere." I lean back in my chair and smile. "I think this residency could be good for you in more ways than one, and my offer stands on introducing you to some likeminded women. No pressure, no expectations, and certainly no headlines. Just...possibilities."

Her eyes meet mine, and I catch a glimpse of the woman behind the platinum records and magazine covers. "Possibilities," she repeats. "I like the sound of that."

FORTY-SEVEN
RUBY

"Are you sure you can't stay just one more day?" Mom asks, collecting the dessert plates from the table. She's wearing her favorite navy cardigan—the one with the little embroidered flowers along the hem that she's had forever. Even at sixty-two, she's still beautiful, with laugh lines that deepen when she smiles and green eyes exactly like mine.

"Mom, I've already extended my stay four times," I say with a laugh, helping her clear the table. "If I don't get back to the office tomorrow, things will start falling apart."

I've brought my laptop and technically been working remotely, but I've been half as productive as normal. Instead of my usual fourteen-hour days, I've managed maybe five or six hours before getting distracted by long walks with Mom, conversations with Dad about his patients, or simply sitting in the garden, allowing myself to enjoy the moment.

Dad gets up to rinse the dishes at the sink. At sixty-five, he's still handsome with his salt-and-pepper beard and kind eyes behind wire-rimmed glasses. The kitchen smells of his famous apple crumble—one of my favorites since I was a kid.

"Well, it's been really nice having you home again," he says, shooting me that warm smile that always made everything better when I was growing up. "We've miss you."

I feel tears welling up again. They come so easily these days, and I don't fight them. I cross the kitchen and wrap my arms around him, not caring that his hands are wet from the dishes. "I've missed you both so much."

I step back and smile through my tears. "Honestly, I'd love to stay longer, but work is piling up, and I've already pushed back three client meetings."

The truth is, something else is pulling me back too. Someone. The thought of Athena sends a flutter through my stomach that reminds me of being sixteen again, writing a crush's name in my notebook margins.

"Well, next time, don't leave it so long," Dad says.

"I won't. And you two absolutely have to come to Vegas. My home is open again."

"Careful what you say now, you won't get rid of us." Mom smiles. "Maybe in September for your birthday?"

"I'd like that." I feel another wave of emotion. All these years wasted, keeping them at arm's length, when their love was exactly what I needed.

The kitchen hasn't changed much in twenty years—the same warm yellow walls, the collection of mismatched mugs hanging from hooks. They keep talking about renovating but never do it, both too busy to prioritize it. This house has always been a constant, even when I wasn't.

I hadn't planned to stay more than a day or two. Just long enough to process Athena's confession, to find clarity in the comfort of my parents' presence. To let them know I loved them even though I'd been absent.

But something about being home—really home—cracked something open inside me, and it's been healing to be here. It's been a week. A week of allowing myself to be cared for, to be loved, to revisit who I was before grief reshuffled my identity like a deck of cards.

I watch as Dad hands Mom a plate to put in the dishwasher, their movements in sync after almost forty years together. He bumps his hip against hers, and she smiles without looking up.

"You two are still so sweet together," I observe. "I love that."

Mom glances at Dad with a warm smile. "We've had plenty of practice."

"I always thought I'd have what you two have. The forever kind." The words come out before I can stop them, and I immediately regret it. It sounded way too melodramatic, and I don't want them to feel guilty for looking happy in front of me.

Mom flinches as she turns to me. "Honey, you still can. Just because it wasn't forever with Claire doesn't mean you can't find it with someone else." I know she's referring to Athena. I've mentioned her a few times during my stay, though I haven't revealed too much.

"Yeah. Maybe you're right," I say. I glance at the clock on the wall for an excuse to escape, then see it's almost midnight. We've been sitting at the table after dinner, talking for hours, lost in conversation.

"Anyway, I should probably head to bed. Need to get up early to drive back if I want to beat the traffic." I kiss my parents goodnight and climb the stairs to my old bedroom, now transformed into Mom's art studio.

The walls are covered with her watercolors—landscapes mostly, scenes from their travels and the view from the back yard. My twin bed still sits in the corner, made up with fresh linens, a small concession to the room's new purpose. An easel stands by the window, a half-finished painting of the bay at sunset.

I've slept in this bed every night I've been here, though they offered the guest room.

Each day, I've called Miranda to extend my absence. "Take all the time you need," she said. "The team has everything covered." And each evening, I've found myself unable to leave, caught in the warm embrace of my childhood home.

I sit on the edge of the bed and check my phone. A message from Athena waits for me, sent an hour ago.

I signed with Zara Nova today. She's starting her residency at the Olympus in November. Wish you were here to celebrate.

I read the message twice, an unexpected twinge of jealousy tightening my chest. Zara Nova, the world-famous, beautiful, and talented Zara Nova. She has that irresistible magnetism that draws everyone to her. The thought of her spending time with Athena all week while I've been away makes my stomach knot uncomfortably. Zara Nova may be straight, but I imagine many women making an exception for Athena.

Did Athena find her attractive? Of course she did—who wouldn't? I try to picture their meetings. Were they alone? Did they share drinks after discussing business?

I shake my head, taken aback by my own thoughts. I've never been the jealous type, but something about Athena makes me feel possessive in a way I've never experienced before.

I trace the words with my fingertip, trying to banish the image of Athena and Zara laughing together over champagne. We've been messaging every day since I left—nothing heavy, nothing that forces me to confront my own feelings. Just light, flirtatious texts that make my heart race and my body yearn.

That's amazing, I type back. *Congratulations.*

Three dots appear immediately, telling me she's online, waiting for my response.

Thanks. How's everything there?

It's been nice. We went through old photo albums earlier. Mom made pot roast. Dad opened a bottle of wine he's been saving for a special occasion. Apparently, me being home counts as special.

It is special, she replies. *I'm glad you're reconnecting with them.*

I smile. *Yeah. But it's time to head home. I'll be back tomorrow.*

Great. Will you come to the club?

My stomach does a flip. *Depends. Will you be there?*

I'll be waiting. The three dots appear, disappear, then appear again. *Wanna play?*

I bite my lip and grin, considering my response. The thought of seeing her, of being in that room with her again, sends a rush of heat through my body. I love the dominant Athena, and God, I long for her.

With you, always, I finally reply. *I'll see you tomorrow.*

I set my phone aside and lie back, imagining her voice in my ear, the exquisite surrender, the way she inhales against my hair. Every night I've been here, I've fallen asleep with these fantasies, these cravings for her control as well as her tenderness.

Has she been in that room with someone else while I've been away? The idea makes my stomach tighten again. I know I'm special to her, but the club exists with or without me, and Athena is still Athena, the object of desire for every woman there.

Staring at the ceiling, I wonder at this unfamiliar jealousy. Perhaps it's part of starting over, these new, messy emotions, and honestly, after years of feeling nothing but grief, even jealousy is welcome. My heart is waking up, demanding more than just survival.

FORTY-EIGHT
ATHENA

The club is already buzzing with activity. Through the security feed on my phone, I watch as the third limousine of the evening arrives, its tinted windows revealing nothing of the passenger inside. Robert, head of security, opens the door to help her out. It's Senator Mitchell's wife. If only he knew what she's up to during her so-called spa trips to Vegas.

I slip my phone into my pocket and scan the lounge, trying to appear composed despite the nervous energy coursing through my veins. Ruby is coming back.

My hands are uncharacteristically clammy, and I discreetly wipe them against my white silk pants. This isn't me. I don't get nervous, especially not in my own domain where I control every variable. Yet here I am, checking my watch for the third time in five minutes, wondering when she'll arrive.

I doubt I'm fooling anyone. Members have noticed how I single Ruby out, how my eyes follow her across the room, how I'm different with her than with anyone else. It's embarrassing, honestly, how transparent I've become.

I make my rounds through the lounge, touching base with members while my senses remain attuned to the entrance, waiting for Ruby to walk through. When I spot Victoria Mitchell entering the main lounge, I approach her with a welcome smile. She's dressed impeccably as always, her bleached bob freshly cut.

"Victoria, what a pleasure. It's been a while," I say, kissing her cheek.

She sighs dramatically. "Darling," she says in her southern drawl, "you have no idea how hard it's been to get away lately. Charly's been dragging me to every fundraiser between DC and California. I'm exhausted."

"Sounds like you need a proper break," I reply. "Can I get you a gin and tonic?"

Victoria smiles and points to a waitress who's already making her way toward us, carrying a crystal tumbler. "Your staff is as impeccable as ever."

The waitress arrives. "Double shot with two slices of cucumber and a pinch of black pepper, Mrs. Mitchell."

"Just the way I like it." Victoria accepts the drink with a grateful nod. She takes a sip and hums with pleasure. "Best service ever. How do they always remember?" Victoria spots Donna across the room and brightens. "Ah, there's Donna. She promised we'd share a doobie over drinks and gossip. I can't wait to catch up." She turns to me, eyebrows raised in invitation. "Care to join us?"

I'm about to accept—Victoria's stories about Washington's inner circle are always entertaining—when movement at the entrance catches my eye. Ruby.

"I'm sorry, Victoria. Next time?"

Ruby stands just inside the entrance, a vision in a knee-length red wrap dress. She looks stunning and everything I rehearsed evaporates.

Ruby's eyes find mine across the room, and she smiles as she approaches. I'm struck by how much I've missed her, and I want to pull her into my arms, to kiss her properly, to show everyone here that she's mine. But I hesitate, unsure of what she wants, so I settle for a kiss on her cheek, letting my lips linger against her skin longer than necessary.

"You're killing me," I whisper in her ear, hoping I sound more composed than I feel. "Can I get you a drink?"

Ruby pulls back slightly, biting her lip as her eyes search mine. "I'll need something strong," she murmurs, a slight huskiness in her voice.

I place my hand at the small of her back, guiding her toward the bar. The contact is innocent enough—anyone watching would see only a hostess escorting a guest—but I feel her muscles tensing under my touch. I signal the bartender with a subtle nod. He knows exactly what to pour. We stand close, facing each other.

Ruby takes a slow sip of her Scotch, her eyes never leaving mine over the rim of the glass. A small stain of amber liquid lingers on her lower lip, and I have to force myself not to lean forward and taste it.

"So...Scotch for truth," I say.

Ruby's lips curve into a smile. "Ask me anything." She reaches out to straighten my collar, her fingers brushing against my neck.

"Did I freak you out? Is that why you left?"

There's a subtle catch in her breath, a momentary tensing of her shoulders. Her fingers pause on my collar as if she's been caught off guard, didn't expect me to be so direct. For a beat, I wonder if I've made a mistake bringing it up.

But I'm tired of dwelling, of wondering, of obsessing over those five words that sent her running across state lines. If she runs again, so be it.

"I'm sorry if I did," I continue. "I just need to know that you're still comfortable with me before we go into that room. Trust is everything, right? We need to be honest with each other."

Ruby nods, her expression softening. "Yes, it freaked me out a little," she says quietly. "But I'm here. You haven't scared me away." Her gaze drops to my lips again. "I have feelings too. I'm just figuring out how to navigate them."

My heart beats faster as her words sink in. The admission I didn't dare hope for, delivered so simply.

"Thank you." My hand moves of its own accord, sliding from the small of her back to curve around her hip. "For your honesty. I know it's not simple." I tighten my grip on her, needing to anchor myself in this moment.

Ruby lets out a soft sigh. "As I said, I'm still figuring things out, but I know one thing."

"What's that?"

She inches closer, aligning her body with mine. "I want you to myself."

My hand moves lower, fingers tracing the curve of her behind through the fabric of her dress. I feel her slight jolt, followed by the way she subtly leans into the touch.

"If it wasn't clear already, let me make it crystal clear right now," I say. "I'm yours and only yours. You won't find me in that room with anyone but you, and you won't find me flirting with other women."

Ruby's eyes widen slightly, her lips parting in surprise at my directness.

"But," I continue, unable to resist teasing her a little, "as I'm a big scary casino boss, I want something in return. That's how this works, right? Quid pro quo."

"Quid pro quo," she repeats, her hand sliding inside my blazer and around my waist. She lifts the fabric of my top from the waistband of my pants and finds my skin, her fingers trailing up and down my back. "What do you want?"

I lean in and brush my lips against her ear. "I want you to spend the night with me." When I pull back to look at her, a flush spreads across her cheeks.

"That's quite a lot to ask for," she says with an amused smile.

"Maybe." I shrug, returning her smile with one of my own. "But I'm a hedonist. I want it all."

FORTY-NINE
RUBY

"I'm not going to blindfold you today." Athena looks me up and down. "I want you to see yourself in the reflection of all those mirrors. I went easy on you last time, but today, I want you to watch." She trails a finger down between my breasts. "Don't worry, though. You'll enjoy it."

I swallow hard. *Did* she go easy on me last time? It didn't feel like that. Part of me is glad I'm not blindfolded, but seeing myself is very confrontational. I'm cuffed to the ceiling, stripped to my black lingerie, and I'm so aroused I can barely stand still.

"Tell me what the safe word is," she says.

"Pause."

"Good Girl." She brings her lips close to mine but doesn't kiss me. And then, in a whisper, she adds, "You're mine, Ruby."

I smile, meeting her eyes. For a split second, all theatre falls away and it's just us, connecting.

Athena steps back, her eyes never leaving mine as she circles me slowly. The mirrors reflect her movements, creating an endless loop of her predatory grace. I see myself in every angle—vulnerable, exposed, waiting.

"I want you to see what I see. I want you to see the way your skin flushes when you're aroused, how your body responds to me before I even lay a hand on you."

She searches for something in the chest of drawers and returns with a flogger. My breath catches.

"That's what I mean. I heard that," she says. The flogger traces my collarbone, then trails down between my breasts, following the path her finger took moments before. It tickles and the leather feels soft and supple.

She steps closer, her breath against my ear. Her free hand slides around my chest, her fingers slipping into my bra and pinching my nipple just hard enough to make me flinch. The flogger taps methodically against my thigh— once, twice, three times—a silent countdown.

"Why are you here, Ruby? Do you like to be spanked?"

I nod, transfixed by our reflection—her confidence against my uncertainty, her control against my surrender.

"I can't hear you." The flogger stops its tapping, hovering dangerously still.

"Yes," I say, finding strength somewhere beneath my fear. I turn my head to meet her eyes. "And I'm here because I'm yours."

Athena's breath hitches. It's barely audible, but I hear it. For a beat, she stares at me as if she's taken aback, but she composes herself quickly. "Good girl." She moves the crop higher, tracing patterns along my inner thigh. My legs tremble, but her arm around my waist holds me steady.

"Watch," she instructs, and I obey, meeting my own gaze in the mirror. It's not just myself I see. There's our audience, six women fixated on us. "See how your pupils dilate?" Athena continues. "How they darken with want?"

When I focus on my eyes, I realize the comment was a distraction because the flogger hits my behind hard, and I cry out.

My skin tingles and arousal shoots between my thighs. Fuck, it feels good.

"More?" she asks.

I nod, and immediately, she strikes me again. "I can't hear you."

"Yes," I plead through ragged breaths. "Yes, please."

Another strike, harder. Hard enough to leave a mark for days. I suck in a breath, but Athena ignores my reaction.

"Morgan, bring me a Scotch, will you? On the rocks," she says, and Morgan scurries off.

"I thought you preferred it neat." I don't know why the comment escapes me; it's a ridiculous thing to say in the middle of all this, and it's met with another smack. The sting accumulates; she's made sure to hit the same spot each time and now it's burning.

"Don't speak unless I ask you to," she hisses. She sounds serious, but I can see she's suppressing a smile. It's a game, of course, but she's never spoken to me like this before. She unclips my bra at the front, and it snaps open, exposing my breasts. Then she drops the flogger as if she's suddenly lost all interest in it and her hands roam over me, caressing my breasts, my waist, and my hips. Her touch feels heavenly, and I close my eyes and moan, arching against her. She wedges her hands into my panties and strokes my sore behind. "I'm going to take these off, okay?"

I nod, then remember she wants me to speak. "Yes," I whisper.

Athena pulls them down, and I feel so vulnerable now that I can see myself and everyone around me. She was right; she went easy on me last time because this is intense.

The amplified audience in the many mirrors make me feel like I'm in an arena.

She watches me intently. "Are you okay?"

"Yes." *Am* I okay? Just like last time, I keep asking myself that question. All I know is that I want this, so I repeat my answer. "Yes."

"Good." Athena's drink arrives, and she shoots Morgan a wink. "Thank you, honey." She holds the glass to my lips, and I gratefully take a sip, letting the strong liquor calm my nerves a little. She does the same, then takes one of the ice cubes from the glass and holds it before me.

Aha. The ice makes sense now.

"Ever played a game hot and cold?" she asks.

I shake my head, then add, "No."

Athena cups my cheek. "My God, you're so innocent." She runs her thumb over my lips, and I recognize the way she looks at me. She wants to kiss me. "Well, there's a first time for everything," she purrs, lowering the ice cube to my left nipple.

The cold is shocking against my heated skin. I gasp, my body instinctively trying to pull away, but the restraints hold me in place. The ice cube leaves a glistening trail as she circles my nipple, which hardens instantly under the freezing touch. A trail of cold water drips down my body, making me shiver.

"Watch," she commands, and my eyes snap to the mirrors where I can see my body's reaction from every angle —the way my back arches, how my lips part in a silent plea, the goose bumps racing across my skin. She continues to hold it there until my nipple feels numb, until it starts to hurt. I can barely take it anymore. Should I ask her to stop? Use the safe word? It's just an ice cube, but it's starting to feel like countless little needles penetrating my skin.

"The beauty of hot and cold," she says before I have the chance to put a stop to it, "is the contrast. The shock of sensation." She suddenly drops the ice cube and lifts me up, and I wrap my legs around her while she replaces it with her mouth, hot and eager against my cold, sensitive skin.

I'm stunned, hanging from my restraints. Athena is much stronger than she looks, and she's right; the contrast is electrifying. My body convulses with pleasure, and I moan loudly, watching the maddeningly sexy display.

"You like this," she murmurs against my skin. Her tongue feels amazing, and when she sucks my nipple into her mouth, I gasp in delight. She continues until I'm starting to relax and then she uses her teeth, biting playfully and shocking me back into submission.

"Oops." She grins as she pulls away and eases me back down. "I couldn't help myself. I'm a biter." She licks her lips and fixes her gaze on my mouth, then takes a fresh ice cube from the glass. "When I see something I like, I want to eat it."

Athena pushes the ice cube against my other breast and moves it lower, tracing a path down my stomach. My muscles contract involuntarily as the cold water trickles down my abdomen, pooling briefly at my navel before continuing its journey downward.

She shoots me a teasing look as she places it against my inner thigh, tracing it upward until it's dangerously close to my sex before veering away.

"Please," I whisper. I don't even care if it's going to be cold. I need something there. Anything to soothe the agonizing need for release.

The ice stops its journey. "Did I ask you to speak?" Athena's voice is stern, but her eyes dance with excitement. She's enjoying my desperation.

"I'm sorry."

Athena rewards my correction by bringing the ice to my lips, letting me taste the cool wetness. It melts against my mouth while her face comes closer and closer to mine. She cups my cheek and moves the ice cube away, replacing it with her mouth. She kisses me almost tenderly, her lips brushing mine briefly before she deepens the kiss. This doesn't feel like it's part of the game. It feels intimate, almost loving in the way she strokes my cheek, my hair.

I moan and arch into her, welcoming both the kiss and the ice cube that she's now trailing down my body again. The dual sensations overwhelm me, and I whimper against her mouth.

Athena pulls away, blinking as if she's snapping out of it, and I wish I could free my hands and pull her back. I watch as she moves behind me, her reflection showing her heated gaze as she wraps her arm around me and brings the ice lower still, past my navel, down to my sex. The cold against my sensitive flesh tears a cry from my throat—half pleasure, half shock. My hips buck involuntarily, seeking more pressure.

"Still," she commands, placing her free hand firmly on my hip to steady me. "Let it happen."

The ice melts against my heat, water running down my inner thighs. She slides the ice between my folds, and I bite my lip, my thighs trembling, my chest heaving.

Athena watches me with fascination. "Good girl," she praises, her voice husky. The ice is beginning to numb me now, and anticipating the sting that will follow, I bring my thighs together.

"Nuh-uh." She spanks my behind with her hand. "Keep your legs apart."

I flinch when she brings the ice cube to my clit and

holds it there. I'm already regretting begging for it. I can't do this. It's too cold, then too numb, then too painful.

"Safe word?" she asks when I let out a whimper.

I hesitate, then shake my head.

"Good girl." Athena drops the ice cube just as I'm about to change my mind and yell *pause*. It clatters across the floor, and the ice makes way for her warm hand. She cups my pussy, drags her fingers through my wetness, and slowly slips two fingers inside me. Her thumb circles my clit softly, careful not to hurt me now that I'm oversensitive.

I throw my head back against her and moan, welcoming her. Athena's surrendered herself; I can feel it. Her cold hand, the one she's used for the ice cubes, reaches around me to massage my breasts while her mouth is on my neck, kissing me.

The warmth of her touch after the cold is exquisite. She works me slowly, her rhythm matching the increasingly ragged pattern of my breathing. I'm light-headed from all the sensations, rapidly climbing toward release, and I love the way she holds me.

"Come for me," she whispers so only I can hear. "And watch."

I force my eyes open, meeting the gazes of our audience and then my own. It's confronting. My body is trembling on the precipice of release, and I look emotional, both broken and whole. From behind me, Athena is watching me too and I see her eyes are glistening while she kisses my hairline and breathes in against me.

The vision of her unleashes something primal within me, and my climax crashes through my body, violent and unstoppable. I moan loudly, my voice echoing around the room, my body convulsing against the restraints. Athena holds me firmly, her arms around me and her fingers continuing their relentless rhythm, drawing out my pleasure. Through the haze of my release, I see the audience responding—some shifting restlessly, others watching with unabashed hunger. In the infinite reflections, I witness my own surrender from every angle, unable to hide from the truth of my desire.

Athena's hands gentle, holding me steady as my breathing slowly returns to normal. She places a soft kiss on my shoulder.

"Breathe," she says, and I realize I've been holding my breath. I exhale shakily, my legs trembling with aftershocks.

She gestures for Morgan to help her with the cuffs and the relief is immediate, blood rushing back to my fingertips. I lean on Athena, and she holds me in a warm embrace.

"I've missed you," she whispers.

I rest my head against her shoulder and tangle my fingers in her hair, clinging on to her. Even under these strange circumstances, holding her feels so right that I don't want to let go. I feel safe with her, cherished. "I've missed you too."

FIFTY

ATHENA

"Are you sure about this?" I ask. Ruby stands in the doorway of my bedroom, still flushed from our session downstairs. "I don't want you to do anything you're uncomfortable with."

She nods, certainty in her gaze. "Yes, I'm sure. I want to stay with you tonight."

Those simple words hold weight. This is different territory, and even though it's what I wanted, I still feel a nervous flutter as we enter.

I leave the lights off, allowing only the ambient glow from the streetlamps to spill through the windows.

"This will be a first," I say, a smile touching my lips as I see Zeus is already sleeping at the end of the bed. "No one has stayed with me since I got him, so I'm not sure how he feels about sharing me."

"I guess we'll find out," Ruby whispers as if trying not to wake him. "Do you have a first-aid kit?"

I laugh. "Hey, he's not that bad." I close the distance between us and wrap her in my arms. The sensation is still new—holding her without purpose or direction, just for the sake of connection—and her body fits against mine so well. Ruby melts into me, accepting the intimacy. I know I have permission now. That I can do this without her feeling uncomfortable or afraid of getting too close. She chose this, chose me, tonight. I feel her exhale against my collarbone, her muscles relaxing as she leans into me.

"Mmm...this feels good," she murmurs as if reading my mind. She inches back to look at me. I don't know how long she stands like that, but I wait, patiently. Finally, she cups my face and pulls me in to kiss me.

Her lips are soft against mine as my hands slide up her back, feeling the delicate curve of her spine through her dress. Without breaking away, I guide her toward the bed.

Ruby slides my blazer off my shoulders and starts unbuttoning my sleeveless white blouse. Everything ends up on the floor, topped with my hat before I turn her around to help her out of her dress. I lower her zipper, revealing inch by inch the elegant line of her back. My fingers brush against her skin, and she shivers.

"Cold?" I ask.

"No," she whispers, turning back to me. "Just...aware." She slides out of her dress, and it pools at her feet.

I understand what she means. It's just us, discovering each other outside the careful boundaries we've maintained.

Her eyes study me in the dim light as I stand before her in my bra and panties. No woman has seen me naked since Elena, and that realization makes me freeze. The weight of Ruby's gaze makes me acutely conscious of every scar, every imperfection I've kept hidden. My heart pounds, a strange anxiety flooding through me. I've forgotten what this feels like—to be seen, truly seen, simply as a woman with a body marked by time and history.

"You're so beautiful," she says softly as her fingers trace

the lace edge of my bra. I remain perfectly still, allowing her this exploration. It's a strange and scary reversal—me surrendering control, even in this small way.

"So are you," I reply, my voice unexpectedly husky.

Ruby's hands slide to my back, finding the clasp of my bra. She unhooks it, letting it fall away between us. Her gaze is appreciative, almost reverent, while her fingertips ghost across my collarbone, down to the curve of my breast. "Don't be afraid."

The tables have turned. I came into this thinking I would be the steady one, the protector. Instead, she's the one anchoring me as I drift in unfamiliar waters. It's disorienting and humbling.

Ruby steps forward and wraps her arms around me. The sensation of her bare skin against mine grounds and soothes me, and I let out a long breath, closing my eyes as her warmth washes over me.

Something breaks loose inside, an emotion I've held at bay, convincing myself it no longer existed. I bury my face in her neck, embarrassed by the sudden wetness in my eyes. I'm undone by tenderness.

"It's okay," Ruby whispers, stroking my hair. "Let's just go to sleep. I want to hold you."

Her words—so simple, asking for nothing beyond connection—break through the last of my defenses. It's been so long since anyone has offered me that kind of sanctuary. Not since Elena. Not since I learned how easily it could be taken away.

Ruby slides into bed first and I follow.

"Come here," she whispers, opening her arms to me.

I shift toward her and let myself be held. Her arm curves around my shoulder, pulling me against her chest, and I rest my head in the hollow beneath her collarbone.

My arm drapes across her waist, fingers splayed against her hip. It feels good. No. More than good. The weight of her arm around me creates a haven of pressure and warmth, a boundary that protects rather than confines. Against her skin, I find a perfect negative space shaped for me alone.

Zeus shifts at our feet, stretching before settling again with a contented purr. Outside, the desert night envelops the house in silence, and the world beyond these walls feels immeasurably far away.

"Do you know the myth of Baucis and Philemon?" I ask. The question rises from nowhere, although I have an idea where my subconscious was going with it.

Ruby shakes her head. "Tell me."

I shift closer, my leg sliding between hers. "Zeus and Hermes decided to visit Earth in human form," I begin. "They wanted to test human hospitality, so they disguised themselves as poor travelers and knocked on door after door, seeking shelter. But no one would take them in."

"Not even recognizing gods among them," Ruby murmurs.

"Exactly. Until they came to the home of an elderly couple—Baucis and Philemon. They were poor but offered the strangers everything they had—food, wine, their own bed." My hand finds hers, our fingers intertwining. "During the meal, the couple noticed something strange. No matter how much wine they poured, the jug remained full."

"The gods revealed themselves," Ruby guesses.

I nod. "They did. Zeus and Hermes were so moved by the couple's generosity that they granted them a wish. And do you know what they asked for?"

"What?"

"They asked that neither would ever have to live without the other. They requested to die together, when their time came, so neither would know the pain of being left behind."

Ruby's breath catches audibly. I feel her body tense against mine, and I wonder if I've wandered into dangerous territory, evoking echoes of her loss. But she gives me a sad smile and swallows hard. "Continue."

"The gods granted their wish," I say, stroking her cheek. "When they were very old, the gods transformed them into two trees—an oak and a linden—growing from a single trunk, their branches forever intertwined."

"That's beautiful," Ruby whispers, and I see her eyes are shining. "Why did you tell me that?"

I consider deflecting, offering something light. But it's too late; I'm already cracked wide open. "Because it's about love and about finding sanctuary in each other. About recognizing the divine in ordinary moments of connection," I say. "And this feels divine."

"It does." She squeezes me and presses a kiss to the top of my head. "I never took you for a romantic."

"I used to be." I shrug. "I am. It's still there. I can feel it simmering when I'm with you."

We lie in silence, the rise and fall of Ruby's chest a rhythm that calms my racing thoughts. Her fingers thread through my hair.

"I never thought I'd feel this way again," she says. "After Claire...I thought that part of me was gone forever."

I meet her gaze, finding in her eyes a vulnerability that mirrors my own. The moonlight catches the tears gathering at their corners.

"But here you are, making me feel everything I thought was lost." She wipes away a tear that rolls down her cheek and takes a shaky breath. "I love you, Athena."

My throat constricts, emotion rising so quickly I almost choke on my reply.

"I—I love you too," I manage, the declaration catching, revealing more in its imperfection.

Ruby's smile illuminates the darkness. She pulls the covers up, cocooning us in warmth, and tightens her hold on me.

In this bed, in her arms, there is no armor. I am no longer untouchable.

FIFTY-ONE
RUBY

I blink awake slowly, disoriented for a moment until awareness floods back. I'm in Athena's bed. And she's here, curled against me, one arm draped across my waist.

My chest tightens, so sudden and overwhelming it steals my breath. Last night rushes back—the club, coming here afterward, our confessions in the darkness. The words still hang in the air, suspended like dust motes in the morning light, real and undeniable.

A week ago, I was terrified of exactly this. Now I'm here, flooded by a beautiful, fragile hope.

Athena shifts in her sleep, her face softening into a sweet smile. Her dark hair spills across the white pillow and her lips are slightly parted, her breathing deep and even. I've seen her commanding spaces, wielding power like it's an extension of herself, but this unguarded version of her slays me. I study her face, allowing myself the luxury of looking without restraint. She's beautiful in a way that transcends conventional attractiveness—all sharp angles and smooth planes, her olive skin flawless, like some Greek goddess come to life.

I glance at the bedside clock and register with mild surprise that it's already past eight. Friday morning, and my calendar is full of meetings I should care about. My phone is probably exploding with messages from Miranda wondering where I am yet again. It doesn't matter. Nothing outside this room holds any significance compared to the woman beside me.

There's a soft clatter from downstairs—a pan against a stovetop perhaps, or dishes being arranged. Athena's house-keeper must have arrived while we slept. Zeus, who was curled at our feet when I drifted off, is nowhere to be seen.

Athena drifts toward consciousness. Her eyes flutter open like she knows I'm watching, focusing slowly until they lock with mine. For a moment, we just stare at each other, neither speaking. Then she smiles, genuine and unguarded.

"Good morning," she whispers, her voice husky with sleep.

I don't reply with words. Instead, I lean forward and press my lips to hers. She responds immediately, her hand sliding up to cradle my face, her thumb stroking my cheek.

The kiss deepens naturally, and there's no urgency, just a gradual unfolding of sensation. Her lips are soft, yielding in a way that contrasts with her usual dominance.

"I love you," I murmur against her mouth, because I need to say it again in the daylight, need to make it real beyond the sanctuary of darkness.

She pulls back just enough to meet my eyes. "I love you too," she says, and then she smiles again, this time with a hint of mischief. "And I'm very happy you're still here."

"Did you think I'd run again?" I ask, tracing the line of her jaw.

"The thought crossed my mind." Athena's smile broadens, and she captures my hand, bringing my fingers to her lips. She sucks my index finger into her mouth, and I close my eyes and moan, instantly aroused. "But if you try, I won't let you."

She kisses me again, deeper, hungrier, while her hand slides from my face to my neck, then lower, tracing the curve of my spine. I arch into her touch, suddenly acutely aware that we're both still naked beneath the sheets.

She rolls me onto my back, her body half-covering mine. Her tongue slides against mine, and I moan again, my hands tangling in her hair to pull her closer. Her thigh presses between my legs, creating a delicious pressure, and when she breaks the kiss to trail her lips down my neck, I tilt my head back, offering more of myself to her exploration.

"You're beautiful," she whispers, and her hand finds my breast. I gasp at the contact, running my hands down her back, feeling the subtle flex of muscles. Her waist, her hip, her thigh...

Her reaction is intense; I can tell she's not used to being touched anymore. She trembles beneath my fingertips, a subtle vibration that betrays her vulnerability. When I trace her behind, she inhales sharply, her eyes fluttering closed for a moment as if overwhelmed by the sensation. There's an unfamiliar hesitancy in her reaction, a momentary tensing before she surrenders to my touch.

I gently shift us around so she's on her back and lace my fingers through hers, bringing our hands over her head as I kiss her. I feel both need and hesitation in the kiss, but she relaxes more and more until finally, she closes her eyes and sighs as I cover her body with mine.

She whispers my name, moaning as I place a trail of kisses down her neck. I let go of her hands and move down, kissing and caressing her breasts. Her back arches as my tongue circles her nipple, her breathing becoming ragged. I lose myself in the taste of her skin, and every response from her body emboldens me.

Her fingers thread through my hair as I move lower, pressing kisses all over her abdomen and along the inside of her thigh. When my mouth finally finds her sex, she gasps, her hips rising to meet me. I take my time, exploring her with my tongue, learning what makes her moan, what makes her grip the sheets.

I feel privileged to be her first in so long. To witness her surrender. I can feel her thighs trembling, hear the catch in her breath when I find just the right spot. Her hips move against my mouth, seeking more pressure, and I grasp her thighs, holding her steady as I continue my gentle assault.

She tastes delicious and I savor every moment. Her breathing grows increasingly erratic, her moans louder, less controlled. I can feel her approaching the edge, her body tensing beneath me.

When she comes, it's with a cry that seems torn from deep inside her. Her body arches off the bed, taut as a bowstring, before collapsing back into the sheets. I move up to hold her, cradling her against me while she shudders through the aftershocks.

She buries her face in my neck, her breathing ragged. I feel wetness against my skin and realize she's crying. Silent tears that speak volumes about how long she's denied herself intimacy.

"It's okay," I whisper, stroking her hair. "I've got you."

Athena turns on her side to face me and we lie tangled together in silence. Her tears have left a dampness on my shoulder, but they've stopped now.

"Are you okay?" I whisper, inching back to meet her eyes.

"Yeah. It's...you know..." She wipes at her eyes and frowns like she's surprised to feel tears. I'm sure many would find it hard to imagine Athena Stavros crying, but to me, she couldn't be farther from the intimidating standoffish woman in white.

"I know," I whisper back. And I do. I know how she feels and understand her fears like no other. "It's a lot."

We're both navigating this strange territory of second chances, relearning what it means to be open, to trust, to love. I press my forehead against hers and breathe her in. Her arms tighten around me as if she's afraid I might vanish, and I hold her just as fiercely.

We gravitate toward each other again, our bodies seeking connection as naturally as breathing. Her lips find mine in a kiss that starts gentle but quickly deepens. The taste of salt from her tears mingles with the sweetness of her mouth as she rolls me beneath her, reclaiming her dominance. Gone is the hesitation, the vulnerability replaced by a fierce hunger that matches my own. I arch up to meet her, my hands mapping the contours of her body with newfound familiarity.

We move in synchrony, a sensual dance of giving and taking. In this sacred space between heartbeats, we're no longer two broken souls but something whole and complete.

FIFTY-TWO
ATHENA

The Aston Martin hugs the curves of the desert road as we climb higher into the hills. Ruby sits beside me, her auburn hair flowing in the wind. I press the accelerator, surging forward as we reach a straightaway, and Ruby's laughter fills the car—a sound I've been chasing all evening.

"I don't remember much from the last time I was in your car," she says, her hand gripping the door as we take another curve. "I was drunk and asleep for most of it."

"You were exhausted," I remind her, reaching across to squeeze her knee.

"Well, I'm wide awake now." She grins as I accelerate again. "And I love this. I love seeing you like this."

I can't help showing off a little, maneuvering through bends, feeling lighter than I have in years. Allowing Ruby to see me, to touch me, to know me completely was terrifying, but now I feel liberated. She stripped away my defenses and left me stronger.

I turn onto the unmarked dirt path that leads to my favorite viewpoint. The car's suspension absorbs the uneven terrain as we make our way up, and Ruby glances at me, eyebrow raised.

"Should I be concerned that you're taking me to a secluded spot in the desert at eleven at night?"

"Only if you're afraid of stars." I bring the car to a stop at the edge of the overlook and kill the engine. Silence envelops us—pure, undiluted desert quiet.

Ruby looks up and smiles. Above us, the night sky unfurls in all its glory, an explosion of stars, the Milky Way a luminous smear across the black canvas, all undimmed by city lights. Below, the desert stretches into darkness, silver-brushed by moonlight. Ancient rock formations stand like sentinels, their shadows pooling in valleys.

"It's beautiful," Ruby whispers, her face still tilted upward. "I've never seen the stars like this."

"You've never been out here? You live so close."

She shakes her head. "Never. I thought about it sometimes, but..." She trails off. "I'm glad I'm here now."

I lean in to kiss her cheek, then get out and move to the trunk. "Are you hungry?"

"Starving," she admits. "I didn't eat after my late lunch."

"That's what I thought. I bet you forget to eat all the time." I pull out a large picnic basket, a thick blanket, and an insulated bag. Ruby watches in amusement as I unfold the blanket and spread it near the edge of the overlook.

"That's so sweet," she says, helping me smooth the corners. "Are you going all Greek on me now? Feeding me like your mom?"

"If I were going 'all Greek on you,' we'd have a feast for twenty, and I'd be telling you that you're too skinny while forcing third helpings onto your plate." I set the basket down and open it, then arrange myself cross-legged on the blanket. I pat the space beside me and Ruby settles there.

From the basket, I produce containers of food, the rich aromas escaping as I open each one.

"What is all this?" Ruby asks.

"A little bit of everything," I say. "Souvlaki, gyros, spanakopita, dolmades, salad, and fresh fruit for dessert." I arrange everything on the Parthenon's fine bone china plates that I've brought along. "The street food court at the Olympus is excellent."

Ruby laughs when I pull out two crystal wineglasses and hand her a bottle of red. "I don't think anyone's ever brought Baccarat crystal to a picnic before."

"I had no idea where to find plastic cups at the Olympus, and everyone was busy preparing for tonight's event." I shrug sheepishly. "So I...borrowed some stuff from the Parthenon."

"Chef Dimitris must love you right now." Ruby opens the wine and pours it. She bites her lip and smiles as she hands me a glass. "There she is again."

"Who?"

"The romantic. The one who sets up a picnic under the stars. The one who knows myths about intertwined trees." She takes my hand, her fingers sliding between mine. "I like seeing her."

"She's been hidden away for a while." I squeeze her hand. "But she's finding her way back." I lean forward to kiss her and when I pull away, her eyes remain closed for a beat longer, as if savoring the moment. "Tell me about your day."

Ruby sighs, helping herself to some of the food. "Chaotic. Everyone wanted to know where I was this morning."

I arch a brow. "Did you tell them what you were up to?"

"I said I had an important personal matter to attend to," she replies with a smirk. "Which wasn't a lie."

"Very diplomatic."

"I am a lawyer." She shakes her head in amusement. "Miranda has been giving me these concerned looks lately. I've been slacking a bit—coming in later, leaving earlier. Taking actual lunch breaks sometimes."

I laugh. "They're worried because you stopped working seventy hours a week?"

"Pretty much." Ruby laughs along. "I suppose there's nothing wrong with bringing it back to fifty. I've decided to hire more people. I realize I've been working my team way too hard too." She swirls her wine thoughtfully. "Another assistant to help Miranda, another paralegal, and I'm even thinking of bringing Sarah on. You met her."

"Claire's niece?"

"Yeah. She's an associate at Gibson Dunn. Brilliant lawyer, super ambitious, and best of all, I trust her." Ruby's face softens. "If it works out, I may be able to leave now and then to have dinner with you before the clock strikes midnight." She takes a bite of food, and her eyes widen with pleasure. "At the Greek food court," she adds. "Oh my God, this is so good I could eat it every single day."

"Whenever you want. Just come and pick me up from my office."

"I'll hold you to that." Ruby leans into me and I drape an arm around her shoulder. "So how about you? How was your day? Break any kneecaps or collect any protection money, big, scary casino boss?"

I laugh and nudge her with my shoulder. "Please, that's Tuesday's agenda. I'm more of a 'make them an offer they can't refuse' on Fridays kind of boss."

"Noted. I'll update my calendar."

"Actually, I've been busy too," I continue. "I've had tons of internal meetings regarding the announcement of Zara Nova's residency."

"That's so exciting. It must be huge for the Olympus."

"It is. Do you like her music?"

"I love her first two albums. Haven't kept up with her latest stuff," Ruby admits. "I haven't really listened to much of anything in the past couple years. I've got a lot of catching up to do."

"Well, I'll take you to her opening night. Introduce you properly."

Ruby's face lights up with an excitement I've rarely seen from her, a girlish enthusiasm. "You would do that? I'd love that so much."

"Of course. One of the perks of dating the big, scary casino boss," I joke. "VIP access included."

"Oh, I'm definitely keeping you around," Ruby grins, settling more comfortably against me. She reaches for a piece of spanakopita, then breaks it in half and offers me a share. Small gestures. New habits. Humble beginnings.

FIFTY-THREE
RUBY

The doors slide open, and I step out of Athena's private elevator. She sits behind a massive black marble desk, phone to her ear. She looks up and her serious expression transforms into a warm smile.

"I'm sorry. I'll have to call you back tomorrow." She gets up and steps around her desk to greet me. "There you are. How was your day?"

"Long," I admit, letting my bag slide to the floor. "But better now."

I turn in a slow circle, taking in her office for the first time, and whistle through my teeth. "I need your decorator for my firm. This is spectacular."

Athena laughs. "My decorator was me, actually. With some help, of course."

I wander to the windows, looking down at the casino floor thirty-eight stories below. Tiny figures move among the tables and machines, waitresses weaving through the crowd with trays of drinks, dealers shuffling cards.

"Wow," I breathe. "It feels fucking powerful being up here. Like watching your own private kingdom."

Athena comes to stand beside me, her shoulder brushing mine. "That was the idea. Though I rarely think of it that way anymore." She turns to me, head tilted in consideration. "Have you ever seen the whole Olympus?"

"Just the Parthenon." I shoot her a flirty smile. "Will you give me a private tour?"

"That can be arranged, Counselor." In one smooth motion, Athena lifts me onto her desk and steps between my legs. "Let's start with my office, shall we? This is my desk. It's Greek marble and as sturdy as they come. I had it stress-tested to support the weight of my ego, so we should be perfectly safe." Her hands slide around my waist as she leans in to kiss me properly this time. I melt into her touch, my hands finding their way into her hair, dislodging her white fedora that falls forgotten to the floor. We're getting carried away, but I can't bring myself to care. My legs wrap around her waist, pulling her closer.

A sharp knock at the door breaks the spell. Athena chuckles as she steps back, wiping traces of my lipstick from her mouth.

"Yes?" she calls, her voice steady despite the flush in her cheeks.

"Ms. Stavros, the event planning team needs your sign-off for the event tonight." Maria's voice comes through the door.

Athena sighs, shooting me an apologetic smile. "I'm busy at the moment, Maria. Ask Mark to sign it off, will you? Tell him I'm handing over control tonight."

"Of course, Ms. Stavros."

"Athena Stavros is handing over control?" I arch a brow. "I'll be damned."

Athena laughs as she retrieves her hat from the floor. "Trust me, it's a work in progress. My therapist calls it growth, but my staff calls it a miracle. It took me three years and one cracked molar from grinding my teeth before I could let someone else make a decision around here." She smooths her hair and puts her hat back on. "Perhaps we should start that tour. The knocking rarely stops when I'm here. If it's not Maria, it's someone else."

Heat still pulses between my thighs, my body buzzing with a desire that's become wonderfully familiar these past weeks. I've developed a Pavlovian response to her—one touch and I'm ready to abandon all my self-restraint. But the anticipation is its own kind of pleasure, the slow simmer that will make tonight's release all the sweeter.

"Show me your empire," I say, sliding off the desk. "I want to see everything."

"Let's start with the food court," Athena says, pulling me back into the elevator. "I'm guessing neither of us has eaten since lunch."

I laugh, squeezing her hand. "Am I that predictable?"

"I recognize the signs of a workaholic," she says. "Unless you prefer to sit down?"

"No, I want more of that street food we had last week. I've actually been thinking about it."

The elevator descends smoothly, its glass walls revealing floor after floor of the Olympus's grandeur. Hotel rooms, the spa floor, an indoor garden terrace. We glide past it all, suspended in our crystalline bubble. I press my hand against the glass, suddenly aware of how exposed we are. Guests look up, their faces tilting toward us, eyes following our journey.

"This is...intense," I murmur. "Everyone can see us."

"Really?" Athena steps closer and puts a hand on my back. "I thought you liked being watched."

We step out into the atrium where two imposing security guards flank the private elevator entrance, subtle nods acknowledging Athena as we pass.

She leads me through the casino, and I notice her glancing around frequently, an almost imperceptible tension in her shoulders.

I take her hand as we walk, and she stiffens momentarily. Her eyes dart around, scanning the faces of staff members and patrons alike.

"Sorry," I say, letting go of her hand. "Are you uncomfortable with this?"

Athena stops and turns to face me. "No, of course not," she says, but her voice catches slightly. She takes my hand again. "I'm just...I'm not used to this." She hesitates. "My staff has never seen me with a love interest. They don't even know I'm gay." She laughs and shakes her head. "It's stupid, I know."

"Hey, it's not stupid. We don't have to—"

She cuts me off, cupping my face in her hands. "No. I want this. I want you. I'm done hiding."

Over her shoulder, I spot a man approaching with an iPad, his stride purposeful, eyes focused on Athena's back. He's dressed impeccably in a tailored suit, with the air of someone who carries significant authority.

He clears his throat as he draws near, and Athena turns.

"Hey, Mark," she says. "Did Maria not tell you I'm signing off for the day?" She continues before he has a chance to reply. "Don't worry about doing the rounds tonight. I'm showing Ruby around, so I've got this."

"I ehm... she called me but I was in a meeting, so I haven't spoken to her yet." Mark's eyes shift between us, lingering on our intertwined fingers. A flicker of surprise crosses his face before he masks it with professional neutrality.

Athena clears her throat, and I feel her hand going clammy in mine. "I'm sorry. Where are my manners? Ruby, this is Mark, my operations director." She pauses, a subtle tension in her jaw before it relaxes into resolution. "Mark, this is Ruby Walsh, my..." She pauses and lets out a nervous chuckle. "My partner." She utters the word "partner" more like a question, like she's testing the word out.

"Oh?" He recovers quickly, extending his hand to me. "Well, that explains why she's been leaving early lately. A pleasure to meet you, Ms. Walsh. Enjoy your tour." With a respectful nod to us both, he disappears into the crowd.

Athena blows out her cheeks. "Wow," she murmurs. "Now he knows."

"That was uncomfortable for you, wasn't it?" I ask after Mark is out of earshot.

She takes a deep breath and nods, then contradicts herself with a shake of her head. "Yes. No. Both." She shrugs. "It's a big deal. First Demetria, now Mark. By tomorrow, the entire staff will know and then..."

I study her expression, suddenly struck by the magnitude of what just happened. In all my focus on my own journey, I've somehow missed how Athena's reality is transforming alongside mine. For a woman who's spent her life hiding this part of herself, each revelation is its own kind of rebirth.

"Are you worried your mom will find out?"

"If I'm out and openly dating a woman, even if it's just in Vegas, she'll find out one way or another," Athena says as we continue our walk toward the food court. "I'm not exactly a celebrity, but there are charity galas and events where I get photographed or mentioned in those society pages my mother loves to read." She gestures to a trio of well-dressed older men being escorted to the high-limit area.

"It's a small world. The wealthy Greeks all know each other, and they love to gossip. They also love to gamble, and when they do..." She gestures around us. "They come here."

"I've really complicated your life," I say. "I'm only now realizing to what extent."

"No." She smiles and waves it off. "No, no, no. Absolutely not. You haven't complicated my life, you've enriched it. And whatever happens, happens. I'll deal with it when the time comes."

FIFTY-FOUR

ATHENA

I'm sitting in Ruby's kitchen, watching with fascination as she chops mushrooms. She insisted on cooking for me and wouldn't accept my help. Although it's adorable, it's hard not to step in as I've never seen anyone chopping the way she does. The way she holds the knife alone is enough to question if she's ever cooked a meal in her life. Mushrooms and burrata on toasted ciabatta with a side salad. Not exactly complicated, but she's making it look like a science experiment.

"Be careful, I don't want you to hurt yourself," I warn her. "Do you want me to turn on the grill for the ciabatta?"

"No, I'm fine. Just stay there and relax. I've got this." She chuckles as she fiddles with the buttons on the oven and shoves in a whole loaf of ciabatta without slicing and oiling it first. "I'm determined."

I'm about to step in anyway when my phone buzzes. Demetria's name lights up the screen, and I smile, welcoming the distraction before Ruby can accuse me of being a control freak. I've been talking to Demetria more regularly since her visit—quick texts, voice messages exchanged, and late-night calls.

"It's my sister," I tell Ruby, who nods encouragingly. Our relationship is still new enough that these small domestic moments feel significant—standing in her kitchen while she cooks, taking personal calls in her space, the casual intimacy of our daily routines intertwining.

"Hey, Dem," I answer. "What's up, sis?"

"Athena!" My sister's voice is breathless with excitement. "I have news," she starts in Greek. "Big news."

"Oh? Everything okay?" I wedge my phone between my ear and my shoulder so I can open the bottle of wine I brought.

"More than okay. I'm getting married!"

"You're what?" The wine bottle nearly slips from my hand. I set it down carefully, exchanging a glance with Ruby, who's paused her chopping and studies me curiously.

"She's getting married," I whisper to her, then focus my attention back to Demetria. "To Julian?"

"Of course to Julian. Who else?"

I clear my throat and try to inject some enthusiasm into my voice. "Sorry. That was a silly question. And congratulations, I'm super happy for you both." My little sister is getting married to someone I've never met, and I'm not sure how I feel about that. But it's my own fault, I suppose. I haven't exactly been around much. "I'm just surprised," I continue. "When you were here last month, you didn't mention it once."

"Well, he asked me, and I said yes." Demetria pauses. "You really are happy for me, right? I need you to be supportive, Athena."

"I am, I promise," I lie, my eyes widening as I meet

Ruby's gaze. "But I'd better plan a trip to meet him first. When's the wedding? Do you have a date yet?"

"It's next week," she says with a chuckle. "At Mom's yacht club in Santorini."

I blink rapidly as I process this. "Next week? Dem, you can't be serious. Why so soon?"

"It's not that soon," she says defensively. "Julian and I have been dating for six months."

To me, that sounds incredibly rushed, but I keep that thought to myself. Despite the shock, it somehow doesn't surprise me all that much. Demetria has always been incredibly impulsive. The youngest who dared to take big risks because everyone was always there to protect her and clean up the mess when things went south. I'm not worried about Julian getting his hands on the family money; that's all under my control, and Demetria gets a generous payout every month. No, I'm worried about her heart, about becoming stuck in a life she regrets with a man she doesn't know that well. But who am I to judge? I haven't known Ruby for long, but it feels right, like I've made a choice for life. Perhaps it's the same with them.

"We just decided—why wait? Life is too short for long engagements," she continues. "And I'm not worried about the short notice. No one will want to miss a Stavros wedding. Our guests will bend over backwards to be there, no matter what, because it's going to be epic!"

"I have no doubt. The yacht club? Mom must have pulled a lot of strings to make that happen. How many guests are you inviting?"

"Their capacity is three hundred, so we're keeping it intimate," Demetria says in all seriousness. "Two-hundred-and-fifty guests for me and Mom and fifty for Julian, although he probably won't even hit that number.

"Right. Three hundred at the yacht club. I hope you have a good wedding planner." A wedding with three hundred guests might not seem intimate to some, but when it comes to Greek weddings, it is, indeed, a modest number.

"I've got the best of the best. She's flown over from New York, and she's used to working under pressure on last-minute events." Demetria pauses. "Which brings me to the next topic. Money. I need funds for the wedding. And for some of Julian's guests who can't afford to attend unless we pay for it."

"Sure. Let me know how much and I'll take care of it." Since being in charge of the Stavros family fortune, I've never turned down a request for money. My responsibility is to keep my mother and sister comfortable and give them whatever they need, no questions asked. If this wedding turns out to be a mistake, so be it. In most cases, when people suddenly inherit a lot of money, the funds are quickly drained by reckless spending, and I'm proud I've done the opposite.

"Thank you!" Demetria's voice grows louder. I imagine her bouncing up and down the way she does when she gets excited. "And I have one final request."

"Of course you do," I joke. "Tell me."

Ruby has abandoned her cooking entirely, leaning against the opposite counter to watch me. From her expression, I'd almost think she understands Greek.

"Well, I was wondering," Demetria says, dropping a pause for effect. "If you'd be my maid of honor."

"You know I will." My smile widens. I may not be convinced about this impromptu wedding, but I can't change her mind, so I'll be there with bells and whistles. "Thank you. It's an honor."

Demetria's delighted squeal makes me hold the phone

away from my ear. "Perfect! Oh, and bring Ruby as your plus-one. Don't worry, I haven't told Mom," she quickly adds. "But she's been talking about her, and she wants her to come."

I frown. "What? Mom's been talking about Ruby? Why?"

"Because she liked her, obviously. She said Ruby was refreshing and a positive influence on you. High praise from our mother, as you know."

I glance at Ruby, who's raised her eyebrows at the mention of her name. "I'd love to bring her, but it's short notice so I can't promise anything."

"Look, bring her, don't bring her. It's up to you. But the invitation stands, and I'd love to have you both there." There's a muffled sound in the background, and Demetria's voice grows distant for a moment. "Yes, darling, just a minute!" She returns to the phone. "I've got to run—Julian's waiting to finalize the guest list. I'll text you all the details, okay? Love you!"

And then she's gone. I set the phone down and look at Ruby. "So," I say, pouring us both a glass of wine. "Want to come to a wedding next week?"

Ruby looks baffled. "Your sister's getting married? Just like that?"

"Apparently so. Demetria has always had a flair for the dramatic and impulsive. She's always been like this—deciding something in an instant and making it happen, consequences be damned. Once, when she was twelve, she decided she wanted to be a ballerina. Within twenty-four hours, she'd convinced our parents to enroll her in the most prestigious dance academy in Greece."

"Did she stick with it?"

I laugh. "God, no. She quit after a month. But that's Demetria—all passion, no patience."

Ruby's hand finds mine on the countertop. "And she wants me to come too?"

"She does. And supposedly, so does my mother. I'm still processing that particular revelation, which is...interesting." I shake my head. "Anyway, you're hereby invited as my plus-one to my sister's wedding in Santorini next week. I know you're busy, but—"

"Are you serious? Santorini? With you?" Ruby grins. "Of course I want to come!"

I take a long sip of wine to hide my face, trying not to let Ruby see the mild panic setting in. I'm about to bring someone home.

Luckily, my moment of internal crisis is interrupted by dark smoke rising from the grill. Ruby whirls around with a yelp, yanking open the oven door to reveal charcoal ciabatta. The smoke detector joins the chaos with its high-pitched wail as Ruby frantically waves a dish towel beneath it, her face a perfect portrait of culinary defeat.

"Well," she says, coughing through the smoke. "What do you feel like? Thai or Italian for takeout?"

FIFTY-FIVE
RUBY

The car glides through the private section of Athens airport, Athena beside me as we head toward the waiting jet. Despite our fourteen-hour journey, she looks immaculate and fresh, while I feel the weariness of international travel in every muscle.

"The jet will take us directly to Santorini," she says, noticing my gaze through the window where a sleek white aircraft with gold trim awaits.

"The private jet," I clarify, still processing this reality. "From Athens to Santorini. Because a commercial flight would be...what? Too pedestrian?"

Athena shoots me a look that's half amusement, half defensiveness. "It's a thirty-minute private flight versus waiting seven hours for a connecting commercial flight or taking a ferry that would waste an entire day."

I think back to her minor meltdown in Vegas when she couldn't secure a private charter for the whole journey. My definition of comfortable travel has always been business class on international flights, but Athena exists in a different stratosphere of wealth. Even flying first-class commercial—

something I've done only once before—was, in her words, "settling."

The driver pulls up alongside the aircraft where our luggage is already being loaded. Athena's shoulders remain tight, her fingers drumming against her thigh as we come to a stop.

"Are you okay?" I ask, covering her restless hand with mine.

"Yeah, I'm fine," she replies too quickly, then sighs. "I'm just...this is all very sudden. The wedding, bringing you home..." She trails off, staring out the window.

"Having your worlds collide?" I offer.

She nods, turning back to me. "I won't lie. I'm nervous. But I want you here, so please don't doubt that. It's been this crazy secret fantasy of mine ever since I was a teenager. Bringing my girlfriend home, celebrating things together..." She as we get out of the car. "But they're good nerves, I promise."

The stairs of the jet are lowered, and a flight attendant appears at the top.

"Ms. Stavros, Ms. Walsh," she greets us in accented English. "Please come on board. We're ready for departure."

Stepping into the cabin feels like entering another dimension. The interior gleams with polished wood and cream leather, more luxurious living room than aircraft. A small dining area with four seats sits at one end, while plush couches line the other. There's a separate bedroom visible through an open door at the rear.

"This is..." I struggle to find words that don't make me sound like a wide-eyed tourist.

"It's our family jet," Athena says casually, as if everyone has one.

"Would you like champagne before takeoff?" the attendant asks.

"Why not?" she replies, and I nod in agreement. If there was ever a time for champagne, it's now, on a private jet, heading to a Greek island. We settle into the wide leather seats, and within minutes, we're taxiing toward the runway with a glass of champagne in hand.

"To our first trip together," I say, raising my glass.

"And to many more," Athena adds, clinking her flute against mine. Her eyes soften as she looks at me. "I'm really glad you're here, Ruby. Thank you for coming."

Soon we're climbing through fluffy white clouds into the brilliant blue Mediterranean sky. Athens sprawls beneath us, a concrete metropolis of beige and terra-cotta buildings densely packed across hills, stretching all the way to the glittering blue coastline. The Acropolis stands proud at the city's heart, a golden crown atop its ancient hill, while modern highways snake between neighborhoods like silver ribbons.

"It's beautiful," I murmur, pressing my face to the window like a child. "I can't believe I've never been to Greece before. All those trips to Europe, and I always chose Paris or London instead."

"You chose the cities of mortals," Athena shoots me a playful smile, "when you could have visited the land of gods. It's okay, you're forgiven. You're here now to redeem yourself."

The flight attendant appears with a light breakfast spread—fresh yogurt with honey and walnuts, warm pastries filled with cheese and raisins, and slices of ripe fruit that burst with flavor.

"A word of warning," Athena says, watching me savor each bite. "My mother will consider it her personal mission to feed you until you can barely move. It's the Greek way." Her eyes crinkle with amusement. "When a Greek mother says 'eat,' it's not a suggestion—it's a command."

I laugh, helping myself to a pastry. "I've already had my preview in Vegas, remember? Your mother's moussaka, the pastitsio, all those containers of food she sent over." I take a bite and sigh with pleasure. "Trust me, I know exactly what I'm getting myself into, and I'm here for it."

According to the captain's announcement, we're passing over Kea, one of the Cycladic islands. I gaze down at the land rising from the azure sea. "It looks so wild and untamed. Different from what I expected."

"The Greek islands are incredibly diverse. Some are lush and green, others volcanic and stark." Athena's voice takes on a softer quality when she talks about her homeland. "That's Kythnos coming up next, and beyond it, Serifos. My auntie had a summer house there when I was young."

"It must have been idyllic, growing up in Greece," I say.

Athena's gaze turns distant, reflective. "It was...intense. Beautiful and complicated. My father had very specific ideas about how his children should be raised—especially me, his oldest daughter. Frankly, his expectations were immense, and he trained me to take over his company one day. I never carried on his legacy, as I had no interest in shipping, but I sold it and reinvested successfully. I have no idea if he'd be proud of me or scold me for that. In the end, I had to make a decision, and I chose to take myself far away from Greece so I could live my life freely." She shrugs. "But yes, parts of my childhood were idyllic. My best memories are by the sea, away from life."

As we continue our journey, Athena points out more islands dotting the Aegean—each with its own mythology, its own character. The champagne settles warmly in my system, creating a pleasant haze as I watch the sea change color beneath us—deep navy to turquoise to almost translucent aquamarine near the shorelines. Fishing boats appear as tiny white specks against the vast blue canvas and I catch glimpses of ferries leaving foamy trails as they connect the scattered islands.

As we prepare for landing, I look out at the approaching island—a crescent of steep cliffs rising from the sea, topped with clusters of white buildings. They cling to the volcanic slopes, stacked in tiers that follow the natural contours of the land. The white walls catch the sunlight, creating a striking contrast against the deep blue sea and darker volcanic rock. I see villages, narrow paths winding between homes, courtyards tucked into unexpected corners, hotels perched on cliff edges, boats dotting the harbor below, and those iconic, blue-domed churches I've seen in countless travel photos.

"Oh my God," I breathe. "It's even more beautiful than the pictures."

Athena watches me with undisguised pleasure. "Wait until you see the sunset. It's what inspired all those myths about gods and mortals falling in love."

FIFTY-SIX
ATHENA

The car winds its way up the narrow coastal road, each turn revealing another breathtaking vista. I alternate between watching Ruby and the familiar landscape—both equally captivating in their beauty.

"Almost there," I tell her as we round the final bend. "Just up ahead."

The iron gates of my family's Santorini home swing open at our approach. Bougainvillea spills over the white stone walls in vibrant cascades of fuchsia and purple, a riotous welcome home. The driver pulls into the driveway and cuts the engine.

"Athena! You're here!" My mother emerges from the house, arms outstretched, wearing a flowing blue kaftan that billows around her in the breeze.

I get out of the car and barely have time to straighten myself before she envelops me in a tight embrace.

"Mom, it's good to see you."

She pulls back, holding me at arm's length to inspect me. "You look tired. The commercial flight was too much, wasn't it? You two need to eat and rest up for tomorrow."

"I'm fine," I assure her, turning to help Ruby from the car.

My mother's attention shifts. "Ruby! Welcome to our home." She embraces Ruby with the same enthusiasm she showed me, if not more.

"Thank you for having me, Sophia," Ruby says. "Your home is absolutely stunning."

"Thank you, sweetie." She links her arm through Ruby's, and I'm amused by my mother's immediate adoption of her. "Athena, Nikos will get your luggage. Come, come."

Nikos—the driver—nods and begins unloading our bags. I pause to thank him, then hurry to catch up. It's ironic. I'm the one who owns a casino, yet my mother has more staff than me.

Following them toward the house, I hear them chatting away like they're old friends and take a moment to see it from Ruby's perspective. The architecture is traditional Cycladic—smooth, curved walls, arched doorways, and blue-painted shutters framing windows that capture fragments of sea and sky. The main house wraps around a central courtyard with an olive tree at its heart.

"This house has been in our family for four generations," I explain to Ruby as we pass through the courtyard. "My parents renovated it when I was young, and eventually, we moved here from Athens. My great-grandfather built it. Back then, coastal land in Santorini was cheap, but now..." I shake my head and chuckle. "People would kill to get their hands on our land."

"The original structure was much smaller," my mother adds. "Each generation has expanded it, but we've maintained the traditional style."

We enter the main living area—an airy, open space with

whitewashed walls and limestone floors. The ceiling soars overhead, crossed by dark wooden beams, and the furniture is a careful balance of traditional Greek elements and modern comfort. Floor-to-ceiling windows frame the spectacular view like a living painting.

Ruby stops in her tracks, momentarily speechless. "Oh my God," she whispers, moving toward the windows. "This is...I don't even have words."

The view that has captivated her—that still captivates me every time—stretches beyond the infinity pool. The Aegean is a vast expanse of deep blue dotted with sailboats and small islands in the distance. White villages cling to the coastal cliffs like scattered sugar cubes, while the sun accentuates every curve and angle of the landscape.

"It's something, isn't it?" I say, coming to stand beside her. "No matter how many times I see it, it still makes me pause."

My mother beams with pride as she gestures to the outdoor seating area. "Please sit and enjoy the view. You must be tired from the journey." She pours lemonade into tall glasses beaded with condensation, then rushes inside and returns with a cake.

We settle on the cushioned sofa, and I notice how Ruby seems to sink into the moment—accepting the glass, smiling at my mother, her body language relaxed despite being so far from home. She belongs here, I realize. Not just in this place, but in my life, in all its facets.

"This cake is delicious," she says after taking a bite. "Did you make it?"

My mother looks pleased. "Yes. It's a lemon zest and almond cake. An old family recipe." She serves herself a small piece. "I can teach you how to make it."

"I'd love that." Ruby smiles playfully at my mother.

"But for now, I'm sure you have better things to do. Are you ready for the big day tomorrow?"

Mom rolls her eyes the way she does when she's about to fire off some dramatic monologue, but the moment is broken by the sound of an approaching car, and she springs to her feet. "Ah! That must be Demetria and Julian! Finally!"

Moments later, Demetria emerges, her dark curls whipping in the breeze, wearing an oversize white linen top over flowing palazzo pants. Behind her, a tall man with sandy hair and horn-rimmed glasses steps out.

"There's my maid of honor!" Demetria exclaims, rushing toward me. Her embrace is fierce, almost desperate, and I hold her a beat longer than usual, sensing something beneath her exuberance.

"And Ruby!" She moves to hug Ruby next. "I'm so glad you could come. Welcome to the family madhouse!"

Julian approaches more slowly, hand extended. "It's a pleasure to meet you, Athena," he says in slightly accented English. His voice is soft, almost shy. "Demetria has told me so much about you."

I shake his hand, studying him. He's nothing like Demetria's usual type—not flashy or overtly confident. Instead, there's a quiet intelligence in his eyes, a thoughtfulness to his demeanor. "Likewise," I reply. "Though I feel at a disadvantage since I'm only just meeting the man my sister is about to marry."

Julian nods and smiles goofily. "It has all happened rather quickly, I know. But when it's right..." He glances at Demetria with undisguised adoration, who, in return, has zeroed in on the cake.

"Is that your almond cake, Mama? God, I've been craving this!" She cuts herself a generous slice—not even a slice, more like a chunk—then cuts another piece and adds it to her plate.

That's when I really look at her—beyond the initial excitement of our reunion. Her face is fuller, her cheekbones less pronounced. The oversize top suddenly seems less like a fashion choice and more like a strategic garment. My eyes narrow as I catch her unconsciously resting a hand on her lower abdomen.

Oh.

"Demetria," I say, rising from my seat. "I just quickly need your opinion on my outfit for tomorrow. Could I show you my options inside for a moment?"

She looks confused, as I've literally never asked her for fashion advice, but follows me into the house. Once we're in the kitchen, out of earshot, I turn to face her.

"Seriously, Dem?" I whisper-hiss. "Is this why you're rushing the wedding?" I place my hand gently on her belly, feeling the slight but unmistakable curve there. "You're pregnant?"

Demetria gasps. "How did you know?"

"Half a cake and a top that could double as a tent?" I shake my head, but I'm smiling. "How far along are you?"

"Almost thirteen weeks. I didn't know. I only found out right after I came back from Vegas," she admits. "It wasn't planned, but...I'm actually excited about it now. Julian is too."

"Was it Mom?" I ask, lowering my voice further. "Did she pressure you into getting married?"

Demetria hesitates, which is answer enough. "Look, it doesn't matter," she says. "I'm pregnant and I love him, and he loves me. It's happening a little faster than expected, but I'm okay with that."

"You're okay with a shotgun wedding?"

"Yeah. Believe it or not. Julian's a good guy and steady in all the ways I'm not." She smiles softly, her hand unconsciously returning to her belly. "I know it seems crazy—especially with my track record. But when I told him about the baby, Athena... you should have seen his face. He wasn't freaking out. He was thrilled."

I'm not convinced but all I can do is be supportive. I reach out and squeeze her hand briefly. "As long as you're sure. I don't want you to do anything you'll regret just because Mom worries about reputation."

The evening air is fragrant with lemon and oregano as we're gathered around the long table on the terrace. Flickering lanterns cast a glow over the feast spread before us: platters of grilled fish, lamb souvlaki, roasted vegetables, and countless small dishes I'm still learning the names of. My wineglass has been refilled so many times I've lost count, and the conversations ebb and flow around me in a blend of Greek and English, courtesy of Athena's extended family, with the occasional French between Julian's parents and his best man.

I'm seated between Athena and Ariana, her nine-year-old niece once removed. Ariana's sister, Delphi, is currently teaching Julian's best man, Phillipe, Greek. He's butchering the pronunciation, which sends the girls into fits of giggles.

"Ef-cha-ri-sto!" Phillipe declares triumphantly, raising his glass. "Did I say that right?"

"Almost!" Ariana calls out from beside me. "But you say it like this: ef-KHA-ri-sto." She emphasizes the middle syllable, her small face serious with the responsibility of her teaching role.

Phillipe repeats the word, still getting it wrong, and the girls dissolve into laughter again.

Across from me, Julian's parents sit quietly, smiling politely but looking slightly overwhelmed. The Beaumont couple are elegant and reserved, a stark contrast to the boisterous Stavros clan. When Julian's father hesitantly reaches for more bread, Athena's mom immediately leaps up to pile more food onto his plate, ignoring his protests.

"You must eat!" she insists. "Tomorrow is a big day! No one leaves my table hungry!"

Demetria and Julian sit at the far end, hands intertwined on the table. Her glow is unmistakable now that Athena has told me in confidence about her pregnancy. I've also noticed Sophia is pouring alcohol-free wine into Demetria's glass. Clearly, this is not a thing until they're married.

Athena's aunt, Ana, is engaged in animated conversation with her son and daughter-in-law, their hands flying as they speak rapid-fire Greek. Every few minutes, Ana turns to include Julian's mother in the conversation, switching to broken English before inevitably slipping back into Greek as the discussion intensifies.

"I warned you," Athena murmurs in my ear. "Total chaos. Are you regretting coming yet?"

I turn to her with a smile. "Not even a little. This is wonderful. All of it."

And it is. The noise, the laughter, the constant flow of food and conversation—it's overwhelming in the best possible way.

"More wine?" Athena's cousin Christos offers, already tilting the bottle toward my glass.

"No thank you, I've really had enough," I say.

When he tries again, Athena steps in. "She said no, Christos." Athena places her hand over my glass. "Are you

trying to get my..." She hesitates for the briefest moment. "...
my friend drunk before the wedding?"

"Just being hospitable," Christos grins, unrepentant.
"Everyone should be a little tipsy before a Greek wedding.
It's tradition!"

"It is not tradition," Sophia corrects from across the
table, wagging her finger. "Do not listen to him, Ruby. He is
a terrible influence."

"The worst," Ana agrees, reaching over to lovingly swat
her son's arm. "Just like his father."

This sets off another round of lively debate, half in
Greek, half in English.

Athena suddenly looks into the living room, then
glances around the crowded table with a puzzled look. She
says something to her mother in Greek, her tone questioning.

Sophia replies, gesturing toward the living room where
one of the staff members is transforming the sofas into
sleeping quarters.

Athena's brow furrows. "But Mom, that's ridiculous,"
she continues in English. "Ruby and I can share my room,
and the twins can take Ruby's room. Right, Ruby?"

It takes me a moment to process what's happening. I've
been so absorbed in the warmth and joy of the evening that
I hadn't considered the sleeping arrangements with so many
people here.

"Of course," I say quickly. "I didn't realize you were
short of bedrooms. I'd be more than happy to share with
Athena."

Sophia looks from Athena to me and back again, then
whispers something to Athena in Greek.

Athena's expression darkens and she stares at her
mother for a long moment. Then she responds in rapid-fire

Greek. She sounds angry and continues even when her mother tries to hush her.

A silence falls over the table. The Greeks stare at Athena and Sophia, their expressions ranging from shock to uncomfortable curiosity. The non-Greeks—Julian's gang and me—exchange confused glances, aware we're missing something significant.

Athena pushes back from the table, and without another word, she strides into the house. I hesitate only briefly before following her, feeling every eye on my back as I go.

I find her in the kitchen, leaning against the fridge.

"What's going on?" I ask softly, keeping my distance. I've never seen her like this—unguarded anger bleeding through her usual composure.

Athena doesn't answer immediately, and I watch as she consciously tries to calm herself.

"My mother thinks we shouldn't share a room," she finally says.

I frown. "Why?"

"She thinks it's inappropriate."

I stare at her, still buffering, until suddenly the pieces click into place. "Because I'm gay?"

Athena nods, a muscle working in her jaw. "She knows, Ruby. I think she knows we're together. She just chose to ignore it." She shakes her head and reaches for my hand, lacing our fingers together.

I glance toward the terrace, suddenly aware of how exposed we are. "It's probably best if you don't touch me like this here."

"I don't care." Athena's grip tightens. "She knows. God knows how long she's known, and still she continued trying to set me up with men. The point is, she's not oblivious. She's choosing to deny who I am. Who we are."

"But she's never said anything to indicate that she knows you're gay, right?"

"No. That would require us actually talking about it." Athena lets out a bitter laugh. "We don't do that in my family. We don't discuss uncomfortable truths. We just pretend they don't exist."

I lean closer, lowering my voice. "Maybe this is your way in. Maybe it's time—"

"For what? A dramatic coming-out at my sister's wedding? That would go over well."

"No, of course not," I say. "But a conversation. A real one, just between you and your mother. She invited me here, Athena. She likes me. That has to count for something."

Athena looks at me, her expression softening slightly. "You don't understand Greek mothers. They can love you fiercely and still never accept certain parts of you. They can invite your 'friend' to family events while deliberately denying the nature of your relationship."

From the terrace comes the sound of renewed conversation, gradually rising in volume. Life continuing despite our momentary drama. Demetria's laugh rings out, musical and carefree.

"Tomorrow is your sister's day," I remind her. "Whatever happens between you and your mother, it should happen after the wedding."

Athena sighs, the fight draining out of her. "Is it my sister's day, though? Because from where I stand, it looks more like my mother's day. It wasn't my sister's idea to get married, and she's always made fun of mom's yacht club and the women who hang out there. Now she's going to have her wedding there, and all mom's friends are invited." She shrugs. "But you're right. I'll let it go for now."

"Hey." I touch her cheek, drawing her gaze to mine. "I'm here for all of it. And if you want me to talk to your mom..."

"Thank you. But this is something I have to do myself." She leans into my touch, her eyes closing briefly. "Let's go back outside. I promise I'll keep the peace before the wedding." She lets out a sarcastic chuckle. "Besides, it'll be interesting to watch my mother dig herself out of this hole. People will surely be asking why it's 'inappropriate' for us to share a room."

I can't help but laugh along. "Okay. That sounds uncomfortable."

"It will be," she says. "But Mom brought this on herself. If she wants to play the denial game, she'd better be ready for the championship round."

FIFTY-EIGHT
ATHENA

I pause at the threshold of the living room, which has been transformed into an impromptu bridal salon. Our normally calm space is now a whirlwind of activity and loud chatter. The furniture has been pushed against the walls to make space for five ornate full-length mirrors arranged in a semicircle. Portable styling stations festooned with white and pink ribbons, fresh flowers, and enough products to stock a small beauty supply store crowd every available surface. The air is thick with competing scents of hairspray and perfume, and it's making me nauseous.

A few bridesmaids in various states of preparation are sitting behind the stations, others are drinking champagne and animatedly talking, all dressed in matching pale pink dresses. Makeup artists and hair stylists flit between the women, wielding brushes and curling irons like weapons.

Demetria sits in the center on what can only be described as a makeshift throne—our grandmother's antique Louis XV chair that normally resides in the formal living room, now decorated with fresh white roses. She's sipping something that's supposed to look like champagne and laughing as a stylist arranges her dark curls into an intricate updo. Her bridal gown hangs from a stand nearby, protected by a garment bag.

I haven't slept. Not really. After last night's confrontation, Ruby insisted on sleeping in the guest room—"to keep the peace," she said. I'd almost protested but knew she was right. This house has enough tension without adding more fuel to the fire. So instead of the comfort of her body against mine, I spent hours staring at the ceiling, replaying my mother's words in my head. Every creak of the old house made me wish I could sneak down the hall to Ruby's room, but I stayed put, trapped in my childhood bed with my very adult frustrations. I opened an email from Demetria with the table plan attached and my frustration mounted.

When I finally drifted off around dawn, my dreams were a jumble of memories—Elena, my father's funeral, my casino opening, Ruby's face the night we met. I woke disoriented and irritable, reaching for a body that wasn't there.

And now, several hours and one too many family interactions later, I have to wear pink. Soft pink, to be precise—a color I've actively avoided since childhood, when my mother dressed Demetria and me in matching outfits that made us look like twin scoops of strawberry ice cream. All to ensure I don't upstage Demetria, the allegedly virginal bride in white, whose pregnancy we're all pretending not to notice.

The men are getting ready in the east wing of the house —Julian and his groomsmen safely segregated from all this feminine energy as tradition demands—while we navigate this absurd charade. The irony would be comical if it weren't so infuriating.

I refused the billowing soft pink bridesmaid dress that would have made me look like an escapee from a 1980s prom night. Instead, I brought my own pantsuit with a satin wrap jacket in the palest blush and matching pants—a compromise that honors the color scheme without compromising my dignity. The outfit hangs in my closet upstairs, waiting, while I steel myself for the inevitable battle about hair and makeup.

My mother and Aunt Ana are already dressed and coiffed to perfection, looking like they're attending a royal wedding. Mom's wearing a powder-blue dress with an elaborate lace overlay, her hair swept up in a style that surely required an engineering degree to create.

She spots me hovering in the doorway and rushes over, her Chanel No. 5 arriving a split second before she does. Her face is a mask of forced cheerfulness, the kind she wears when she's determined to maintain appearances despite whatever chaos might be unfolding beneath the surface.

"Athena! Finally. Where were you? Everyone is almost ready, and you haven't even started." She surveys me with the critical eye that has made me second-guess my appearance since adolescence. "They're waiting to do your hair—we've saved you a place next to Ruby." She gestures toward where Ruby sits, a makeup artist applying something to her eyes.

I see her, and my heart does that ridiculous flutter that still catches me off guard. Ruby looks relaxed, smiling at something the makeup artist has said. She's in her element here, comfortable in a way I never am around beauty rituals and feminine traditions. She catches my eye and gives me a subtle wink.

"No, Mom," I say, stepping farther into the chaos. "I've already done my hair, and I don't need makeup. I prefer it simple." The thought of sitting in that chair while some stranger tugs at my scalp and covers my face in products I never use makes my skin crawl.

My mother's smile doesn't falter, but her eyes narrow slightly, the way they always do when I'm not following her script. "Don't be ridiculous. The hairdressers are geniuses— they've worked with celebrities. Your hair needs..." She makes a vague gesture toward my head, somehow implying with one hand movement that my entire appearance requires professional intervention. "And where's your dress?"

"My hair is fine," I insist, resisting the urge to touch it self-consciously. I own part of the Vegas Strip, but some- how, my mother still manages to make me feel like an awkward teenager. "I brought my own pantsuit. I'll change and be ready in twenty minutes. I just came to get a coffee."

"Pantsuit?" Her voice rises almost an octave, drawing the attention of several bridesmaids, who quickly pretend they weren't eavesdropping. "But all the bridesmaids are wearing the same pink dresses! We ordered you one too." She gestures to Demetria's friends.

"I'm not a bridesmaid, I'm the maid of honor," I reply, trying to keep my voice level despite the growing tension headache behind my eyes. "And my outfit is perfectly appropriate."

My mother sighs, the sound heavy with disappoint- ment. "At least let them do your makeup. Look at what they've done for Ruby." She points across the room. "Doesn't she look beautiful?"

I turn toward Ruby again and smile. She's wearing a deep-emerald dress, the color complementing her auburn hair and making her eyes seem even more vibrant. The fabric drapes her body in a way that's both elegant and sensual, revealing just enough skin to be alluring without crossing into inappropriate territory. Her hair has been styled in loose waves, and her makeup brings out the delicate structure of her cheekbones and the fullness of her lips.

She looks up, catches me staring, and returns my smile —that private smile that's reserved just for me, the one that makes the corners of her eyes crease slightly. Of course she looks beautiful. She's breathtaking.

Something inside me snaps, and all the tension from last night, all the pretense, all the years of half-truths and strategic omissions—they collapse at once.

"What do you want me to say, Mom?" My voice comes out louder than intended, cutting through the cheerful chatter. "I don't get it. Yes, Ruby looks beautiful." The room falls silent as every head turns toward me, conversations dying mid-sentence. Demetria's eyes widen, her hand frozen with a champagne flute halfway to her lips. "To me, she's the most beautiful woman in the world, but that's not what you want to hear, is it?"

My mother's face goes slack with shock, and her eyes widen as she takes a half-step backward, bumping into a makeup table and sending a collection of brushes scattering.

Even the hired photographers have stopped clicking, their cameras lowering slowly as they register the unfolding drama.

I take a deep breath, feeling light-headed with a strange mix of terror and relief. The secret I've guarded for so long is out there now, impossible to take back. I lower my voice with effort, trying to regain some control, but the words keep spilling out.

"So you can save yourself the effort of seating me next to your friend's single son at dinner," I continue, meeting my mother's stunned gaze. "I'm only interested in Ruby." The words feel both foreign and completely natural on my tongue. "And you know it, don't you? You just pretend you don't. Just like you pretend your adult daughter is still a virgin."

I gesture toward Demetria, who's instinctively placed a hand over her slightly rounded abdomen, her eyes darting between me and our mother like she's watching a tennis match where the ball might explode at any moment.

"And in a few days, we'll all celebrate that she got pregnant on her wedding night," I continue, unable to stop now that I've started. "Why all the pretending, Mom? What decade are we living in?"

My mother's face has drained of color. She opens her mouth, but no sound emerges, perhaps for the first time in her life rendered completely speechless. Her hands flutter uselessly at her sides before she clasps them together tightly, her knuckles turning white with the pressure. Behind her, Demetria stares at me. Her stylist has frozen with a section of hair held aloft.

"I'm not saying anything that people here don't already know," I continue. "Literally everyone in this room knows Demetria is pregnant, and we're all pretending otherwise. The way we're all pretending I'm not gay." I look around at the silent audience, meeting several pairs of averted eyes. "It doesn't make sense, Mom. It's got to stop."

No one seems to know what to do. The makeup artists exchange glances, silently communicating about whether they should continue working or flee the scene. Demetria's bridesmaids studiously examine their manicures, their shoes, the ceiling—looking anywhere but at the family drama unfolding before them. Only Aunt Ana seems completely unfazed, taking a long sip of her champagne like she's watching a particularly entertaining episode of her favorite soap opera.

My mother's eyes fill with tears. Not the dramatic kind she's prone to when she wants to make a point—those strategic tears she deploys to win arguments or extract promises—but genuine, shocked tears that make her makeup begin to run in dark rivulets down her cheeks. She looks smaller suddenly, more fragile than I can ever remember seeing her. The formidable matriarch who has ruled our family with absolute authority since my father's death seems to diminish before my eyes, her shoulders slumping under the weight of the truths she can no longer deny.

"How dare you," she whispers, but there's no heat in it. Just hurt and perhaps the realization that her constructed version of reality has just crumbled beyond repair. "Today of all days."

"I'm sorry for the timing," I say, and I mean it. Some part of me knows I should have found a more private moment for this confrontation, that dropping this bomb in a room full of witnesses on Demetria's wedding day is not my finest moment. "But I'm not sorry for the truth."

Ruby gets up and crosses the room to stand beside me. Her hand finds mine without hesitation.

"Mrs. Stavros," she begins. "I love your daughter. That's the simple truth of it."

The words hit me with unexpected force. We've said them to each other in private, whispered them in the dark, but hearing her declare it so openly, in front of my family and strangers alike... It's intense.

Ruby takes a deep breath, her expression softening. "When my wife died, my mother said something to me I'll never forget. She told me she was worried about me—that she always thought Claire would be the one to make sure I was okay, and Claire wasn't there anymore." Her voice trembles slightly, but she steadies it. "My mother worried because that's what mothers do, isn't it? They want to know their children are okay when they're not nearby to check on them."

My mother stares at Ruby, caught off guard by this unexpected turn in the conversation.

"I can promise you, Mrs. Stavros," Ruby continues, squeezing my hand, "that I will take care of Athena. I will be by her side through good times and bad. I will take that worry off your shoulders." She pauses, her gaze unwavering. "Isn't that what every mother wants? To know their child is loved and cared for?"

My mother's gaze drops to our joined hands, lingering on our interlaced fingers, then rises to meet Ruby's eyes again. Something passes between them—a silent communication I can't quite decipher. Then, to my astonishment, she nods once, slowly, a gesture of acknowledgment if not quite acceptance.

I wait for her to say something. I think she's trying, but no words come out.

Demetria rises from her chair, her expression carrying the particular exasperation that only siblings can inspire—the look that says *I could kill you right now, but I also understand why you did it.*

"All right, everyone," she says to the room at large, clapping her hands together in a gesture so reminiscent of our mother that it would be funny under different circumstances. "The show is over. I'm getting married in four hours, and I'd like my hair to be symmetrical. So let's all get on with it, shall we? I'm not pregnant and my sister is not gay." She grins at her audience, then points to me. "And my sister needs some waterproof mascara. Don't argue with me, Athena. I'm the bride."

The room erupts into nervous laughter, a collective release of held breath. Demetria returns to her chair, settling back while she shoots me a smile. Her hand still rests protectively over her belly—but openly now, without shame, the way it should have been all along. Only when I touch my cheeks do I realize I've been crying.

The yacht club gleams white against the deepening blue of the Aegean as the sun begins its descent toward the horizon. The Mediterranean is dotted with distant islands and passing sailboats the way I imagined it's been for hundreds of years. The ceremony took place on the seaside terrace of the Santorini Yacht Club, where an ancient stone arbor was draped with cascading white roses and delicate greenery, the shimmering waters spread before us like a living painting. Now, as evening settles in, we've moved to the dining hall with its soaring ceilings, marble columns, and crystal chandeliers.

I marvel at how seamlessly the day has progressed despite this morning's dramatic revelation. Like a stone tossed into water, Athena's declaration caused momentary ripples before the surface smoothed once more. The wedding proceeded as planned—beautiful, emotional, and perfect in its authenticity. Demetria was radiant in her flowy, bohemian dress, designed to hide her tiny baby bump. Julian couldn't take his eyes off her as they exchanged vows.

The club is as exclusive as Athena described—a modern architectural structure nestled in a protected harbor on the eastern side of the island, accessible only by a winding private road that keeps tourists at bay. Founded in the 1920s, its membership remains a closely guarded privilege passed through generations of wealthy families. The main building curves around a sheltered cove where yachts bob at anchor, and inside, the decor balances old-world opulence with subtle nautical touches.

I sit at the large round table designated for immediate family—a placement I'm told is significant—watching Athena squirm beside George, the recently divorced son of her mother's oldest friend. He's handsome enough, with dark curls and the confidence of a man who's rarely heard the word "no." For the past twenty minutes, he's been visibly trying to impress Athena.

Athena nods politely, but I can tell she's not in the slightest interested in his bragging. She looks stunning in her pale-pink pantsuit, but when I first saw her in it, I couldn't help but giggle, as I've only ever seen her in white. Earlier, she whispered that she felt like "a stick of cotton candy with arms and legs" and kept adjusting the sleeves as if the color might somehow rub off on her skin if she stayed still too long.

My own dinner companion, Andreas, has been far less persistent since our illuminating conversation an hour ago. When he first sat beside me, full of compliments about my dress and hair, I waited for an appropriate moment before telling him I had no interest in men.

To his credit, after the initial shock—Greeks can be surprisingly conservative for a culture with such sexually open-minded ancient history—he relaxed, and our conversation has since flowed naturally. We've discovered a shared interest in art history, and he's been telling me about his favorite museums in Europe.

Across the room, Sophia catches my eye. She's been doing this all evening—sending me small smiles, tentative but genuine. It's as if she's trying to telegraph that she likes me, that she accepts me, without actually saying the words. Earlier, during the ceremony, she squeezed my hand when I teared up during the vows, a gesture that surprised us both. And at the reception line, she introduced me to several cousins as "Ruby, Athena's *special friend* from America," her emphasis suggesting she was trying to find the right words.

There's a way forward here, I'm certain of it. Not an easy path, perhaps, but one we can navigate together.

The banquet has been extraordinary, an endless procession of dishes that showcase the best of Greek cuisine, and as the staff begins clearing the plates from the main course, the band takes their position at the corner of the dance floor. The sun has nearly disappeared, leaving behind a canvas of pinks and purples in the sky.

I catch fragments of conversation around me in Greek. I may not understand the words, but I recognize the tone of gossip when I hear it. All day, there have been whispers and glances, conversations that falter when Athena or I approach. News travels quickly in small communities, and by now, most guests know about this morning's revelation. I've seen the looks—some curious, some disapproving, some surprisingly supportive. An elderly woman I'm told is Athena's godmother patted my hand earlier and said something in Greek that made Demetria laugh and Athena blush furiously. When I asked for a translation, Demetria just said, "She approves of Athena's taste."

Demetria and Julian rise from their seats at the head

table to applause. The band begins a slow, romantic melody as they move to the center of the dance floor. Julian takes her in his arms with such tenderness that I feel a pang in my chest. Their first dance is beautiful, and they move together as if they've been doing this for years, not months, her white gown swirling around them. When Julian whispers something in her ear that makes her laugh, the sound rings clear across the room, and the guests smile in response.

Other couples begin to join them on the dance floor—Julian's parents, Athena's cousin and his wife, and an elderly couple. Soon the floor is filled with swaying bodies, the single guests remaining seated at the tables, watching.

Sophia's gaze travels around the table until it lands on me again. Her eyes find mine, then deliberately shift to Athena. She gives me a small nod, subtle but unmistakable. An invitation. Permission.

My heart racing, I stand and smooth the front of my dress, then walk over to where Athena sits. George stops mid-sentence, confusion crossing his features as he looks up at me. But I focus only on Athena as I extend my hand.

"Would you like to dance?"

Athena's eyebrows shoot up in surprise, but her lips stretch into a wide smile.

"Yes," she says, placing her hand in mine. "I would love to."

We move together onto the dance floor, aware of the whispers that follow us. Athena's arm slides around my waist and my hand finds her shoulder. The band is playing something slow and sweet, and she pulls me closer. "You look beautiful tonight," she murmurs.

"So do you," I reply. "Even in pink."

Athena laughs, the sound vibrating through her chest

where it presses against mine. "Enjoy it while it lasts. I'm burning this suit the minute we get back to Vegas." She looks around, and immediately, heads turn the other way as if they hadn't just been watching us. "Look at me," she says. "I'm dancing with my partner at my sister's wedding and the world hasn't ended."

"You're still standing. That's the thing about fears—they're never quite as terrifying once you face them. Though I think your mother might need another glass of wine."

I nod toward the family table where Sophia has become the center of an impromptu gathering. Three elegant older women have descended upon her like a flock of well-groomed vultures. They lean in close, gesturing occasionally toward us. Sophia sits rigidly in her chair, her smile fixed in place as she clutches her wineglass like a lifeline.

"I never thought I'd say this, as I could have killed her this morning, but poor Mom." Athena watches her mother with a complexity of emotion. "She's handling the unofficial morality committee of Santorini." She sighs. "Look at her spine, though—straight as a rod. She won't give them the satisfaction of seeing her buckle, even now. That's where Demetria gets her stubbornness from," she adds with a flicker of a smile.

As the song transitions to something livelier, Demetria and Julian appear beside us on the dance floor.

"I'm sorry about the drama this morning," Athena says, looking unusually sheepish. "I didn't mean to come out in the bridal suite, and I shouldn't have mentioned your pregnancy."

Demetria snorts with laughter. "Please! You were right. Everyone there knew I was pregnant—I told them myself. If anything, you've given the other guests something to gossip about besides my weight gain and suspiciously rushed wedding." She pats her barely-there bump. "Twenty years from now, everyone will still be talking about the day Athena Stavros wore pink *and* danced with a woman." She grins at me. "Welcome to the family, Ruby."

SIXTY

ATHENA

I close my suitcase, listening to the distant sounds of laughter drifting up from the terrace. Ruby stands by the balcony doors, gazing out at the sea, and for a moment, I simply watch her, memorizing the curve of her profile against the backdrop of sea and sky.

"I'm going to miss this view," she says without turning around. "The desert has its own kind of beauty, but this..." She gestures toward the panorama before her. "This is something else entirely."

I move to stand beside her, my hand on the small of her back. "We can come back whenever you want. The house is always here."

Ruby leans into my touch. Last night, she slept in my room, in my bed. No sneaking around, no pretending.

"Do you think your mother will ever fully accept us?" Ruby asks.

"I think she already does, in her own way," I say. "Acceptance for her doesn't look like rainbow flags and pride parades. It looks like making sure you have the right pillow and that you're included in family affairs." I brush a strand of hair from her face, letting my fingers linger against her cheek. "Rome wasn't built in a day, and my mother's worldview won't change overnight. But we're still speaking, so I'm counting it as a win."

We're interrupted by a knock on the open door, and Nikos stands there. "Ms. Stavros, the car is ready whenever you are."

"Thank you, Nikos. We'll be down in a moment."

We gather our bags and make our way downstairs. As we step out onto the terrace, I'm greeted by the sight of my mother, Demetria, Julian, his parents, and his best man enjoying a leisurely lunch. Aunt Ana is there too, gesturing wildly while she dominates the conversation.

Demetria spots us first and waves us over. She's still in her silk pajamas, looking more like my sister than the elegant bride of yesterday.

"We're off," I announce, setting our bags down by the door.

Julian rises from his seat to give us a hug. "Thank you both for being here. It meant the world to us, and it was great to meet you."

"Are you sure you can't stay longer?" Demetria asks. She gestures to the empty chairs. "We're just having lunch before Julian's parents leave, and we're not going on our honeymoon until tomorrow."

"Unfortunately, we can't," I reply. "We both have work, but we'll stay for longer next time."

Demetria pouts playfully, then brightens. "Well, I guess I'll have to be satisfied with gaining such a fabulous sister-in-law." She beams at Ruby. "Or should I say, future sister-in-law? I'm not quite sure what the protocol is when there's no ring yet."

Ruby blushes but laughs, taking Demetria's teasing in stride. "Whatever you want to call me, I'm honored."

Aunt Ana rises from her chair, coming over to embrace me. "Goodbye, sweetheart," she says, kissing both my cheeks. "You've certainly given us something to talk about."

I can't help but smile at her tone—half-scandalized, half-delighted. Ana has always thrived on gossip, especially when it involves her wealthier sister's family. This week must be like Christmas for her.

Ruby moves to the table. "I wish we could stay today," she says with a sigh. "The sea looks so clear. I'd love to take a dip, but I have some very big deadlines coming up."

My mother rises from her seat, smoothing down her linen dress as she approaches us. "Then we'll see you soon," she says. "You're always welcome here." She pauses, and then—remarkably—a small, almost humorous smile plays at the corners of her mouth. "And you can sleep in Athena's room next time."

The significance of her statement is not lost on anyone present. It's as close to a blessing as my mother can manage.

Ruby's eyes widen briefly before she recovers with a playful smirk. "Well, guess what? I already did," she replies, the hint of mischief in her voice sending a ripple of surprised laughter around the table.

Even my mother chuckles, and I close the distance between us to hug her.

"Thank you, Mom," I say. "For everything." The words carry more weight than their simplicity suggests.

I'm grateful for her love, for her acceptance, reluctant as it may be. For the cracks in her walls of denial, for her willingness to grow beyond the boundaries of her upbringing. For choosing love over tradition, for welcoming Ruby into our family.

My mother hugs me back longer than she ever has. Then, with the dignity that has carried her through all of life's challenges—my father's death, raising two headstrong daughters alone, navigating the expectations of Greek society—she straightens her shoulders and dabs at her eyes with a handkerchief embroidered with our family monogram.

"Your father would be proud of you," she says softly. The words catch me off guard, piercing straight through my defenses. "He always said you were the strongest of us all." She touches my cheek briefly. "I will need some time to get comfortable with this, Athena. But you are my daughter, and I love you. Nothing changes that."

I step back and swallow down the lump in my throat. In this family, we navigate our emotions through the safe channels of ritual and propriety. Some habits die hard, even in moments of revelation.

She nods once, a sharp dip of her chin, and steps back into her role.

"We need to leave now if we're going to make our flight," I say, and Demetria jumps up and envelops me in a fierce hug. I place my hand on her belly, smiling down at the small bump. "Make sure you eat well. We need Junior to grow strong and healthy."

"Junior?" Demetria laughs. "We're thinking Hunter for a boy, Juliet for a girl."

My mother's gasp is audible. "Hunter? Juliet?" She shakes her head vigorously. "Absolutely not. The baby will have a proper Greek name. Perhaps Alexandros after your father, or Sophia if it's a girl."

So much for my mother's newfound restraint. Her moment of emotional vulnerability lasted all of five minutes before she snapped back to her usual self—opinionated, unstoppable, and utterly convinced of her rightness in all matters.

Julian tentatively raises a hand. "Actually, we were hoping to honor my grandmother—"

"Your grandmother?" Aunt Ana interjects. "What was her name?"

"Juliet," Julian says, stating the obvious. "I was very close to her."

My mother's eyebrows shoot upward. "Ju-li-et?" She pronounces each syllable as if testing a questionable food. "I don't know."

"It's French, Mother," Demetria sighs. "Julian is French."

"The baby is half-Greek," my mother counters. "And a Stavros."

"What about Dimitri for a boy?" Julian's father suggests, clearly attempting diplomacy. "It's similar to Demetria and has roots in both cultures."

"Or Chloe for a girl," Julian's mother adds. "After Julian's aunt. That's a Greek name, isn't it?"

"Chloe is acceptable," my mother concedes as if granting a major diplomatic concession. "But I still think Sophia is better. Six generations of firstborn daughters in my family have been named Sophia."

"Five," Aunt Ana corrects. "You're forgetting that great-aunt Calliope broke the tradition."

"She did not! Her full name was Sophia Calliope."

As Aunt Ana and Mom launch into what promises to be a detailed family history debate, Ruby and I back away slowly, collecting our bags without a word. By the time we're sliding into the back seat of the car, the debate has evolved into a full-blown argument because I can hear them even at the front of the house.

"They may still be arguing when we land in Vegas," I say as Nikos pulls away from the villa. "But Demetria will do exactly what she wants anyway."

SIXTY-ONE
RUBY

Athena sits beside me in the limo, her fingers laced with mine on the leather seat between us. She's been quiet since our plane landed, perhaps processing everything that's happened in the whirlwind of the past few days. I understand. She's come out to not just her staff but her entire family, danced with me at her sister's wedding, and gained her mother's tentative acceptance—milestones she never thought possible.

As we turn onto the winding road leading to The Ridges, I squeeze her hand, drawing her attention back to me. "My place or yours?"

She meets my eyes and smiles. "It's up to you."

I consider for a moment, though the decision has already made itself. "I prefer your house. Besides, Zeus will be anxious to see you. We can't leave him alone another night."

Athena chuckles. "I knew it. You do love him."

"I never said that," I protest, but my smile betrays me.

She leans forward to address the driver. "We'll go to my house," she says.

I rest my head against Athena's shoulder, suddenly aware of how exhausted I am. "I'll have to get up earlier tomorrow to swing by my place and change for work."

"You could always consider bringing some of your clothes over permanently," Athena suggests casually. "So you don't have to worry about that anymore. It would be practical."

I lift my head to study her face, taking in the neutrality of her expression, the way she's trying to make this sound like a simple logistical matter rather than what it truly is— an invitation to further intertwine our lives. "Sure," I say with a teasing grin. "Practical."

We both know what this is. Not just convenience, but a step. A small one, perhaps, but significant, nonetheless.

The car pulls up to Athena's gate. Home. As the driver retrieves our luggage from the trunk, I turn to Athena. "Are you busy tomorrow? I thought maybe we could have lunch at that new place on Charleston."

"I can't do lunch," she says. "I'm meeting with Zara Nova and her manager. But dinner would be perfect."

I arch an eyebrow. "Again? If she were queer, I'd be jealous."

Athena gives me a look I can't quite interpret, then glances toward the driver who's taking our suitcases to the front door. She lowers her voice. "Well, about that... Can you swear this stays between us?"

"Sure." My curiosity piqued, I lean closer. "Just pretend I heard it in the club and that nasty-ass NDA applies."

"Let's talk inside," she says, nodding to the driver as he places the last of our bags by the door. "Thank you. Have a good night."

I raise my hand as he retreats to the car, then follow Athena into the house, pulling our luggage behind us. The moment the door closes, I drop everything. "Okay, spill. What about Zara Nova?"

Athena sets her keys in the crystal bowl on the entry table. "She's bisexual," she says, her voice still low though we're alone now. "She hasn't had the chance to date women since college, and she wants to explore that side of herself."

"What?" I gasp, momentarily stunned by this revelation. "Okay, that's truly NDA-worthy information."

"I know," Athena agrees. "She's understandably concerned about discretion, given her public profile, so I was thinking of introducing her to someone from the club. My members are discreet, so it should be safe for her."

"That's actually brilliant," I say. "Will you take her to the club?"

Athena shakes her head. "No, I don't think so. I don't know if I can trust her yet, and she has paparazzi following her everywhere she goes. It would be too risky."

A soft meow comes from the landing, and we both look up to see Zeus padding down the stairs, his golden eyes fixed on Athena, tail rising in greeting. He quickens his pace, letting out another vocal meow.

"Hello, my little prince," Athena coos, immediately dropping to her knees to greet him. "Did you miss me? Has Asha been taking good care of you?"

Zeus butts his head against her hand, purring so loudly I can hear it from where I stand. He weaves between her knees, rubbing himself against her in undisguised affection. Then, to my surprise, he breaks away from Athena and approaches me, repeating the same greeting ritual against my legs.

I crouch down too, running my fingers through his soft fur. "Hello to you too, baby. Are you coming up to bed with us tonight?"

He purrs louder, pressing his head more firmly into my palm. This strangely majestic creature, who once seemed so aloof, has decided he likes me. Maybe he knows I'm not just visiting anymore.

A yawn catches me by surprise, and I cover my mouth with the back of my hand.

"Tired?" Athena asks.

"Exhausted," I admit. "It was a lot in such a short time span, but it was worth it." I rise to my feet. "It was so special to see where you come from, to meet your family. To witness that side of you."

Athena stands as well. "I honestly never thought that would happen, ever." Her voice catches slightly. "Not in that way. Not with you by my side, openly." In the soft light of her entryway, with Zeus winding figure-eights around our ankles, her eyes well up. "You've changed my life," she says, the words coming out in a rush as if she's been holding them back. "Because of you, I don't have to hide anymore. I can be myself—all of myself—for the first time."

"You've changed mine too," I tell her, stepping closer until our bodies nearly touch. "If it wasn't for you, I'd still be locked in that office until midnight, moving through each day without feeling anything. Existing but not living.

"I love you," I say, the words still new enough to send a thrill through me. "And I love that we found each other. That we recognized something in each other that needed healing."

Athena's hand rises to cup my cheek, and she strokes me with her thumb. "I never expected you," she whispers. "Nothing has been the same since I met you."

She kisses me then, slow and tender, her body curving into mine. When we break apart, she takes my hand and leads me toward the stairs, toward the bedroom that no longer feels like just hers, Zeus already bounding ahead of us as if to ensure we follow.

In this quiet house on the edge of the desert, with the lights of Vegas glimmering in the distance, I've found something I thought was lost forever—not just love, but possibility. The chance to build something new from the ashes of what came before. Not to replace what was lost, but to honor it by living fully again.

Perhaps that's what healing looks like in the end—not the absence of scars, but the creation of new patterns around them. This is where we begin again. Not at the start, but somewhere in the middle of our stories, carrying all that came before, yet open to what lies ahead.

EPILOGUE

ONE YEAR LATER

I smile as I cradle Hunter in my arms. He's warm and solid, his dark curls—so like Demetria's—nestled against the crook of my elbow. His eyes study my face with that peculiar solemnity only babies seem capable of. Almost seven months old and already sizing me up.

"What's your verdict, little man?" I whisper, bouncing him gently. "Do I pass inspection?"

He blinks slowly in response, his tiny mouth forming a perfect "o" before his chubby fingers find the gold chain around my neck. I carefully detach his grip. One thing I've learned about babies—they're stronger than they look.

"You're a menace, you know that?" I murmur, touching the tip of his button nose. "Just like your mother. Grabbing everything that catches your eye."

Ruby's mother is setting the long outdoor dining table. Martha Walsh looks in her element, arranging silverware while humming along to my playlist. It's been sweet watching her these past three days—how easily she slips between doting grandmother-figure with Hunter and spirited conversationalist with my mother.

The sound of laughter drifts from the kitchen where Ruby and my mother are preparing an array of side dishes for tonight's dinner. The unlikely friendship that's developed between them continues to amaze me. Two years ago, I couldn't have imagined my mother willingly spending time with my partner, let alone giggling together over cooking mishaps. Yet here we are—Sophia Stavros, pillar of Greek Orthodox tradition, teaching my partner the fine art of making authentic tzatziki.

Out on the terrace, Ruby's father and Julian have appointed themselves guardians of flame and meat. David Walsh gestures with a pair of tongs while Julian nods seriously, absorbing whatever barbecue wisdom is being imparted.

Hunter lets out a string of babbling sounds, his tiny hands reaching up to pat my cheeks.

"Is that so?" I reply, pretending to understand his nonsensical commentary. "Well, I completely agree. Men and their obsession with fire is prehistoric, but we humor them because the end result is usually delicious."

I'm still not entirely comfortable holding him, afraid I'll break this perfect, fragile creature. But Demetria insists that I need the practice and keeps depositing him in my arms. She and Julian are great parents, especially for two artistic souls who once swore they valued freedom above all else. They were delighted for everyone to babysit while they went out in Vegas last night, not returning until the early hours—a rare night of freedom they clearly needed.

Julian's show in New York received rave reviews, but they decided to settle in Santorini, both agreeing it was a better environment for Hunter to grow up in. I'm sure the fact that my mother—the trusted babysitter—lives nearby had something to do with it too; I can tell Demetria is used to being heavily dependent on her.

"You're quite the little diplomat, aren't you?" I say to Hunter as he yawns widely. "Bringing everyone together like this. We would all move mountains for you."

Hunter responds by drooling on my white shirt just as Ruby emerges balancing two enormous bowls of salad. She's wearing denim shorts and a green T-shirt, looking relaxed in a way that still feels like a small miracle.

"Look at you two," she says, setting the bowls on the table. "You're a natural."

"I think that's overstating things considerably," I reply. "We've reached a temporary truce. He doesn't scream, I don't panic."

Ruby laughs and moves closer, leaning down to plant a kiss on Hunter's forehead. "Hey there, little nugget." She smooths a hand over his curls, then straightens to meet my eyes. "You look cute with a baby, you know that? It suits you."

Something warm blooms in my chest. We've talked about children. Ruby wants them, I'm open to it because it's important to her. But seeing Ruby's expression, the softness in her gaze as she looks at Hunter, then at me...it makes it easy to imagine us as starting a family.

"I'm just the backup," I say, deflecting as I always do when feelings threaten to overwhelm me. "The emergency aunt when everyone else is busy."

"Mm-hmm," Ruby murmurs, clearly unconvinced. She brushes a strand of hair from my face, tucking it behind my ear. "I'll grab the rest of the salads. Then I need to run home quickly to get more wine. I think we demolished most of the bottles last night."

"No need," I tell her. "I brought some over earlier. They're already in the wine fridge."

I'm struck by how seamlessly we've built our life together. The club runs like clockwork and everyone knows we belong together. We still play there, exploring boundaries and desires, but it's in our bed, in our home, where we make love.

Ruby has moved in with me officially, but she's kept her house as well. We're using it as a guest house, which has proven useful with both our families in town and when we're not expecting visitors, we rent it out privately. The office has been securely locked, ensuring no one can see the comings and goings on the driveway when club members arrive.

Demetria appears with Sarah and Erik in tow. "Look who I found!"

Sarah and Erik have been over regularly since moving to Vegas a while back—Erik for his new position in marketing at a major casino group, and Sarah, now a junior associate at Ruby's firm.

"Oh wow," Sarah says, taking in the scene before her. "I didn't realize the entire extended family would be here!" Her eyes widen at the sight of Hunter in my arms. "And the baby! He's so cute. Can I hold him?"

"If you can pry him away from Athena," Demetria says with a grin. "She's been hogging him all afternoon."

"I have not been 'hogging' him," I protest, even as I instinctively tighten my hold. "He's been perfectly content where he is."

"Translation: 'Back off, he's mine,'" Ruby stage-whispers to Sarah, who laughs.

I roll my eyes but carefully transfer Hunter to Sarah's waiting arms. She coos at him immediately, and Erik leans in, making ridiculous faces that somehow charm Hunter into a gummy smile.

"Man, we are not ready for one of these," Erik says.

"Speak for yourself," Sarah replies, not taking her eyes off Hunter. "I wouldn't mind..."

My mother emerges from the kitchen, wiping her hands on a dishcloth. "Ah, the young couple has arrived! Good, good. Now we are only waiting for..." She pauses, glancing at me. "Who else is coming, Athena?"

"Zara," I reply. "She should be here any minute and she may or may not bring a plus one."

"Zara?" Demetria asks. "Who's Zara?"

"Zara Nova. The singer," I say.

Demetria chuckles, assuming I'm joking. Then her eyes widen comically as realization dawns. "Wait. Seriously? Why didn't you tell me? I would have made more of an effort!" She gestures down at her outfit—yoga pants and a loose t-shirt with visible baby food stains on the shoulder.

"Don't worry," I assure her. "I told her it was super casual so please don't make a big deal out of it."

"Zara Nova is coming to dinner?" Sarah frowns as she looks up from baby Hunter.

"Who is Zara Nova?" my mother asks, joining the conversation.

As if on cue, the gate buzzes again and moments later Zara steps into the backyard, radiant in a simple pink jumpsuit, her dark curls piled on top of her head. She's carrying a bottle of champagne and wearing oversize shades.

"Sorry I'm late," she calls, her smile brightening as she takes in our gathering. "Traffic on the Strip was a nightmare." She leans into me, then adds in a lower voice, "My date couldn't make it."

"Let me guess," I murmur. "Stuck in Washington?"

"You know it," Zara sighs dramatically. "She sends her love, of course." She moves through our gathering, charming Ruby's parents, accepting a glass of wine from Julian, bending to coo at Hunter. It's been a privilege watching her find her footing over these past months, both professionally and personally.

My mother introduces herself to Zara, then claps her hands together as she addresses the group. "Please, sit, everyone!" she announces, claiming the head of the table with the authority that comes naturally to her. "Sit, sit! The food is getting cold!"

Platters of grilled meats and vegetables sit at the center of the table, surrounded by bowls of colorful salads, rice, dips, and baskets of bread.

There's a flurry of movement as everyone finds a place. I end up between Ruby and Sarah, with Hunter's high chair positioned nearby. Wine is poured, water glasses filled, plates passed.

Ruby's hand finds mine under the table, warm and familiar against my palm. I glance at her, taking in the subtle lines around her eyes, the way her whole face illuminates when she smiles. Love still catches me by surprise sometimes—how completely it has transformed my life, how vastly different my world looks now.

My gaze travels around the table. My mother is in deep conversation with David Walsh about Greek versus American medical practices. Demetria helps Julian feed Hunter while Martha plates for them. Sarah and Erik listen raptly as Zara tells them about her planned world tour, and Ruby beside me, simply sits contently, like me, enjoying the moment.

This tableau before me represents everything I once feared and now cherish. I'm a partner, daughter, sister, aunt, friend. The path that brought us here was neither straight nor smooth, but standing at this destination, I wouldn't change a single step.

———

Don't miss Zara Nova's story in The Residency. Coming Fall 2025

AFTERWORD

I hope you've loved reading Hedonism as much as we've loved writing it. If you've enjoyed this book, would you consider rating it and reviewing it? Reviews are very important to authors and we'd be really grateful!

Sign up to Lise Gold's monthly newsletter and get a free novella! **https://bit.ly/2GclQzf**

ABOUT THE AUTHOR

Lise Gold crafts sapphic romance under her own name and sapphic erotica as Madeleine Taylor. A globetrotter with roots in London to Norwegian and English parents, her childhood across four countries shaped her boundless curiosity and love for diverse settings. When researching her novels, Lise can often be found in far-flung destinations, notebook in hand.

In 2018, after fifteen years in design, Lise traded sketches for full-time storytelling and never looked back. When away from her writing desk, she cherishes sun-filled days, good food and wine, and adores animals of all kinds. She lives with her beloved dog in their London home.

ALSO BY LISE GOLD

Lily's Fire

Beyond the Skyline

The Cruise

French Summer

Fireflies

Northern Lights

Southern Roots

Eastern Nights

Western Shores

Northern Vows

Living

The Scent of Rome

Blue

The Next Life

In The Mirror

Christmas In Heaven

Welcome to Paradise

After Sunset

Paradise Pride

Cupid Is A Cat

Members Only

Along The Mystic River

In Dreams

Chance Encounters

Songbirds of Sedona

Red Rock Ranch

Mistletoe Motel

The Turning Tides of Us

Madeleine Taylor (sapphic erotica)

The Good Girl

Online

Masquerade

Santa's Favorite